Larissa Lai is the author of two novels—*When Fox Is a Thousand* (Press Gang 1995, Arsenal Pulp 2004) and *Salt Fish Girl* (Thomas Allen Publishers 2002). She was an active cultural organizer through the 1990s and holds an MA in Creative Writing from the University of East Anglia and PhD in English from the University of Calgary. She is currently an Assistant Professor in Canadian Literature at the University of British Columbia in Vancouver, British Columbia.

Books of Merit

salt fish girl

salt fish girl

A NOVEL

larissa lai

Thomas Allen Publishers
Toronto

National Library of Canada Cataloguing in Publication Data

Lai, Larissa, 1967–
    Salt fish girl / Larissa Lai. – 1st ed.

ISBN 10: 0-88762-382-4   ISBN 13: 978-0-88762-382-0

I. Title.

PS8573.A3775S24   2002   C813'.54   C2002-902552-4
PR9199.3.L2815S24   2002

Cover and text design: Gordon Robertson
Editor: Katja Pantzar
Cover images: Morgan Mazzoni (top), Tim Hall (bottom), courtesy Getty Images
Author photograph: Chick Rice

Sections of earlier drafts of the novel have previously appeared in the magazines *absinthe*, *Filling Station*, and *Tessera*, and in the anthologies *Take Out*, *Carnal Nation*, and *First Hand*.

"Fan Tan Fanny," by Richard Rodgers and Oscar Hammerstein II
Copyright © 1958 by Richard Rodgers and Oscar Hammerstein II Copyright renewed

Williamson Music owner of publication and allied rights throughout the world. International copyright secured. All rights reserved. Reprinted by permission.

Published by Thomas Allen Publishers,
a division of Thomas Allen & Son Limited,
145 Front Street East, Suite 209,
Toronto, Ontario M5A 1E3 Canada
www.thomasallen.ca

The publisher gratefully acknowledges the support of The Ontario Arts Council for its publishing program.

We acknowledge the support of the Canada Council for the Arts, which last year invested $20.1 million in writing and publishing throughout Canada.

We acknowledge the Government of Ontario through the Ontario Media Development Corporation's Ontario Book Initiative.

We acknowledge the financial support of the Government of Canada through the Canada Book Fund (CBF) for our publishing activities.

Printed and bound in Canada

14 13 12 11 10   4 5 6 7 8

For my grandmother, Tsui-Pun Wai-Chee

"I don't like rain. I don't mean that thunder scares me. You know very well what I mean I mean that sometimes I wish I was a fish with a settled smelling center."

— *Gertrude Stein,*
"Farragut or A Husband's Recompense"
in Useful Knowledge

Contents

salt fish girl

Nu Wa

Bank of the Yellow River,
pre-Shang dynasty

THE BIFURCATION

In the beginning there was just me. I was lonely. You have no idea. I was lonely in a way even the most shunned of you have never known loneliness. And I was cold, which is not the same as cold-blooded, no matter what they say about me. It was not a philosophical, mountaintop sort of loneliness, the self-inflicted loneliness of a sage in his dark cave. It was a murkier sort of solitude, silent with the wet sleep of the unformed world. The materials of life still lay dormant, not yet understanding their profound relationship to one another. There was no order, nothing had a clear relationship to anything else. The land was not the land, the sea not the sea, the air not the air, the sky not the sky. The mountains were not yet mountains, nor the clouds clouds.

But wait. Here comes the sound of a river, water rushing in to fill the gap. Here comes the river. Husssssssh. Shhhhhh. Finger pressed vertically against lips, didn't I tell you? Of course I have lips, a woman's lips, a woman's mouth already muttering secrets under my breath. Look, I have a woman's eyes, woman's rope of smooth black hair extending past my waist. A woman's torso. Your gaze slides over breasts and belly. The softest skin, warm and quivering. And below? Forget modesty. Here comes the tail, a thick cord of muscle undulating, silver slippery in the early morning light. Lean closer and you see the scales, translucent, glinting pinks and greens and oily cobalt blues.

I know that eye, the eye that registers fear first, and then the desire to consume. What kind of soup would my flesh make? What would you dream after tasting?

Worried you, eh? Never mind, I was telling you about the river. Shhhhhh. Here it comes. Curve and slither, form and motion we both understand.

In the beginning there was me, the river and a rotten-egg smell. I don't know where the smell came from, dank and sulphurous, but there it was, the stink of beginnings and endings, not for the faint of heart. I was lonely. I scooped up a clot of mud from the riverbank and rolled it cool and brown between my palms. It was slippery and hard to control. I poked and prodded it. I jabbed and jerked it. I laid it in the palm of one hand and I stroked and smoothed it with the fingers of the other until it began to look a little like me. I gave it a thick, smiling mouth. I gave it a stubby little tail so it wouldn't get too arrogant and think itself better than me. The mouth contorted into a rude shape. I pinched it back into place. I gave the thing some eyes so it could see who it was dealing with. The eyes opened and gazed at me insolently and the mouth contorted again, then settled in an insipid smirk. I laid my thumb into a little indent beneath the waist, and, in a fury, pressed until the tail split in two. The mouth opened. . . oohhhh. The thing went limp. I smoothed the rough bits between the dangling flaps of bifurcated tail, trying to conceal the damage I had done, pretend it was part of the original design. Oooohhhh, sighed the thing. It began to breathe.

Can you understand me? I asked it. Do you speak my language? I wanted to tell it about my loneliness and how delighted I was to have its company. I wanted to ask its forgiveness for my moment of wrath.

The thing stared at me. It pointed at my tail and started to laugh. Furious, I dashed it to the ground, where it crumpled and then lay still. I scooped up another clot of mud and rolled it between my palms. But as soon as I gave it a mouth and eyes, it too began to laugh at me. I split its tail. I dropped it unceremoniously into the river and began another. All day I worked, varying nose length and eye colour, shoe size and heart size, hoping to create one that would treat me with a little respect, but always with the same result. I worked until I was so exhausted I could not keep my eyes open a moment longer and then I slumped down beside the wreckage of my monstrous creations and fell asleep.

I woke to the sound of sighs and laughter. The things had survived my fury. The crushed ones had healed, the ones I dropped into the river had swum to shore. They were rolling two by two in the mud, moaning and giggling and stroking one another at the point of damage, the point at which I had split the tail. They're a bit disgusting, I thought to myself, but I don't feel lonely any more. I showed them how to build houses and plant rice and tried to get them to treat me a little better. When they saw that I could help them, they made an effort, but they weren't very clever and so they relapsed, frequently, into rudeness and insolence.

I wondered how long they would last, with the few meagre agricultural skills I had taught them. In a few years, they discovered they could cultivate some riverside plants in their gardens and eat those along with rice. I brought them pigs and chickens and taught them how to fish. They were brutal creatures with no qualms about laying a knife against a pig's throat when they were hungry. They roasted the pig whole in a deep pit. Later though, I found a neat plate of roasted pork sitting on a rock by the river, presumably meant for me.

They made it into a habit. Every feast day they left me a plate of roasted pork. Later, they marked it for me by burning sticks of aromatic wood beside the plate. I began to grow fond of them and worried about their mortality.

As they aged they slowed down, grew pale and thin. Their glossy black hair lost its sheen and whitened. They developed sores in their mouths and infections in their ears. Their eyes glazed over and some of them went blind. They hobbled about in obvious pain, their sores running with pus and blood. I grew despondent and listless. I could not bear to watch. One day an old woman came to me, her clothes tattered, her hair streaked with ghostly white strands. "What is wrong with us?" she said. "You made us. Now help us." My despondency grew into a full-blown depression. I slithered off into the hills and found myself a dark cave.

In the dark I dreamt about their origins, searching for a key. I remembered their mischievous eyes, their rude smirks. I remembered my fury and how I had wished to destroy them. I remembered how I had split their tails, and how they had learned, awkwardly, to walk, rather than gliding along low to the earth as I did. I remembered the pleasure they derived from stroking one another between the legs.

There was something to this if I could just . . . And then I had it! Suppose I gave this instinctive activity a dual purpose, suppose it were not just for pleasure, but also for procreation. Not that I have anything against pleasure myself, leave that to Confucius; he'll be along soon enough. But why not give the behaviour a secondary function? Delighted, I slipped and slithered back to the little river settlement. I made the strong ones into women and the weak ones into men. I taught them how to kiss.

They were pleased with my latest invention. They kissed and stroked and stimulated one another until their hair resumed its original glossiness and their cheeks and eyes grew bright. They copulated in their little river shacks and I politely averted my eyes, not wanting to embarrass them. They became so absorbed with one another that they forgot about me altogether, except for those who could not have children. These built temples and burned incense for me. They laid out plates of pork and whole steamed chickens and sweet round oranges laced with tears of longing. I helped them when I could, but after a few thousand years there were so many of them, I could not help them all, though I revelled in the success of this latest project.

But the more of them there were, the more preoccupied they became with their daily lives and the less time they had for me. They left food and burned incense for the gods of agriculture and war and only occasionally for me. Because their affection for me diminished so gradually, I didn't realize how resentful I had grown, or how lonely. The first emotion I recognized in myself was envy. I longed to walk amongst them, experience the passion I had invented without having ever felt it. You might think it odd, to envy the beings one has created. I can't explain it, except to say that it happened and that it consumed me with such a burning longing that I could think of nothing except how I might walk among them unde-tected and experience their joys and sorrows.

I returned to the riverbank, to the precise spot where in my loneliness I had scooped up that first handful of mud and prodded it into shape. The mud was cool against my belly. I glided down the slippery bank to a bend in the river where the water pooled. At the end of the pool, water flowed be-tween two jagged rocks. I followed the bank. It dropped off sharply and I skidded down the drop. Beside me, the water gushed. The narrow stream had become a thin rope of wa-terfall. At the bottom was a cold green lake. I slithered to the far end and slipped into it. The water was very clear. I lay beneath the surface. It was still as glass, a veil above which the dry world shone like a painting on the ceiling of a chapel, except that it moved. Storm clouds gathered furiously up there and it seemed amazing to me that things could be so still and quiet here below when there was so much violence up above. The surface held flat and unmoving until the boat approached. Its wake shot ripples through the stillness. Slowly, the boat glided across my transparent roof, a dark looming shape, dry and full of mystery. It shut out the troubled blue-grey light. A paddle dipped rhythmically in the water, first on one side then the other, a dark wing repeatedly breaking the surface. Suddenly, over the ledge, a face appeared. It was a young man's face, all angles. The eyes were dark and contemplative. I couldn't know then that it was not the kind of face young men usually wore in public. It was a private face, a lonely face, the kind of face men reserve only for reflective surfaces. I shivered and the shiver travelled down the full rope length of my body, making the underwater weeds in which I hid shudder also with an animal sort of motion. The young man noticed, and his eyes changed. He was no longer watching himself, but looking into the water. He had seen me.

The boat passed overhead and its shadow moved slowly away into the distance. The sky opened up overhead again and light streamed down in long blue shafts. But I no longer felt content. I found myself longing for the shadow. A storm broke and it began to rain. The surface broke up so that what lay above became indecipherable. I swam along a steep ledge down one side of the lake, which went so deep it might have been bottomless. Light did not penetrate to this dark cold place and so I found my way by feel. My fingers brushed against the jagged edge of an opening. I reached down and groped in the dark. I peered over the ledge. There was a faint light in the cave, and at its bottom lay an enormous green fish with scales as big as my hands and eyes older than the world. Patiently, her gills gaped open and closed.

"I saw a young man's face," I told her, "I want to go up into the world as a human being."

She said, "I can give you legs, but the bifurcation of your tail will be very painful."

"I don't care," I said. "I'm not afraid of pain."

"Open your mouth," she said.

I felt a stream of water flow into my mouth like a finger. It pressed something smooth and round into the back of my throat. I thought I would choke. I thought I would swallow the round thing, but it nestled firmly just where the water had nudged it, as though there were a small round gap in my mouth I had not noticed before. I felt no pain there, but in the tip of my tail I did. An unpleasant heat at first and then a terrible burning sensation. There was the sound of flesh ripping, and then I felt it, my body beginning to split in two. I screamed. She placed her hand over my mouth. "The pearl will keep you alive forever," she said. "But you will never again be without pain." The ripping continued up my long spine. The vertebrae cracked in two and the strands of the spinal cord were wrenched apart. The agony was unbearable. I opened my mouth again and clamped down on the hand that still covered it. She shrieked and let me go. Fast as I could I slithered away from her, up out of the cold dark depths to where there was still light and plant life, up to the far side of the lake, leaving a trail of blood in my wake.

I pulled myself onto a big flat rock to examine the damage. The separating continued and where my tail had torn in two the flesh dangled limp and useless. I reached down and tried to press the halves together again, but they didn't quite fit. Already they were rounding a little. I watched in horror as my bright scales flaked off one by one to reveal vulnerable flesh beneath, greyish pink and much too soft. I picked the scales up off the cool surface of the rock and tried to press them back to my thin skin, but to no avail. The split tip of my tail opened and flattened and the ends separated in four places. My feet were translucent, pale and veined. I had no faith that I'd be able to stand on them. I stroked my new appendages with cold hands, trying to soothe away the burning pain. I turned on my rock. Behind me on a nearby rock sat another woman, also stroking her legs and marvelling at their newness. Her face was remarkably like the face I had seen gazing down at me from the boat.

Miranda

*Serendipity, a walled city
on the west coast
of North America,
2044*

FIRST SYMPTOMS

My mother was a sixty-three-year-old woman the year
I was born. I have a picture of her, taken the week before
my conception, posing at her vanity, where she often sat
in those slow grey days. The dark wood vanity is tidy and
unadorned except for a clean lace doily carefully arranged
in the centre. To one side an array of elegantly cut perfume
bottles glitters. My mother is smiling in the photograph.
Her hair is black, but you can tell it has been dyed because
the shade is so unnaturally dark. It has been carefully
permed in smooth, neat waves, and pinned at the back

with discreet black pins. She wears a close-fitting dress patterned with irridescent dragonflies and draped modestly with a gauzy wine-red shawl. Perhaps she and my father were on their way out to meet some old cabaret friends at the New Kubla Khan—that famous club, a legend in my family long before my birth. People said her career was made and broken there. That she was admired there by men and women alike. And there my father had first given her that ridiculous bunch of white chrysanthemums and stayed to conceive my eldest brother, Aaron. Around her neck, she wears a pearl choker, which gleams softly in the late afternoon sunlight that trickles through the flower-shaped holes worked into the lacy curtains, sunlight enhanced by another, artificial light, that the discerning viewer could source with a little careful scrutiny. In the mirror behind her you can see the headless reflection of the photographer, a tall thin man in a well-cut suit. Where his head should be a brilliant light flares—the old Nikon's powerful flashbox doing its job.

From her sad smile and from the faded way her eyes shine you can tell she thinks of herself as old. Certainly she has no premonition of my arrival, at least not in this photograph. About my father, because you can't see his head you can't tell. Maybe he knows something she doesn't, but I doubt it. But if you look really carefully into the brilliance of the flash reflected in the mirror behind my mother, you can see the outline of the camera's lens, and in the centre of that lens is a teensy black squiggle. It might just be a hair on the negative, but I like to think of it as a twinkle in my father's eye, a wriggly little premonition of my coming. When we look at the photograph together, no one notices the squiggle but me. No one really even notices the reflection of the man in the mirror. Once, when my parents weren't around, I pointed the squiggle out to my brother Aaron, but he just laughed and said, "It's not possible, stupid. When you look in a camera you look through the viewfinder. Your eye won't appear in the lens." I never mentioned it again.

On the day of my conception, there was a scent in the air, a strange scent, that over the years was to become very familiar. But on this day it wasn't yet. Seated at her vanity, fingering the trappings of long-forgotten glory, the bottles and tubes, the boxes and cases out of which beauty refused any longer to leak, my mother caught her first whiff. At first she couldn't place it, and it struck her as unpleasant, like the reek of cat pee tinged with the smell of hot peppers that have not been dried and are on the verge of going off. The scent was ever so faint at first—the merest molecules brushed her nostrils and set them tingling. A breeze wafted through the room, and the same scent rode in on it, but more strongly this time. When it was stronger, oddly, it did not seem so unpleasant. There was something intriguing about it, something vaguely familiar in a subtropical kitchen sort of way. A cross-draft pushed through the barely open window to the right of her dresser, and brought with it another dimension of the same odour, intriguing, yes, and familiar too, and also illicit—the smell of something forbidden smuggled on board in a battered suitcase, and mingled with the smell of unwashed underwear. My mother's curiosity was piqued. She stopped fiddling with the worn tortoiseshell compact her elder sister had given her on the long-ago night of her cabaret debut. She laid both hands flat on the vanity top and breathed the odour in. Durian, such as she hadn't tasted since she was a small child and her grandmother smuggled one in from Hong Kong, once upon a time before the absolute power of the Big Six and our family's fortunate installation at Serendipity. Durian, like the one she begged her husband for only last week, when they saw some growing— strangely, for this is not their climate—near a beach in the Unregulated Zone, where law-abiding corporate citizens like them are not supposed to go. She wanted it so badly, she would have taken the risk, but my father said that wild things weren't safe. She knew that. She wanted it anyway.

My father entered the room holding in both hands that heady fruit in its spiky, leather-hard shell. My mother turned to him with a look he had not seen since another night, long ago, before their wedding, when he had first burst into her dressing room at the New Kubla Khan, eyes shining with boyish passion and terror, the night of the white chrysanthemums and my brother Aaron's conception. She turned to him and her eyes brightened and her mouth grew moist. Her dyed hair suddenly caught the light, and the dark strands gleamed with a brilliance that, while neither youthful nor natural, was nonetheless lively.

"Durian," he said. "Come eat." He stood in the doorway and did not move. She rose from the worn seat of her ancient vanity, and on her dainty, small, now lithe feet, practically wafted up to him and pressed her warm lips to his. He dropped the durian in surprise. As they tumbled to the floor, it tumbled between them, its green spikes biting greedily into their flesh, its pepper-pissy juices mixing with their somewhat more subtly scented ones and the blood of the injuries it inflicted with its green teeth.

As for the precise nature of my conception in this incident, what shall I say? That the third gender is more unusual and more potent than most imagine? That my conception was immaculate, given the fact that my mother was a good eight years past menopause? I can tell you none of these things because I know nothing about them. From time to time I get an inkling, enough to sense that there was something I knew before this moment, but whatever it was flooded away from me in that instant, before I could grasp a sense of what it was that was leaving.

But as a result of this incident, my mother's belly swelled watermelon round. The child, however, that emerged from her womb nine months later did not smell watermelon sweet.

If the truth must be told, I stank. Vaguely at first, of pepper and cat pee, but as I grew the smell intensified, so sour and acrid that no amount of roll-on deodorant, however liberally applied, could take the odour away.

"I don't mind," said my mother. "I think she smells quite delightful."

My parents took me home from the Serendipity Memorial Hospital to a house full of secrets. I was a reeking bundle, which gave them something to talk about, something on which to focus their discontent and give it a voice. My sour body stank up the whole house. The unpleasant cat pee odour oozed from my pores and flowed into every room. It swirled around the coffee table, glided smoothly over the couch and poured over the rug. It crept up the foot of my father's favourite armchair and dribbled over the fat armrests. It coiled round the loveseat where my mother liked to curl on rainy afternoons rescrolling through her favourite murder mysteries and penny romances. It gushed into the kitchen and ran over the counters. It sneaked through the narrowest cracks into all the cupboards, leached through airtight lids into cookie jars and flour canisters, rice buckets and spice bottles. It crept under bedroom doors into the private rooms of each family member—my mother's sewing room, the master bedroom, and downstairs to the rec room and the rooms that adjoined it. It flooded my father's study on the right, and on the left it gushed down three steps to the landing and wafted under the closed door of my brother Aaron's secret quarters where he had lived once with his lovely wife, Donna, before she drowned. It was a room I wasn't to see for many years, but that doesn't matter yet. What matters is the smell. It got into everything, the lacy curtains in all the upstairs windows, the faux zebra rug on the living-room floor, the gingham cloth on the kitchen table and the plastic-covered taupe linen one in the dining room. It infused the marital bedspread, the shirts, jackets and neatly pressed trousers that hung in my father's closet, the floral dresses that hung in my mother's. It got into the linen closets and suffused the clean sheets, pillowcases, face cloths and plush bath towels. There was no escape from that terrible odour. It crept into people's underwear drawers so that my intimate odour became that of all my family members as well. So all-permeating was the smell that you'd think those who loved me at least would stop noticing it after a while, but that was not the case.

I had just been born. How could I possibly understand anything about the secrets of the house I had been born into? How could I have guessed that my birth was the spring of my parents' love for one another? That foul odour of cat pee and pepper not only infused the external fabric of our house, it seeped into the skin of all my family members. It rushed up their nostrils and in through their ears. It poured down their throats when they opened their mouths to speak.

At the age of sixty-five my mother fell in love with my father for the first time. I didn't know how lonely that love-seat in the corner had been in the decades prior to my birth. I had no inkling of the hours of solitude my mother had spent curled there reading her trashy novels, or how many times my brother Aaron had walked past her, casting glances full of fury against her self-pity. In my earliest memories my mother and father sit together on that couch whispering to one another like teenagers. Or he sits in his armchair reading aloud while my mother sits at his feet gazing up in rapture. I crawl over the zebra-striped carpet pushing old toy cars inherited from Aaron's long-ago childhood. From the back of the house comes the occasional sound of clanking metal—Aaron tinkering with one of the antique automobiles he bought from time to time.

So engrossed were my family in their new-found state of bliss that they didn't notice changes happening in the outside world. My father forgot to cut the grass. My mother no longer weeded the flower beds. The house hadn't been painted since three years before my birth. Now, as I approached my fifth birthday, the paint had begun to peel, but my parents didn't notice. The hedges needed trimming. The plum tree in the front yard badly wanted pruning. My parents, who once upon a time in their unhappiness had meticulously attended to these things, ceased to notice, or if they noticed they were delighted by the riotous exuberance of life around them and gave no thought to containing it. The hedge climbed higher and part of it began to spread over the roof of the house. The plum tree scattered its fruit messily over the lawn, where it rotted, giving off a sickly sweet smell that no doubt combined unpleasantly with the sour odour already pouring from the windows of the house. But one or two of the plum stones took root and the following spring little seedlings poked up warm and sleepy past the rapidly springing grass.

One day, when I was around four, there was a knock on the door. It was the next-door neighbour, Mr. Burke, a tall, burly man with a thick red moustache, meticulously trimmed, just like the lawn outside his house. I didn't hear what he said to my father—something about garbage disposal, and grass. His face was the stern, cold face of someone who had been brewing resentment for a long time and was trying to be gracious by holding it back. My father could have blasted him for his icy contempt, but instead he nodded gravely and diplomatically. Yes, he had been putting out his garbage, no, the compost bin was in perfect condition, of course he would cut the grass and see to it that the hedge got a trimming. When he closed the door, he shot my mother the first unkind look I had ever seen him give her. In response she sighed an ancient sigh, the kind that comes only from repeated disappointment. It was the first window into their old life that I caught.

I looked up from the eyepiece of my sturdy toy micro-scope, where I had been examining a cell scraping from the inside of my cheek. It was marvellous how translucent the cells were, how you could see the lines of their fragile walls, the round yolks of nuclei and the fat cigar-shaped mitochondria. My parents were great fans of toys that revealed the world in its minutiae and its enormity (I had a telescope too), especially old-fashioned ones that called up a simpler, more elegant past. They weren't so good with things on a human scale. My mother retreated to her bed-room. I heard the sounds of an ancient, scratchy CD-ROM starting up on an equally decaying laptop. My mother belonged to that embarrassing era of sleek technology when everyone believed in the goodness of the world. Though such things generally bored me beyond belief, for some reason I felt compelled to go and spy on her. I think it was more because of that terrible sigh I had heard her breathe than because I was interested in her schmaltzy en-tertainments. I tiptoed down the unvacuumed hallway carpet to her bedroom door. I eased it open a crack. She sat steely-faced at her vanity. She had propped the com-puter up in front of her mirror and was watching a CD-ROM of herself, much younger, dressed in a shimmery sequinned red cheongsam, hair pinned and piled high on top of her head, singing a Nancy Kwan cover. "*Fan Tan Fanny was leaving her man . . .*" A balding man in a baby bonnet sat scrunched up in a mesh playpen at the left rear of the stage. In the foreground my mother loaded a tiny suitcase with long ruffled evening gowns in brilliant colours. The camera panned over the audience. Was that my father, sitting there in the audience on the second level near the back? The camera zoomed in, not at my father, but onto the face of a very handsome dark-haired man in the pit. He wore a white suit and had a pink rose stuck through his lapel buttonhole. His eyes were full of my mother. If you looked closely (as I couldn't then, from my illicit vantage point) you could actually see two tiny reflections of her in each of his dark irises. "*Fan Tan Fanny kept waving her fan . . .*" The camera panned back to my mother in her slinky dress, desperately attempting to force the tiny suitcase shut. An array of long-legged, cheongsammed Asian women fluttering fans made of playing cards poured down a fake white marble staircase behind her. "*Goodbye, Danny, you two-timing Dan / Some other man loves your little Fanny,*" sang my mother, clutching the closed but bulging suitcase. "*Bye-bye!*" The screen went black. "You've tuned into Running Dog TV," boomed the disembodied voice of the announcer, "broadcasting to you from the East Neighbourhood at the very borders of Serendipity. I could throw a stone into the Unregulated Zone. Very dangerous, ladies and gentlemen, very very dangerous. But you're always safe when you're watching Running Dog. Tune in tomorrow at eight for the latest from the Miss Aimee Ling at the New Kubla Khan." The sound diminished to nothing, and clips from the evening's entertainment flashed silently over the screen. My mother remained fixed in front of her vanity table. In the mirror, her face was still and hard as a mask, but because of the light that flickered from the computer screen, I could see the glitter of tears silently running down her cheeks.

My parents' romance was over, but that doesn't mean that the foul odour that emanated from my pores diminished in the least bit. What it meant was that my durian stink ceased to be a source of sensuality and became instead an irritant of the worst sort, because it was always present. It began to nag at people.

And it was just at that moment that I had to begin school. It was a blustery September and all over Serendipity leaves whirled in the air and giant Saturna apples tumbled from trees and smashed on the streets and sidewalks. The air smelled like apple cider. I remember noting the distinct difference between that smell and my own, though were anyone to have asked me at the time, I would have said I smelled nothing at all. On the first day the teacher sat me between a blonde girl with glasses and a frail, dark boy. She gave us all spelling books. She wrote the words for our first spelling test on the board: *run can dog big sit pat*. I couldn't have cared less. What I did notice was my classmates leaning away from me. They whispered and chattered to one another intently. I couldn't hear a word they were saying. They didn't chatter to me. The teacher gave them all a detention for being unruly. At recess, I hung around the edges of a small group playing a clapping game, hoping to be invited in, hoping the girl with dark curls would teach me the rhyme. But the kids ignored me. I moved onto a group that was skipping. "Go away, Cat Box," said a girl with pretty red shoes. "Kitty Litter," said the dark-haired boy I sat next to. "Pissy Pussy," said the girl who sat on the other side of him. I slunk off to the edge of the playground, my head down, examining the scruffy tufts of grass and the gaps of dirt between them. At the end of the day, when the bell rang, I alone left the classroom and went to meet my mother at the front gate. All the other kids had to stay an extra twenty minutes.

When I saw my mother I knew right away that she had been crying. She had carefully retouched her makeup, thinking I wouldn't notice the puffiness around her eyes, but I saw it. She smiled when she saw me. "How was your first day?" she asked.

"It was great," I lied, to comfort her.

"I'm glad," she said. "My day was terrible."

"What was so terrible about it, Ma?" I asked, my eyes filled with concern.

I must have looked quite cute, because she laughed, and a brightness returned to her eyes. "Never mind," she said. "I'll tell you when you're older."

"How much older?" I demanded.

"When you're ten, maybe."

I was only five. Have I pieced these things together from memory, or did I really think about them then as I do now? When we approached the house I could see that a lot of work had been done on it. The hedge was half-trimmed, the plum tree had been partially pruned. There were cans of eggshell-blue paint lined up on the porch. When we came into the main hallway and looked into the living room we saw my father rocking furiously in his rocking armchair. "I don't care, Aimee," he said. "We've got to do something about it."

"What's that, Stewart?" my mother said.

"That smell," he said. "We have to take her for treatment."

My mother shot him an ice-cold glare. "Go to your room, Miranda," she said. "I need to talk to your father about something in private."

Obediently, I shuffled down the hallway and into my room.

"Close the door!" my mother yelled.

I closed it, but then I eased it slightly open again. She didn't notice. I heard her speaking softly to my father in a voice full of fury. "We agreed that we wouldn't make her feel self-conscious about the smell, didn't we? It's hard enough that she's the only Asian child in her class, and surely she is aware of that. I won't have you working your neurosis out on her."

"Who are you to talk about neuroses?" my father snapped. "You're the one that married the wrong man! If you're still so in love with that callous, shallow son of a bitch why don't you go look for him? Hear he's a famous doctor at Painted Horse now."

"How dare you?" my mother said. "When Aaron was born we made an agreement, didn't we? I've kept my side of the bargain even though it's harder for me than it is for you. What do you know about anything?"

"What do you know?" he said. "You have no idea how hard my life is . . ."

I couldn't bear it any more. Softly, I clicked my door shut. I crawled into my bed and pulled the pillow tightly over my head.

I didn't hear them fighting again for a long time, although there was a tension between them now that hadn't existed before. My father finished trimming the hedge and pruning the plum tree. He dragged Aaron away from his beloved garage long enough to give the whole house a lovely coat of delicate eggshell-blue paint. On sunny afternoons the house blended into the sky, giving the curious impression of a free-floating brown tile roof. There was no further talk of my smell.

Things continued much the same at school. The other kids ignored me, and I wandered the perimeter of the playground watching the grass fade and puddles forming in the rain.

In the springtime, my mother gave me a bag of pretty blue marbles with fish and flowers floating inside them. For a while, other kids played with me, until all the marbles were lost, which didn't take long—perhaps less than a week. I felt quite forlorn the day I lost my last marble. I walked up the back steps of the school and sat down at the top one. Quietly I sang a few lyrics from one of my mother's cabaret songs to comfort myself.

> *Here's a song for Clara Cruise*
> *A pretty girl who loved her shoes*
> *Redder than a red red rose*
> *The patent leather showed her toes*
> *She fell in love with them on sight*
> *The soles they made her feet so light*
> *The pretty shoes of Clara Cruise*
> *She danced in them throughout the night*

My voice was coarse and out of tune. I closed my eyes and imagined I was her, wearing a long red cheongsam and crooning to an admiring television audience of thousands. Of course I could never admit this fantasy to anyone, supposing I had anyone to admit it to. Television was a thing of the past, having long since been replaced by Interactive Electronic Books, or ebbies for short.

It was, in fact, through new technologies that I learned anything at all about the world. I knew little about my father's job as a tax collector until he bought a Business Suit for home use. It came in a large cardboard carton, just my father's height. It was wide, heavy and awkward. The delivery man helped him struggle down to the basement with it. I went downstairs to watch while he unpacked it. It was a large black suit made of some shiny synthetic material, elastic and tight-fitting. There were pieces for every part of the body—a torso piece, two leg pieces, detachable sleeves, boots, gloves, a hood, a terrifyingly anonymous black mask in the exact contours of my father's face but without features or colour. The Business Suit came with a sturdy stand in black steel, which my father stood in the far corner of the room near an electrical socket.

"What's it for?" I asked.

My dad said, "So I can go to the Office in the evenings."

"I don't like it," I said. "It's ugly."

"I know it is, Miranda," said my father with an air of lonely stoicism. "But when you see me at work, I hope you'll be proud of the part I play in the life of our community."

The last thing he drew out of the box was a cheap video monitor, which he placed on the floor a short distance away. It came without accessories so we laid it flat on the floor. To watch it, I had to stand over it and look down as though into a fish pond. "You can't have it on all the time," he said. "Because some of the things I do are not suitable for children's viewing. But when I put on the suit, what you see in front of you is not real. If you want to see what I'm really doing you have to look at the video screen."

"Okay, Dad," I said, my eyes wide.

"Shall we give it a go then?" he said, smiling.

I watched as he stepped into the torso piece and drew the leggings over his thin knees. I helped him adjust the sleeves and attach them to the armholes round the back where it was hard for him to reach. I climbed on a chair so I could help him tuck the bottom edges of the hood into the top part of the torso piece and helped him pull the zipper closed around the neck. I watched in awe as he pulled on the tight-fitting boots and then zipped the Business Suit up the front. Last, he placed the dark mask over his face, obliterating his own features. He tucked the edges into the hood and then zipped it shut. I suppressed a gasp of horror. He looked like an executioner.

"Okay, Miranda," came his muffled voice from behind the mask. "Turn on the video monitor." As I reached to do so, he flipped a switch at the console on his wrist. The shadowy shape of my father began to move. He didn't go anywhere. His motions were the motions of a mime. His steps fell back on themselves. His arms groped forwards like those of the sleepwalkers I sometimes saw in ancient movies rented for Spying except that his were dumb and clumsy and lacking in precision.

The flimsy video monitor crackled and fizzled to life. I turned away from the dark form of my father zombie-walking in his Business Suit. On the screen I saw a man striding across a burning landscape. Crumpled buildings and burnt-out trucks and tanks were scattered everywhere, all smouldering dully. Inside some, tongues of dying flame still flickered. There was the sound of hammers clanking and sirens blaring and people calling for help. The man was tall and strong and solitary. As he approached, his face came into focus. It was my father, but a much younger, stronger, more heroic version of him, both like the man I knew and entirely without the soft, gentle, bookish demeanour with which he carried himself through family life. A woman and child appeared at his feet. Their clothes were ragged. The woman's cheek was bleeding. The child was screaming and scrabbling with its sharp desperate little claws for her breast which jutted through her torn clothing just a bit too sexily for one so abject. My father helped the woman to her feet. He unhooked a canteen from his belt and gave it to her to drink. Suddenly a flock of something like birds swooped towards them—round discs with razor-sharp edges that screamed like crows. My father's eyes turned red and shot lightning bolts at them. He raised his arm. It was a gun, shooting rapid machine-gun fire. He continued to walk and as he put each knee forward a spray of bullets shot out. The birds were subdued. The swooping became a slow tumbling. They flickered, lost their solidity, became a thin stream of digits. My father opened his mouth wide and swallowed them.

I forgot about the man in the dark rubber suit and watched the video screen for hours as my father helped the helpless and swallowed increasingly long streams of razor disc birds that turned into numbers when he opened his mouth. The Business Suit made tax collecting into a marvellous adventure. I thought perhaps that when I grew up, I'd like to be a tax collector too. After a while his belly began to swell and his movements slowed. In a dark door-way in a bombed-out street, he stumbled, clutched the wall. His belly was round as a football. Two policemen appeared beside him in the doorway and dragged him into a dark room. It was a dungeon. Two other taxmen were already handcuffed to the wall. The policemen pushed my father's arms over his head and handcuffed him beside them. With heavy truncheons they began to beat him. My father leaned towards the wall and I thought I saw a stream of numbers erupt from his mouth just as the picture fizzled and the monitor went dead. I looked up. My father was still moving in that dark suit. I could hear him behind the mask retching. It was clear he was suffering. But he was not suffering so much that he had forgotten me. He had flicked the switch on his wrist console.

I knew I was supposed to go upstairs and help my mother with dinner, but I couldn't bear to leave him. I squatted on the floor and watched the shadow shape wince from the policemen's blows. I watched as he doubled over, then fell to the ground still retching. He lay there for a long time, motionless.

Though I was utterly terrified to do so, I approached the prone figure. I tugged at the zipper that held the mask to his face and peeled it back. I pulled the mask away. His eyes were closed. The muscles around his mouth flinched involuntarily. I reached to his wrist to flick the switch that would turn the Business Suit off, but as I did so, the opposite rubber hand grabbed mine with startling violence. His eyes slammed open and his face contorted in fury. "No!" he said. "Don't you ever do that. You must never ever interfere with the Business Suit."

My father had never shouted at me before, and I was frightened. "Why do you do it?" I squeaked.

My father's face softened and he became his gentle self again, more or less. "The bank promised adventure," he said. "It doesn't hurt all the time." He sighed. "Remember I asked you to leave?"

I nodded. But then I said, "You don't need to protect me."

"Run along to your mother now," said my dad.

I felt I'd betrayed him deeply by witnessing what I'd witnessed. Perhaps this was the beginning of my troubles with loyalty. Even long afterwards I couldn't decide what would have been the right thing to do.

Weeks passed and my spelling improved, though my relationship with classmates did not. One night I awoke with a terrible thirst. I climbed out of bed to get myself a glass of water. As I passed the stairs that led down to the basement, I could see a light coming from the bottom. I heard a disturbing whimpering noise. Though there was no sense to the sounds, it was clearly my father's voice. I knew I wasn't supposed to interfere, but the sound was even more terrible than the one I had heard him make when the Receivers General were extracting taxes from him. If I could not save my mother from her inarticulate discontent, I thought, perhaps I could help my father. I tiptoed down the steps and into the rec room. My father lay crumpled on the floor in his Business Suit. I turned to where the monitor sat and turned it on. A gang of spindly tall children with mutilated faces were holding my father's head down in a cesspool and beating him with spiky iron balls on chains. They stuck their long sharp fingers into his pockets, into his mouth and ears. A free flow of digits streamed up their fingers, up their arms, shoulders, cheeks, into their own mouths. I banged furiously against the screen. "Stop it!" I screamed. "Get away from him! Get away!" I'm sure now that it was a coincidence that they did.

They ran off howling like animals. Slowly my father pulled himself out of the cesspool. Painfully, achingly he stood up. His first steps were the lopsided steps of a cripple. He staggered towards a cluster of buildings on the horizon. He unhooked a canteen from his hip and took a long drink. His stride evened out and he grew tall and heroic again. I looked up at the rubber-clad figure attached to the stand. There he was, complacently strolling along in the Business Suit.

I returned my gaze to the monitor. My father was walking through the dark streets of a crumbling neighbourhood in a city I didn't recognize. Certainly it was not Serendipity, where all the storefront windows gleamed with cleanliness, behind which beautiful things were displayed. The glass of these shop windows was for the most part broken, the bicycles and radios, the Spy Goggles and portable orchestras that lay behind them long since stolen. Some of the signs above the shops were in English. I could make out the letters of the alphabet I was still learning. But some of the signs were in other cryptic languages I had never seen or heard of. The strange shapes of the characters frightened me. There was something ominous and heavy about them. The image of my heroic father patrolling these streets did, however, comfort me. He slipped into the doorway of one of them, one with a terrible other-language sign above it. I shivered in my cold spot on the basement floor, still squatting intently over the monitor. My nightdress was made of flannel, but it wasn't warm enough. Now he was talking to a tall Asian man in a dark blue jacket. The man took several jars down from the shelves and showed their contents to my father. Inside were roots and herbs in strange muted colours, browns and dark greens and greys. Unlike the food we ate at Serendipity, which was always vibrant bright and regular in shape and colour, these were strange, twisted and misshapen. My father shook his head. He stepped out onto the street and continued walking.

Presently he came to another shop, with strange writing over the door. There was a woman in a white lab coat behind the counter. She too showed him the dark, misshapen contents of large jars, which she pulled down from a high shelf. The herbs and roots looked every bit as unpleasant as the ones the man had shown my father. There was something grey with long tendrilling roots, something dark brown and striated, something moth-green and skin-like. But this time my father nodded enthusiastically. The woman smiled and closed the jars. She put them back on the shelf. My father left the shop and began walking back the way he had come. He would leave the Business Suit soon, I thought. Quickly, I flicked off the video monitor and ran upstairs to my room.

In the morning, when I came down the hallway and into the kitchen, my mother and father were already there, hunched over the kitchen table, their heads close together. At first I thought this was a good sign, that a little of their recently departed affection for one another had returned. But then I could hear they were arguing, their voices low but full of venom. I didn't enter the kitchen but hid in the shadows of the hallway.

"No one goes there these days but thugs and desperate people," my mother was saying. "It's not like when we were young, Stewart. It isn't safe for you or Miranda."

"I should never have brought you that evil fruit," said my dad. "Only barbarians eat those kinds of things. You know if it doesn't have a Saturna sticker it isn't safe. Everything has been affected by these modified pollens. If it grows wild in the Unregulated Zone you have no idea what kinds of mutations have occurred."

"You sound like the bloody *Saturna Telegram*," said my mother. "If the Unregulated Zone is such a terrible place, how can you possibly dream of taking her there?"

"Aimee," said my dad, "I know the *Telegram* is propaganda. But sometimes propaganda contains a grain of truth. The thing is, it's done now. It's not that I want to take her out there. It's that we don't have a choice."

"Serendipity has a perfectly good medical system," said my mother. "Why not make use of it?" She reached into the fruit bowl in the middle of the table, chose a Saturna Gala, and, humming to herself, absently began to peel the fruit. (At the time, it didn't strike me as odd that one apple was amply large enough to feed the four of us. That didn't occur to me until many years later.)

"Because," my dad said, raising his voice to drown out her annoying humming, "I don't want to risk them finding out what we did. There are rumours about children like her at the Office. They aren't nice rumours."

"You are not taking her into the Unregulated Zone," my mother said. "I have nothing against Chinese herbal medicine, but it's not worth the risk. If we lived at Painted Horse we'd have access to other kinds of medicine. But we don't. We'll survive."

I woke late one Saturday shortly after hearing that conversation to the sound of my mother singing an old cabaret tune and rummaging through her closet. The hangers clanked against one another and gauzy materials rustled deliciously. In my dreams I was beautiful like my mother. In the daytime, though, it was a dark sullen face that greeted me in the mirror. When I look back on photographs of that time, I realize that I was not an unattractive child, but my social stature, such as it was among the Serendipity six-year-old set, was worse than that of the ugliest girl in my class and so I saw no loveliness in the face I confronted every morning. I longed to be beautiful like my mother, still glamorous at her twilight age. I shuffled shyly into her room. "Where are you going today, Mom?" I said.

She stopped, mid-tune, to answer me. "Going to play mah-jong with some of my old cabaret friends," she whispered. "Don't tell your father. He thinks I'm going to a Tupperware party with Mrs. Gould." Bitterly she added, "Which just goes to show how much attention he's actually paid to me all these years." Mrs. Gould had left catalogues the previous week. Tupperware was working on its image. It now produced cases for Spy Goggles, pillboxes especially for Spicer's Six-Day Antidepressant System in addition to its usual sandwich boxes and water jugs, but it still wasn't my mother's cup of tea. "What do you think? Red flowers or blue houndstooth?" She laid two dresses on the bed.

"Red flowers, of course," I said, pointing and shuffling just a little closer.

She recoiled from my approach, ever so slightly. Reached behind her for a cut glass bottle on her vanity. Liberally she sprayed perfume behind her ears. "Red flowers it is," she said. And doused the dress as well.

I sighed—was it my mother's ancient sigh?—and retreated to my room.

That old song started up again in her chocolatey voice. I sniffed the backs of my wrists. The smell was strong, but not unpleasant. I didn't understand what the big deal was. After my mother had left and the echo of her song had faded from the house, I slipped into the kitchen and poured myself a glass of milk. I took it out to the back step, under which I kept a stash of *Forbidden Tales* comic books. My favourite was *The Snow Princess,* about a young Nordic royal kidnapped by an evil sultan and forced to live with him in a tent in the desert. She always escapes. The fun of the book was that it allowed me to participate in devising the means of her emancipation. My favourite so far was a version in which she made a carpet of her own hair, which blended with the colour of the sand, so that the sultan didn't see her levitating until she was high above him in the sky, blue as her eyes. My mother thought the *Forbidden Tales* were cute, but my father hated them. He said they were unwholesome. My mother said, "They are part of our collective unconscious." My father said, "They are socially destructive stereotypes." I didn't know what they were talking about. I just liked the stories. There was a part of the book where you could help the princess decide what to wear for her kidnapping and then for her escape. The array of outfits was astonishing, ranging as it did from brassieres and hot pants to tiaras and long flowing dresses. But for the most part I was much more interested in the mechanics of escape. This time, I dressed her in a red flowered dress like my mother's and helped her escape with a short tap-dancing American in a top hat. They danced off into an orange sunset decorated with palm trees and a distant oasis.

As the light faded, an ominous city arose and flooded the screen with its brilliant lights. A woman ran down an abandoned road, past broken shop windows and the bombed-out frames of houses. On her feet she wore a pair of blue and silver running shoes that shone with a dazzling light. "Bloody Pallas," I muttered. I pressed the fast-forward button and the woman scrambled at a fantastic pace down the bombed-out street, which, in spite of its dilapidated state, had a sort of romance about it. I couldn't have been less interested. I leaned on the rewind button until the fjords appeared again and the Snow Princess beckoned anew from within the folds of a white ermine cloak. The sultan was just peeping through the bedroom window for the first time, when there was a tap on my shoulder. Irritated, I pulled my Spy Goggles off. It was my father.

"We're going to see a doctor, Miranda," he said.

"Why?" I said. "Are you ill?"

"Not for me," he said. "For you."

"But there's nothing wrong with me," I said.

My father looked terribly embarrassed. His eyelids fluttered and his cheeks flushed red. "Miranda," he said, "can you turn off *The Snow Princess* for a minute?"

Reluctantly I flicked the switch on the side of my comic book. I took a long gulp from my glass of milk.

"I wish your mother could be the one to have this discussion with you because I know she'd be so much better at it," my dad said. "But your mother doesn't want to, and so I have to do it."

"What, Dad?" I said.

"Well," said my father, "when you were conceived . . ."

"Conceived?"

"You know, when your mother and I decided to have you . . ."

"Aaron said I was an accident."

"Please, Miranda. No doubt this is harder for me than it is for you. We ate this fruit," he said. "I think it has had some kind of effect on your, well, on your . . . body odour."

I was cross with my father. I did not want my smell to be acknowledged. Once you speak something, you make it real, and that was most decidedly what I did not want. But he blurted it all out anyway. I laughed nervously.

"I did some research with the Business Suit," my dad said. "I think I've found someone who can help you."

"I don't want to be helped," I said irritably.

"Please, Miranda," he said. "I know it seems unpleasant now, but trust me, it will be so much better to get this done."

"No. I don't want to go," I said.

But the next hour saw me sitting in a red plastic milk crate on the back of my father's bicycle, heading for the city

gates. One side of the crate had been removed so that my
legs could dangle out the back of my father's bike. I was
frightened. I had never left Serendipity before and had
no idea what to expect. At the city gates we paused. My
father had a few soft words with the guard who came out
of the sentry box to speak to him. I had my back to them,
so I couldn't see or hear clearly what was going on, but I
thought I heard my father fiddling with his wallet, thought
I heard the papery rustle of money changing hands. Then
we were out. For a long stretch we just bumped along
a crumbling highway. Grass and weeds poked out of the
cracks. On one side there grew a thin forest of scraggly
trees, on the other a parched field of tall yellow grass.
A low concrete building came up on the right, though
because of my peculiar backwards-looking vantage point,
I didn't see it until we had passed. I turned my head once
and saw a vast city mushrooming up into a pinkish purple
sky. As we entered it the air grew thick with the smell of
old petrol, sulphur, urine and rotten food. Or at least, that
was what I detected through the haze of my own odour.
The buildings were for the most part empty. Many of
them were crumbling, some from sheer age, and some in
long rows where they had clearly been bombed. Very few
windows had glass in them. The place was beginning to
seem familiar, and at first I found this very spooky. Then I
realized I had seen a version of it in the monitor that was
attached to the Business Suit. It was also the city of the Pallas advertisement, except that it had none of that roman-
tic sheen. It was too dirty and too foul-smelling.

My dad pedalled down a dark alleyway and propped
his bike up against a graffitied concrete wall. He locked it

to a rusted steel girder that stuck out of the concrete. We pushed through a set of peeling wood doors and into a dark room.

The doctor was a thin, businesslike young woman. She sat behind a dark wood desk and observed us over the tops of wire-framed spectacles, her white lab coat gleaming amid the dust and dark wood of the shop. My father lifted me right up onto her desk and explained the problem. She nodded earnestly. She made me stick out my tongue. She took my wrist and prodded around the inside of it for my pulse. Gravely she sniffed behind my ears. Then she nodded at my father to indicate that he was to remove me from her desk. She took out a pad and scribbled a few characters. She pointed us to a narrow doorway that led into the next room. Her husband sat at the counter. Behind him on the wall were jars and jars of the strange dark herbs I had spied in the Business Suit's monitor. My father handed him the prescription. "Fifteen minutes," said the man. We could have gone out onto the street and looked around. I was certainly curious as to what was out there. "We'll wait," said my dad. I watched as the man shook portions of herbs out onto square sheets of white newsprint and carefully weighed them in an old-fashioned Chinese scale, sliding the counterweight up and down a graduated ruler. Through my own odour, I thought the herbs smelled like earth. When he was finished there were seven neat piles of dusty brown and grey herbs on seven white sheets. He slid them off the sheets into plastic bags and heat-sealed them shut. "Five cups of water," he said to my father, "boiled down to one. Every day for seven days."

My father nodded. The man named a price and my father counted out the money without flinching. Then we were back on the bicycle and pedalling away from the city at an alarming rate. My father was worried we might not get home before my mother. The bombed-out buildings and empty windows rolled by quickly. We passed some kids playing clapping games in front of an eyeless church. Further down, outside a dimly lit chip shop, a bunch of older kids were smoking and shoving one another around. One of them, too poor to afford socks, wore plastic shopping bags over her feet. They hung over the edges of her battered boots with an oddly affected grace. The crumbling city grew more beautiful as it receded. Above it, the polluted sky hung a deep purple.

The house was dark when we got back, except for the garage, which was brightly lit. Tinny pop music poured from a portable orchestra in the far corner. As we approached we could see my brother's feet sticking out from underneath his latest acquisition, a late-twentieth-century BMW convertible in mint condition.

"Your mom home?" my dad asked, pulling his bike up beside the tool rack.

"Don't think so," came Aaron's voice from beneath the car.

I followed my father in through the side door. "Go into the kitchen, Miranda, and get that medium-sized stainless steel pot your mom uses for noodles. Bring it down to my study."

"I don't think I can reach."

"Well, use a chair," he said impatiently. Then he scampered down the stairs.

When I came down with the pot, he had a battered old hot plate set up on top of his filing cabinet. He dumped the contents of one bag of herbs into the pot and filled it with water from the bathroom sink. He set it down on the hot plate and turned it on. It made a few slightly alarming cracking and popping noises, but then settled down to give off the required slow, even heat. From the lower drawer of his desk, my father produced a comic book, which he handed to me with a conspiratorial smile. I took the book, even though it wasn't really the kind I like. I settled into the corner of the room with it. Presently, a dark, bitter smell rose from the pot.

I heard a key turn in the front door lock. There would be a confrontation, I thought. I didn't want to witness it. I would have had time to run up the dark stairs and down the hall to my bedroom without running into my mother, but my father grabbed my arm. "Keep quiet and she won't know," my father said.

"It stinks, Dad. Even I can smell it."

"Shhh," said my dad.

I heard my mother open the basement door. "Stewart?" she called. "Miranda? Are you down here?" A switch flicked on and light from the basement hallway poured under the crack between the floor and the door. Then came the distinct sound of my mother's low-heeled just-a-little-less-than-sensible shoes coming down the basement steps.

"Uh-oh," said my father. "Better get into the closet."

"How is that going to help?" I protested, but he grabbed me by the arm and shoved me behind the curtain. I crouched in the dark amongst old files and outdated technologies—an old computer, a game of Virtual Twister, a fondue set, a soft soccer ball, the croquet set with the yellow mallet missing, a boxful of mobile phones from before we all had implants. It was dusty. I suppressed a sneeze.

My mother came into the room. "What in God's name are you doing, Stewart?" she said. "You haven't been where I think you've been, have you?"

"I don't know," said my father sheepishly.

"How can you not know?" my mother said. "Stewart, the evidence is right in front of you. There's no point in lying."

"I thought it would help," my father said. "Burke was here again. And also my colleagues at work, they're talking. Marconi asked about it in the dungeon last week."

"Marconi is an idiot and Burke is a meddler," said my mother. "I can't believe you would take her to the Unregulated Zone behind my back."

"Why shouldn't I? You do all kinds of things behind my back."

"Don't start, Stewart."

"You started. I might have made a mistake with that durian, but I made it because of you. Now you want to take no responsibility whatsoever? You don't care. You don't even want to be part of this family. Why don't you just go away and be with that man, and then at least we can all have it over with."

"I went to see Marsha," my mother said softly. But the fury had gone out of her. My father had used ammunition that worked. I hated it when my parents fought, but there was nothing that frightened me more than my mother's sudden docility at that moment. She clicked back up the stairs in her glamorous-in-spite-of-the-low-heel shoes. When I heard her move into the bedroom, I slipped out of my hiding place and out the door, abandoning my new comic book, the foul-smelling pot and my conniving father. "Hey," my dad said. But I pretended I didn't hear him. I dashed up the stairs and out onto the back porch, now flooded with moonlight.

I fished the *Forbidden Tales* out from under the stairs, pulled on my Spy Goggles and flicked the switch. The Snow Princess didn't care about my smell. It had no effect on whether or not she escaped from the sultan. The foul odour of the Chinese herbs poured out the basement window. Eleven dresses, twenty-nine pairs of shoes and one winged chariot later, my father appeared in the back doorway holding a white bowl full of foul-smelling black stuff. "*Snow Princess* off," he mouthed, silently. His free hand made a cutting gesture at his throat. I gave the Princess a last wistful look and turned the book off. I pushed the Goggles up onto my forehead.

My father held the bowl towards me. It stank worse than I did. I scowled at him.

"Come on, Miranda," he said. "You'll be glad in the long run. Remember the talk we had."

I sighed my mother's ancient sigh and took the bowl. With one hand I plugged my nose. With the other I downed the contents as quickly as possible. The stuff was viscous and indescribably bitter. When it was empty I handed the bowl back to my father.

"Good girl," he said. He gave me a lollipop like the kind sultan gave the Snow Princess sometimes, to lure her down from her tower. I whipped the wrapper off and jammed it gratefully into my gob.

"Much better," I said through the cloying sweetness.

I remained on the back step reading my comic book until a thin sliver of moon rose above my brother's garage. The first stars were just getting bright enough to see. I would have stayed. I enjoyed the serenity of moments like these. But my mother pushed open the screen door and stuck her head out.

"Time for a bath, Miranda," she said.

"Do I have to?" I said.

She nodded. "Comic book off."

Reluctantly, I flicked the switch and followed her upstairs. A sickly floral scent filled the upstairs hall.

"I got you new bubble bath," said my mother. "It comes in a bottle shaped like an angel. Want to see?"

"Not really," I said.

The bathtub was overflowing with white froth. Any other five-year-old would have been delighted, but even then I knew there was a motivation beyond simple love for me.

"No bath tonight," I said.

"All good children bathe before bed," my mother said. "I'll read to you after."

"I hate baths," I said.

But in the end, I agreed to submerge myself in the over-perfumed tub with the proviso that there would be strawberries in my cereal in the morning.

This is what I remember. I undressed and stepped into the tub. The water was warm and soothing. I scrubbed myself with soap. I shampooed my hair and rinsed it by submersing my whole head in water, swishing my hair around beneath the bubbles and breathing out through my nose. Now that I was in the water, it was actually quite pleasant and so I lay back into the heat, closed my eyes and relaxed. Perhaps I dozed because the next thing I knew, the water was cold and my mother was calling to me to get out of the tub and go to bed.

I pulled the plug, stepped out of the water and dried myself on the alligator towel she'd left me. If the skin on my legs felt a little rough when rubbed in one direction, and oddly slippery smooth when rubbed in the other, I didn't register it fully. I stepped into my flannel pyjamas and went to my room. My mother was waiting for me with an old-fashioned book made out of real paper. It was the story of an Italian princess trapped on an island with a nasty, dark sea monster. There were elaborate pen-and-ink drawings illustrating just how ugly he was, with his great, round eyes and droopy whiskers. I felt secretly sorry for him.

Late that night, long after my mother had finished the story and gone to bed, I woke up and trundled to the bathroom to pee. As I sat on the toilet, I noticed something glinting on the floor of the tub, beneath a trace of bubble bath residue. It caught the thin light of the sliver moon, which was visible outside the bathroom window. I finished peeing and reached into the tub to pick it up. It was a fish scale like those I'd watched my mother scrape off the salmon we'd had for dinner that evening. One must have clung to her sleeve and then fallen into the water when she ran my bath. It was both silver and translucent at the same time. That's pretty, I thought, but a bit creepy too. I turned on the cold faucet and swished water around the tub, washing away that scale and three or four more that clung to the cold porcelain.

Nu Wa

South China, late 1800s

THE SALT FISH GIRL

In spite of the pain I must have dozed, because when I looked again the woman was gone. I felt cold and hungry. I slid off my rock, and on uneasy new legs wobbled to shore and slowly made my way towards the nearest town. It was late and most of the people were asleep. But at the third alley, I saw light coming from a doorway. It illuminated a pair of feet that poked out onto the walk. I stumbled over a jagged stone, making a scuffling noise, and a face emerged from the doorway. I recognized it. It was the face of a sickly young woman who in hopes of children often left oranges at my shrine,

before I had given up my divinity in search of baser pleasures.

Eventually the lights went out in the house. I stepped down the alley, as stealthily as I could on my new legs, and pushed the unlocked door open. Beside it was a wide cistern full of water. Without quite knowing what I was doing, I climbed into it. To my shock and horror, my body began to diminish in length. My legs fused together and the pain disappeared. I felt a tightening in the pit of my belly. My body narrowed and shrank. Suddenly the cistern was an ocean, as big as the lake I had recently left. At first I struggled, tried to pull myself up out of the water, but to no avail. Even floating on the surface, half exposed to the air, did not effect a reversal. I let myself drift beneath the surface and sleep.

Later that night, my eyes opened when a shadow fell across the water. It was the woman's face, big and round as a dinner plate. Her hand appeared above the surface, enormous and wielding a huge drinking cup. Before I could understand what was happening, she dipped the cup into the cistern and scooped up a cup of water, and me along with it. Didn't she know that it was unwise to drink unboiled river water? She lifted the cup to her lips and down I went in the first gulp. I glided down her throat and slid into her womb. Nine months later I emerged as a bawling black-haired baby girl.

Except for inexplicable stabbing pains in my legs, my childhood passed peacefully. But when I was fifteen and still many years from marriage, I fell in love with a girl from the coast. She was the daughter of a dry goods merchant who specialized primarily in salt fish. It was, in fact, her father's trade that brought her to my attention. She stank of that putrid, but nonetheless enticing smell that all good South Chinese children are weaned on, its flavour being the first to replace that of mother's milk. They feed it to us in a milk-coloured rice gruel, lumpier than the real thing and spiked with salt for strength.

You might say saltiness is the source of our tension. Stinky saltiness, nothing like mother's milk. The scent calls up all kinds of complicated tensions having to do with love and resentment, the passive-aggressive push-pull emotions of a loving mother who nonetheless eventually wants her breasts to herself, not to be forever on tap to the mewling, sucking creatures that come so strangely from her body and take over her life. Especially from keen observation of her mother before her, she knows that we eventually grow too monstrously huge for the memory of our births, and that we will eventually leave. Why give away too much of yourself, especially intimate bodily fluids, when you know you'll eventually be abandoned, with or without gratitude depending on luck. Give 'em salt fish congee early and you'll forget about 'em sooner and vice versa.

That's the problem with girls. They leave. You can't rely on them. Of course, in these modern times of difficulty and poverty, you can't rely on boys either. Who knows if or when their overseas uncles will call for them, change their names, call them "son" instead of "nephew," and leave you in the dirt? So my mother started me on salt fish congee early. Who could blame her? She was never the type meant for motherhood. If it hadn't been expected of her, if she had had other options, she'd have been an empress or a poet or a martyr. Something grand, and perhaps a bit tragic. She loved those old sages, with their subtle cleverness and sad-girl stories. But leave those to me.

It began with an offer of sweet sesame pudding. My mother said it would be waiting for me when I got back, if only I'd be a good girl and go do the shopping. She smiled sweetly as I pulled on my shoes. Trying to make up for lost time, I guess. But why bother offering me sweet now, when it's salt I'm hooked on. Already she had a bad feeling about my peculiar tastes. Something gooey sweet would do the trick, she thought. Sweets always work on children. She thought she could change me, but it was a bit late for that. While the sticky pot may be a great place for drowning spirits, its dark thickness doesn't entice. Perhaps later, when I've calmed down and my tastes have grown a little simpler. Until then, it's stinky salt fish I'm after.

I walked away whistling because I was happy to have my mother's attention, in spite of the fact that the form it took didn't particularly appeal. I waved at the aunties gathering mulberry leaves in the fields, and at the uncles shovelling silkworm waste into the fish ponds. I didn't know that my mother's motive for offering the black sesame pudding had nothing to do with making up for any neurotic, return-to-infancy, childhood-deprivation fantasies on my part. She had something infinitely more immediate and material in mind. If beneath it all I had a niggling feeling that something was wrong, I ignored it.

Perhaps I shouldn't have. As it turned out my mother *was* thinking about abandonment. She wanted me out of the house that day so she could invite over nosy Old Lady Liu, the go-between, to talk behind my back about matters matrimonial. I know some girls are betrothed at ages much more tender than mine, but still! I was only fifteen. Wouldn't there be plenty of time for that later? Oh sure, I know it's tradition. I know my mother isn't personally to blame, that she is just doing what all good mothers are supposed to do if they want their daughters to live respectable lives. Note I didn't say happy. We all know that joy and sorrow are entirely matters of fate and have nothing whatsoever to do with planning.

So she had only my welfare in mind, but did she have to start so early? It was a cruel trick of patriarchy to make her the agent of our separation, which she so dreaded. Dreaded and longed for, just to have it over with. It was a complicated black sesame pudding she stirred up that afternoon.

As for me, I went to the market with my baby brother strapped to my back and a belly clamouring for something savoury.

As we approached the market, a young woman turned the corner down a dark alley, one strong brown arm bracing a basket of salted dainties atop her lovely head. The scent of the fish, or perhaps her scent, or, more likely still, some heady combination of the two wafted under my nose and caused a warmth to spread in the pit of my belly. I followed her right to the entrance of the market, ignoring the rice-wrap and sweet potato seller whose wares I otherwise would have paused to ponder.

I followed her right to the salt fish stall that she ran with her father. She set the basket down among numerous others filled with tiny blue-veined fish so small it would take twenty to make a modest mouthful, and others filled with long dry flats

of deep ocean fish the length of my forearm and half again.
I bought enough to flavour a good-sized vat of congee and then
breathed deeply to still my mind for the rest of the shopping.

After that I was hooked. The recollection of her bright eyes and
lean muscular arms reeled me in as surely as any live fish
seduced by worms or, perhaps more accurately, by shreds of
the flesh of their own kind. I made it my job to do the marketing in spite of the fact that it fell on top of all my regular
chores, of which there were many—fetching water, feeding
the chickens, sweeping the courtyard, taking care of my baby
brother and chopping all the meat and vegetables for every
meal. I was frugal, had an eye for fresh goods, and was a good
bargainer, so my mother was happy to send me. Besides, my
market morning absences were a perfect time for the go-
between to visit.

So while my mother secretly sweetened up that meddling
old nanny-goat, I managed to see the Salt Fish Girl every
fifteen days, except when she went back to the coast with
her father for more supplies. At first she took little notice of
me—just another skinny village girl with a bad complexion
and bony fingers. She sold me my fish without a word beyond the few necessary numbers and then turned to the impatient aunties eager to get home for their morning congee.

Whether it was because I was such a staunch regular, or
because of the way I gazed at her above the smelly baskets,
over which black flies hovered and dirty hands exchanged
coins, I can't be sure, but she began to recognize me and

put aside choice bits of merchandise in anticipation of my arrival. As she passed me the pungent preserves and took my coins, she stole a quick glance or two and flashed a shy smile through which her crooked teeth peeked endearingly.

A number of months passed in this manner before I worked up the nerve to invite her to come with me when market day was over. Of course I would catch a scolding for shirking my day's duties when I got home, but the adventure would be well worth the bother. In the late afternoon, we walked down to the river together, lay down in the tall grass and played tickling games until the stars sprinkled down from the night sky and covered us like bright, hungry kisses.

Then we separated. I walked home reeking of salt fish, took my anxious mother's scolding with a brave and defiant face, went to bed and tumbled into a deep and contented slumber.

At the new moon, I announced my decision to become a spinster. Tradition allows this if the family is agreeable and there is no protest from the local magistrate. My mother was furious. The go-between had found a suitable husband for me in the neighbouring village. He was the youngest son of a silk farmer, which was a common but respectable trade in these parts. He was blind in one eye, and ugly as sin. He was the only one of the farmer's sons who had been sent to school, and rumour had it that his father wanted to find him a position with the government. My mother had been making arrangements for us to meet that week.

"Forget it," I said. "I've made arrangements of my own."

"I never raised you to be so cheeky, I'm sure," she said.

"True. But aren't you glad I'll be here with you when you grow old, rather than scrubbing undies for my mother-in-law?"

I showed her all the money I had saved spinning silk for other village families, and announced that I would pay for my spinsterhood ceremony myself. I imagine that my mother was secretly pleased, in the mixed way that only a married woman can be, seeing that her daughter has escaped what she could not. She shook her finger at me and made a great scene of bawling me out, but there was something theatrical about it that assured me her anger was just for show. Later, though, before my father came upstairs to bed, I heard her crying softly in her room. I didn't really understand what this meant.

It was harder for the Salt Fish Girl. No spinsterhood tradition was observed on the coast and her father was dead set against her picking up the nasty customs of the locals. He forbade her to see me.

I hadn't expected this difficulty. I had assumed she would follow my example. I hadn't asked myself what I would do if she wasn't able to. Did I still want to enter the sisterhood on my own? It is hard to retract such a grave decision as I had made without losing some credibility. It would be harder for me to make further autonomous decisions regarding my life. Worse still, some of my sisters were upset with me for choosing spinsterhood for less than spiritual reasons. I sat tight and continued to see it through, even as I plotted how to rescue the Salt Fish Girl.

Her father could not stop me from coming to the market. I continued to buy fish from her until one afternoon, in a fury, he closed his stand early and marched her to the mud hut, on the edge of the market district, that they lived in when they were doing trade in town.

Desperation made me bold. I went to his stall the following market day, hoping to see her. I didn't, but the pungent odour of salt fish inspired a plan. Pumped full of fool's courage, I went up to him.

"Where is your daughter?"

"Thank you for your concern, but if you don't mind my saying, it's none of your business."

"That may or may not be the case," I said, more boldly still, "but won't you tell me anyway?"

"She's sick at home, no thanks to you."

"Then tell her I wish from the depths of my heart that she will get well soon and come to see me," I responded politely.

If there had been fewer people standing around watching, he would have reached out and slugged me. I could read the restraint in his eyes. As it was, he refused to sell me any salt fish, but pointed me in the direction of the butcher instead and said perhaps the man with the bloody apron could do something for me.

I thought to stay and argue, but decided I'd better back off for the time being.

The next market day, I passed by his house just as he was leaving. I heard his daughter pleading with him to be allowed out, to be taken along to the market. He refused sternly and locked her in the back room, where she wailed loudly long after he was out of earshot.

An hour later, I approached him at his stall.

"Where is your daughter on this auspicious market day?"

"She's at home with a fever, no thanks to you."

"Tell her I am praying to the Goddess of Mercy for her health and hope that she will come and see me soon."

He grunted.

I tried to buy some fish, but he said I didn't deserve it and would find what I deserved at the execution grounds on the other side of town. I would have spat at him, but there were too many people watching.

The following market day, when I approached him, he lunged at me in sheer fury, grabbed me around the neck and squeezed as hard as he could. I gasped desperately. It took five big men, including the bloody-aproned butcher, to pull him off me. The first thing I could smell when I could breathe again was . . . salt fish. The stink of it made me want to live more than ever.

I walked around the marketplace at a furious pace, trying to come up with a plan. The sky grew dark and the vendors one by one began to close their stalls. My stomach started to grumble. I hadn't eaten since early that morning. I circled the marketplace looking for a cooked-food vendor, but they had all packed up and gone home. The poultry man was busy with his fowl. He had three unsold chickens that he was trying to pack into the same basket, but they squawked and pecked at each other, as though each was to blame for her sister's unhappy fate. Suddenly the basket burst and the chickens ran about clucking madly. One ran farther afield than the rest. On an impulse I took off after it. The poultry vendor, in a hurry to get home, yelled after me, "If you can catch it, it's yours." The chicken led me right to the Salt Fish Girl's back window, where I pounced on it and clutched the squawking thing in my arms.

The Salt Fish Girl leaned out the window dangling a heavy fish hook. Expertly, she hooked me by the scruff of my collar and pulled me, chicken and all, into the house. "You could try to be a little more subtle," she said.

The chicken kept squawking. She drew a fish-gutting knife from her skirt and solemnly slit its throat. Blood spurted up in a long arc, and drenched me in a dark shower.

In the downpour I hatched a plan. "Pack a bag," I said. "We're going to escape."

She gave me a mop and some clean clothes. I sopped up the blood quickly, put on the clean clothes and helped her out the window. With the chicken in one hand and the bloody clothes in the other, I jumped out after her.

We dug a shallow hole in the backyard, buried the bloody clothes and then ran to the river. There, we stole a skiff and floated downstream.

In the morning, finding his daughter missing, the old merchant ran to the police and accused me of kidnapping. The police searched my parents' house and found nothing. They said I had not come home since setting out for market the previous day. Eventually, their questioning led the police to the bloody-aproned butcher and the other four men who had dragged the salt fish merchant off me the day before.

"Perhaps," said the butcher, "he's accusing the girl to conceal something terrible he's done to her. Surely it's at least worth searching his house."

The police made a careful search of the merchant's house and found nothing but baskets and baskets of sweet and pungent salt fish. The merchant shot a scornful look at the butcher, who stood in the doorway. The police were just about to call off the search for the day, when the youngest of them noticed some newly turned soil behind the house. As I had hoped, the bloody clothes were unearthed and identified by both my parents and the butcher as mine. The poor old salt fish merchant stood accused of murder.

Many miles downstream, munching on boiled chicken, I chuckled at the thought.

The Salt Fish Girl asked me why I was laughing and so I told her. But instead of laughing with me, she pulled a long face.

"What's wrong?" I asked.

"I don't want my father to die," she whispered, and began to cry.

It's a bit late for that, I thought. *You should have said so a long time ago.* But I said nothing and put my arms around her. I could feel her heart pounding inside her rib cage. She sobbed and howled so desperately that I said, "We could go back. We'd still be in time to save him."

But she shook her head, and said through her tears, "What's done is done. What happens is what's meant to be."

I held her and said nothing. She continued to weep and eventually sobbed herself to sleep.

And that, I suppose, was the beginning of our quarrels.

Miranda

Serendipity, 2044-2062

THE MEMORY DISEASE

1. The Business Suit

My parents were so anxious about my odour, I didn't dare tell them about the scales, which didn't appear at the bottom of the tub with much frequency anyway. For all the years of my childhood, not a month went by without a secret trip to some doctor's office or herbalist's shop in the Unregulated Zone. Once, I had to drink an infusion made by pouring hot water into a jar packed with live, angry bees. Once I had to drink a soup made from embryonic chickens still sleeping in their eggs and coated in mucusy egg white. I don't know why I should find such things unpleasant. I eat eggs and I eat chicken. Why should I be horrified by the liminal state between the two?

Years passed. Time was measured by the various foul-tasting remedies I took, slight alterations in the bite and weight of the odour, and my mother's various admonitions against my father's growing obsession. Finally, my mother persuaded my father to take me to a Saturna-sanctioned medical doctor and to stop taking me out of the compound and feeding me unproven remedies.

The doctor prescribed two kinds of pills. There were little green ones that made me jittery at night and bad-tempered in the daytime. I took them until my eyes sank into my head and I grew so thin from lack of sleep that my parents feared for my life. There were fat red ones that were almost impossible to swallow. They made me scream and laugh like a hyena at anything anyone said, funny or not. This made my parents very nervous. In the meantime, the strange cat-pee odour that seeped from beneath my skin intensified to the point where my mother too began to worry.

My father roamed Real World in his Business Suit. He spent so much time covered from top to toe in black rubber that his skin took on a deathly pallor. You could see all the veins in his hands and face. Behind his eyes you could see there was a lot of mental activity going on which he did not share with us. Real World was awash with a plethora of ideologically interesting half-truths, in such abundance that only the most obsessed insomniacs could sort them, and even then, any action based on information gleaned was a gamble. My father's eyes took on the sheen of the waking dead. They had a sinister gleam because of all the secrets he was keeping.

When I was twelve, a new boy came to our school. His name was Ian Chestnut. I remember him walking into cyborg science class, and the rustle of whispers that travelled across the classroom. He was small, slender and very fair. I wondered how he'd register with the popular kids, whether they would want him to be one of theirs because his features were so exquisitely lovely, or whether they'd decide he was too effeminate and therefore to be shunned. As it turned out, he wasn't the kind to give them that chance. It was me he approached at recess time, while the pretty girls tried out lip gloss in the bathroom. I sat in the porch of a boarded-up chapel doorway, eating sliced apples my mother had prepared for me that morning and neatly packed into a shimmery yellow Tupperware box. He sat down beside me. "Can I have a slice?" he asked.

I raised an eyebrow. Couldn't he smell my foul odour? "Sure, I guess," I said, holding the box towards him.

He took a slice. "Have you heard the word of God?" he said.

I laughed. "At Serendipity we're taught to place our faith in reason," I said. "I believe spirituality is a personal matter."

"So do I," he said, offended. "I'm not trying to push anything on you."

"Okay," I said. "But no one talks like that here."

He was quiet.

"You want another slice of apple?" I offered.

He took another slice. "You don't need to feel the pain you feel, you know," he said.

"Listen," I said. "It's nice you came to talk to me and everything, but I'm not into all this religion stuff. Do you know how to play twenty-one?" My mother had been going out to play cards or mah-jong a lot lately, and we sometimes practised together. It made me feel very grown up.

Ian shook his head.

"I could show you if you want."

"Okay," he said.

I took a deck out of my back pocket and dealt two for him and two for myself. "This is just practice," I said, "so we can show each other what we have. Later, when we play for real, then you can't show me yours any more."

Ian caught on quickly and we spent the rest of the break gambling for pebbles which we picked up off the ground. At lunchtime, I went to look for him. Secretly, I wondered if I could win his lunch off him. I was terribly curious about what this boy ate. Ian came from the fabled Painted Horse, a Nextcorp town I had heard my parents speak about under their breath in several of their increasingly frequent arguments. But when I got to the lunchroom, Mrs. Sharma was on supervision and had already placed Ian between two of the smaller, more mischievous boys in class, perhaps hoping he would eventually become a moderating influence. I slunk off to my usual corner and ate alone.

The next day at recess he was waiting for me in the boarded-up doorway. "Want to play twenty-one?" he said.

I grinned. "Okay," I said. "Let's use something real for the kitty. Not just rocks. I have peanuts and raisins."

"I have a Snax bar," Ian said.

I was disappointed. I had expected something much more exotic. Still, it was great having someone who was actually willing to spend time with me, though I was suspicious of Ian's motives. I knew a little about the fundamentalist Christianity of Nextcorp from Spying. This was my first experience of it up close, but Ian didn't strike me as particularly menacing. I laid my bag of peanuts and raisins on the concrete between us and dealt him two cards off the top of the pack. Then I took two for myself. A jack and a seven—I hated in-betweenish hands like that, not enough to ensure a win, but enough to make it only too easy to go over. "Another card?" I asked Ian, eyeing him carefully as my mother told me I should always eye opponents, to see if I could gauge from his mood what he might be holding. His eyes twinkled. There was mischief in them.

"Bring 'em on," he said.

I dealt him a card.

He looked at it. "Another one," he said.

I was just handing it to him when a shadow fell across the kitty. It was Mr. Kingsley, the math teacher from grade four, whom I'd hated because he was so strict. "Gambling in the house of the Lord?" he said, tossing a quick glance at the boarded-up door. He snatched the cards out of our hands and took the kitty too. "Who's your teacher now, Miranda?" he said. "Mrs. Sharma, right?"

Mrs. Sharma gave us a detention, though only for twenty minutes. Still, I felt very pleased with myself. I'd finally done something worthy of punishment. The world was opening up.

Ian said his parents were intelligence agents for Saturna. They had recently been discovered by the councillors at Painted Horse. They would have received the death sentence if Saturna had not traded them for two of its own, who had recently been charged with espionage in Serendipity. Ian said he thought his parents were double agents, that they were really working for Nextcorp, and were on a mission right this very minute. Did I want to come over and make my own assessment?

From the outside Ian's house didn't look that different from ours. It was a low-roofed bungalow with pink aluminum siding and a white roof. But inside it was an electronic jungle. The walls, the ceilings, even parts of the floor were covered in screens and consoles. Images and numbers flickered everywhere you looked.

"Look around, don't be shy," Ian's mother said, handing me a glass of brilliant blue liquid to drink. Her teeth gleamed white. Her eyes were both prosthetic and had a terrible piercing intelligence to them. She was immaculately dressed in a stiff, shiny metallic dress. But she had an awful smell about her, like rusting iron only much more intense. Like an ancient battleship left to rot in some forgotten harbour.

"Is that Ian's new friend?" boomed a very manly voice from the back of the house. Presently, a tall, wide man came thumping down the hallway. He wore a sleeveless T-shirt and his arm muscles rippled unnaturally. "Welcome, little miss," he said. His smile was every bit as white as Mrs. Chestnut's. I did my best not to gawp.

"Hurry up and drink your drink," Ian said. "I want to show you something."

I was afraid of the blue drink. Would it turn my eyes funny like Mrs. Chestnut's? Or give me overinflated muscles like Mister's? I took a very small sip and put it down beside a bowl containing unnaturally large pink blossoms.

I followed Ian to his room at the back of the house. Like the other rooms the walls screamed streams of numbers, flashing lights, and screens with small moving images. I realized then that it served no purpose, that it was just wallpaper, tasteless maybe, but benign.

In the far corner, their simple elegance dwarfed by the noisy decor, stood two headless mannequins holding up two children's-size Business Suits in neon green and orange.

"They're Swimming Suits," Ian said. "You move through Real World as though it's under water. The added bonus is that no one can see you."

"Great for spies," I said, fishing.

"Yeah," he said. "Except that it's really hard to control your direction and stuff. They're emotionally guided. Mostly all I ever see is flashes of things."

I felt momentarily ashamed of my boring, antiquated playing cards, in spite of my mother's voice at the back of my mind reminding me of the importance of keeping old games, old stories and traditional values alive. Sometimes it was difficult to hang on to that, especially at moments like this when the glittering technologies of the new world beckoned. "Those are pretty cool, I guess," I said nonchalantly.

"You want to try them out?" he said. "We can go together."

I was a bit scared, but I nodded anyway.

"You take the orange one," he said.

I put my arm inside the right sleeve first. It felt the same on the inside as it did on the outside. For some reason, this surprised me. But I climbed inside the thing and zipped it up. It was a bit tight.

"That's good," Ian said. "You want all the contacts to work."

But the hood was a bit too big and the contours of the face mask were all wrong. The eye seals were too close together, the nose piece was too long, the mouth too small, the ears too low. "It's going to make it hard to see and hear, isn't it?" I asked.

"Never mind, it's just for a short trip," Ian said. "I'll guide you and you'll be all right."

When we were properly sealed inside, he turned the suits on. I was falling and then, splash! I was underwater, swimming down the street outside Ian's house. Ian was beside me. He took my hand. We glided down the road, took the shortcut across the park. The school loomed in the distance, but the colours weren't quite right. My eyes felt blurry and wet, as though water were seeping into the mask. There was a bit of electronic fizzle, which felt like salt water in the eyes. I blinked to clear them. When I opened them again I was crouching on the floor in a wet basement. The wetness was a bit tacky, a bit viscous and reddish brown. It was all over the floor and spattered across the wall. At the far end of the room, three men in chains lay on the floor, bruised and unconscious. I swam towards them. The one in the middle had a black eye and many great, bleeding welts across his back. He was whimpering like a dog. It was my father.

I screamed and kicked, screamed, kicked and gasped.

"Turn it off, turn it off," I yelled. Everything went black and the mask felt tight and claustrophobic against my face. I ripped it off. "Did you see that? Did you see that? Were you there with me?"

"Shhh," said Ian. "You don't need to yell."

"Where were you?"

"You let go of my hand."

"My father . . ." I wailed, and burst into tears.

I think Ian and Mrs. Chestnut made me drink something. I think they were trying to get me to lie down. All I really remember is grabbing my coat and rushing out the door onto the cool streets of Serendipity and hurrying home to my father as fast as I could.

My mother let me in. "You're home early," she said. "Was it all right at Ian Chestnut's?"

"Where's Dad?" I said.

"Downstairs in his study, I think," said my mother. "Mucking around with his silly Business Suit."

I pushed past her and ran downstairs.

My father was there, lying face down on the floor, still as stone in his Business Suit. In the course of the night's journey he must have swept his hand over his desk, because there was a mess of paper, some loose, some clipped, on top of him. I brushed it all away, but as I did so a few words caught my eye—"my daughter Miranda" the paper said. Absently, I stuffed it and the pages attached into my pocket. I rolled my dad over and pulled the mask off his face. I reached to the wrist console. His opposite hand was sluggish, but it tried to push me away. "Don't . . ." he said. "Don't interfere . . ."

"How can I not interfere, Dad?"

He shoved me with aggression I did not expect. My head slammed against the corner of the desk. I heard the sound of rushing water. A coolness flooded from the top of my head down to my feet as though I had suddenly been immersed in water.

When I regained consciousness I was in my own room in my own bed. Both my mother and my father leaned over me, their faces full of concern. My mother said something about a fever. My dad nodded gravely. He tried to get me to drink something blue from a glass, but I was afraid of the drink and refused to open my mouth. That's all I remember.

When I woke again, they weren't there. I felt very hot and very thirsty. There was a glass of orange juice beside the bed. I drank it and lay back down. It wasn't comfortable. There was something in my pocket. I fished it out, and the events of earlier that evening came rushing back to me. ". . . my daughter Miranda . . ." What had my father been writing? I uncrumpled the paper and read:

Dear Dr. Flowers,

I hope you will forgive me for taking the risk of writing to you from one corporation's compound to another. Please trust that my motives are neither political nor financial, but purely of a personal nature. A co-worker of mine, a very old woman who does accounts on the ground floor and claims to be your aunt, informs me that a number of workers living at Painted Horse 1000, including your own daughter, are suffering from symptoms similar to those my daughter Miranda is experiencing. The most immediately noticeable symptom is an odd odour that does not seem to emanate from any particular part of the body, but hangs over the child like a cloud. The neighbours describe the odour as akin to cat urine. Others say she smells of pepper. As for myself, were I presented with such an odour and not told its source, I would say it is a stink of durian, a tropical fruit I recall from my childhood, though none is available in the Saturna compound where I work and live.

The child also has some skin trouble which might simply be an aggravated form of psoriasis unrelated to the odour. As well, she experiences occasional breathing difficulty, particularly when she is asleep.

So far, none of the professionals I have taken her to see has been able to ascertain whether the disease, if this is indeed what it is, is acquired or hereditary. The child is otherwise normal, except for two small fistulas, one above each ear, which she has inherited from her mother.

I am certain some of these disorders are simple enough, and may not necessarily be related. I recount them to you merely for the sake of giving as much information as possible to work with. While the child's odour is a difficult thing for all members of the family to contend with, it is more her long-term health that concerns me. My co-worker, your aunt, suggested that there are some who believe these symptoms to be peculiar to a new breed of auto-immune diseases, related to genetic and other industrial modifications to our food supply, that may prove quite devastating in the decades to come.

I understand that I take a grave risk in forwarding this correspondence to you, as neither of our employers is likely

to view it without suspicion. Let this only be an indication
of my sincerity, and of my great need for your assistance.
   Yours truly,
   Stewart Ching

The letter was scrawled and messy and full of crossed-out
words and hesitations. This, I surmised and feared, was the
rough draft of a letter that had indeed been sent.

   It was terribly upsetting to think that my parents might
know what I dreamt at night. I had no consciousness of
sleep-talking, though sometimes the intensity of my dream
world frightened me. But only sometimes. At other times
it seemed the most natural thing in the world that I should
remember things that went on before I was born, things
that happened in other lifetimes. They happened to me; I
was there, and the memories are continuous. Why should
they be anything but? I did not realize that other people
did not have these memories. I did not think of myself as a
child afflicted by history, unable to escape its delights or
its torments. Because my existence in this lifetime had
been carried out entirely within the narrow confines of
the Serendipity, I did not understand my condition as a
"condition," nor did I know that there were others in
other compounds or out in the Unregulated Zone who
were afflicted with variations of the same bizarre symptoms, and whose bodies reeked of oranges, or tobacco, or
rotten eggs, or cabbage. Or else of silk, of cotton, of coffee, of blood and carnage, of coal, of freshly baked bread,
of machine oil, of dust and rain and mud. The disease had
not yet reached the point of epidemic. In fact, there were
not yet any indications that this strange disorder was causing

any real harm, except, perhaps, at a social level. Its sufferers had not yet begun their compulsive march into the rivers and oceans, unable to resist the water's pull. Their bodies had not yet begun to wash up on the shores like fragments of an ancient rock separated from their seemingly indestructible mass of origin and pummelled smooth by the tide.

What I did know was that my father intended to subject me to some treatment far stranger and more dangerous than anything I had undergone up to that point, and I did not want to go. I did not understand the fierce love that drove him any more than I understood his fears of the rapidly changing world. I was a sheltered child, living out my parents' utopian dream as though it were reality. They did not show me the cracks. And out of loyalty and love for them, when I sensed the cracks, I refused to see them. But of course this unspoken pact could not last.

The second letter was neither signed nor dated:

Our team of medical experts considers your daughter a perfect subject for our current drug trials. Some minor surgery may also be involved. Please understand that because this disease is a new and undocumented one, it will be necessary for us to monitor her progress over the long term. For this reason, it is important that she reside in close proximity to our offices, for up to fifteen years. A parent or guardian will thus be required. If you are prepared to relocate to the Painted Horse Democratic Urban Village located off Highway 10 in the former municipality of Greenwood, British Columbia, we would be happy to take her on as a test patient. The cost of the treatment is 8,000

Painted Horse units or the equivalent in U.S. dollars. Un-fortunately, at this time, no grants to cover these costs are available to non–Painted Horse citizens.

The next letter was only too enthusiastic in its response.

Dear Dr. Flowers,

How can I thank you for your kind offer? My wife and I are extremely pleased that our daughter has been offered a place in your clinic under your supervision. My wife has agreed to make the journey with my daughter. Unfortu-nately, as I am tied to my job, I shall not be able to accom-pany them. It will require some time for us to pull together the necessary resources. I will write you again as soon as they are in place.

I returned to the first letter and read it again. I was shocked. Suddenly, and for the first time, I felt dirty. I felt the shame my father had felt since he had first plucked that dangerous fruit. The patch of sky I could see, where an edge of curtain fluttered away from the open window, was very dark. I looked at my bedside clock. It was just after three in the morning. I didn't want to wake my sleep-ing family, but I was full of a terrible restlessness I could not repress. As quietly as possible, I slipped out of bed and padded down the hallway to the bathroom. Without turn-ing on the lights, I groped for the bathtub. I put the plug into it and turned on the faucets to half strength so that the sound of rushing water was a little quieter than it might have been. I sat at the edge of the tub and waited patiently until it was full. Then I slipped out of my flannel nightdress and into the steamy water. I rolled a face cloth liberally in the soap and began to wash. I scrubbed and scrubbed my skin until it hurt. I applied extra soap beneath my arms, to my feet and between my legs. I shampooed my hair twice and swished the suds into the water. I used a brush for my back and brushed until I felt blood rise to the surface. But the whole time, that foul pepper and cat-pee odour lingered through the scents of soap and sham-poo. It wasn't dirt. It came from the inside. If I stayed in the water long enough, I thought, perhaps it would leach out. I lay back to soak, as though I could soak the empty scent of water into my body. I closed my eyes and sank into the heat.

I didn't sleep exactly, and I wouldn't describe what hap-pened as a dream. I felt a dull ache along my spinal cord that evolved, slowly at first, and then with alarming speed, into a searing pain so sharp that I shot upright. I pulled the plug and as I did so, the pain began to diminish. When the tub was empty, the pain was gone. But in the morning when I went to the toilet, I noticed a dark streak of blood on my underpants. I'm dying, I thought. They are right to send me away. But I didn't really want to go. To leave Serendipity would be a terrible exile, the ultimate pun-ishment for this strange disease over which I had no con-trol. I closed my eyes and imagined a steel table, sharp tools and curved ones with empty gaps the shape of organs. I imagined a bright searchlight and my own body splayed open like a gutted trout. I opened my eyes. I unrolled a long strip of toilet paper and squished it into a thick wad, which I stuffed between my legs. I had to put on a show of health.

"Poor Miranda," said my mother when I came into the kitchen. "You don't look so well. You don't have to go to school if you don't want to."

I sat down at the kitchen table. She put a plate of bacon and eggs in front of me. The eggs jiggled like crazy eyes. Looking too closely at the viscous film that held the yolks in place made my stomach turn. "Can I just have some juice?" I said.

She went to the fridge and poured me a glass. "Maybe you better stay in today, Miranda."

"Why? I'm fine," I said. I dug into the jiggly eggs with steely determination.

I ate as quickly as possible and tried to ignore the feeling of nausea that rose in my throat. I gulped the juice and made for the door. "See ya later, Mom," I said.

I was early for school. Ian was waiting for me near the front entrance. "I think the school used to be a Secret Service building before," he said. "Come and see what I found." I followed him down the corridor at the back of the school where the grade eights had their lockers. There was a narrow hallway that led to an alternative door to the gym, one we never used—with two exceptions I could recall. One was a fire drill. The other was the time we used it as a stage door when we put on a student production of *A Midsummer Night's Dream*. To the right of the door was a boys' bathroom which doubled as a janitor's closet. I'd never really noticed it before. After looking sharply to the left and right, Ian led me through this door. There was a urinal in one corner and a dirty sink in the other. Against the far wall was a big closet. Ian slid the door open. It was full of filthy grey mops and red buckets with the traces of dirty water dried onto their sides. Behind them was another small door, like the door to a safe, raised a metre off the ground. Ian fished a paper clip from his pocket and picked the lock. On the other side lay darkness and a steel ladder. Ian climbed through the hole and began to descend.

"No way," I said. "I'm not going down there."

"Come on," he said. "It's a cool place." His hand poked out of the hole, a gesture of encouragement.

"I don't think so. The bell's gonna go any minute."

"Chicken," he said.

I stepped into the hole and descended into the dark.

It was hot at the bottom. We were in a boiler room of some sort. I could hear water running and the occasional clank of metal suddenly expanding or contracting. My eyes adjusted to the dark and I could see a lot of rusty drums and pipes, some with clocks attached and numbers rapidly indicating the passage of time and the consumption of energy. We walked along the wall to a set of swinging double doors. Ian stood on tiptoe to peek through the windows and then led me out into a clean shiny corridor, the floors done in the same speckled white linoleum that covered the floors upstairs. Like a real spy, he flattened his back against one wall when voices came from the main corridor which ran perpendicular to our little side one. Women's voices, a language I didn't understand. They passed by without our seeing them, dark bodies in blue uniforms with strange curling text in a language I didn't recognize printed in large white letters across their backs. Some carried mops. One pulled a large industrial vacuum cleaner.

"Who are those women?" I whispered to Ian.

"What women?" he said.

I pointed.

"Oh, them," he said. "They're not women. They're Janitors." And then in the lowest whisper possible he said, "Most of them are illegal, you know. And they're primary carriers of the Contagion."

"What contagion?" I said.

"The Contagion," he said. "You know. You have some secondary symptoms. So does my mom. Lots of people in Painted Horse do."

"Never heard of it," I said, but his flippant expression of knowledge registered as a shock.

"Never seen Rudy Flowers' dissections on TV?"

"We don't do TV," I said. Didn't he know what a thing of the past it was?

"He rearranges the organs of the afflicted," Ian said. "They are the new language of God."

My eyes bugged out. "He what?"

"The body is the language of the Third Testament," Ian said.

"Saturna is a secular corporation," I told him. "We don't believe in that kind of stuff."

The sound of footsteps came from around a bend in the corridor. Ian pulled me into a side hallway. Pressed against the wall, I watched another group of Janitors pass, their tired feet scuffing against the floor. In horror I watched their backs as they moved away from us. There were rectangular holes in their uniforms that ran from the tailbone to the base of the neck. The muscle and skin of their backs had been replaced with some kind of transparent silicone composite so that you could see their spines and behind them, their hearts pounding, their livers and kidneys swimming in oceans of blood and gristle. We had studied anatomy at school. I could see that the organs had been shifted, had been carefully arranged like stones in a formal garden, mimicking the asymmetrical aesthetics of nature, but with human intention.

"Who did that to them?" I asked Ian.

"They're under observation," he said. "Must be having some kind of experimental therapy."

My head swirled with this new information. I wanted to ask Ian whether his mother had had Dr. Flowers' treatment, but didn't quite dare. "What happens to them afterwards?" I whispered. But Ian just put a finger to his lips. He didn't want the Janitors to catch us.

I felt very claustrophobic. I didn't care where the corridor led. "It's five to nine," I said. "We'll be late for class."

"For a non-Christian you're awfully obedient," Ian said.

But when I began walking back in the direction we'd come, he followed me.

It was hard to concentrate on classes. My head swam with the events of the past twenty-four hours. I fidgeted in my seat. My legs itched. I scratched them. The durian stench rose around me so thick you could almost touch it. I despaired as, up to that point, I had never despaired before.

When I came home from school my mother took three varieties of ice cream from the freezer. "Sundaes!" I said. "Yes!" And then, "I'll go get Dad. He likes that weird sauce with walnuts in it, remember?"

"Dad's still at work," my mother said. "He can have one later."

I was disappointed. My dad knew how to stack the scoops and drizzle the sauce so that the sundaes looked just like the ones in the advertisements for Sunny Saturdays, a restaurant chain that specialized in burgers and ice cream. My mom's weren't nearly as artfully built. Her scoops slid off one another, the sauce clotted at the top and ran too thin down the sides. It still tasted good though. I sighed and dug into her offering. We ate supper without my father too. "He's working overtime," my mother explained. I shuddered. I knew the reason. It was bedtime by the time my father emerged from the basement stairwell, pale as bread and limping. He was so pale, in fact, that you could see the veins pulsing beneath the skin of his face and neck. He looked more like a man who had emerged from a coffin than a man just home from work. By the sight of him, I could tell that the Receivers General had been heavy-handed with their truncheons today. I felt angry and powerless.

That night when the family was asleep, I again pulled myself up out of bed. My durian cloud followed me, palpable as snow. I moved slowly, praying it wouldn't spill through my parents' bedroom door. I moved half by my own volition and half by a peculiar sort of instinct that I couldn't describe later. I tiptoed down to the basement, again slowing near Aaron's room so that that smell wouldn't suddenly rush under the door and wake him. I slipped into my father's office. In the pale green light that leaked in from the street and through the narrow ground-level window, I could make out his desk, his chair, the ominous black shape of the Business Suit on its rack. I pulled the chair up to it and took the pieces down one by one. I stuck my feet into the leggings. They were way too long, so I made a tuck under the knee and jammed the small fold inside the larger one so it would stay. I pulled on the torso piece and zipped it shut. It was also too big, but there was nothing to be done. The armpieces had to be tucked and folded. My feet swam in the boots. The hood and mask flopped untidily over my face. There was no pulling them tighter. I knew my enterprise might come to nothing, but I had to try. I flicked the suit on. The banging and clanking began. I strode across the fiery burned-out landscape, turning to the left and right to see what was around me. There were holes in the landscape here and there that I hadn't seen when my father wore the suit. Perhaps they occurred because of the folds and loose contacts between the suit and my body. I walked as tall and as bravely as I could. In the distance I saw the razor disc birds gather. I raised my arm in preparation. When they swooped towards me, I pointed a finger. I aimed at their open beaks and poured a long thin stream of digits into their mouths. The birds swelled and flew up into the virtual sky. I could hear them crowing gleefully in the distance for quite some time after they disappeared from sight. But having given them so many numbers I now felt strangely weak. Still, I walked the path as best I could. No doubt I looked lame and patchy, not at all the heroic figure my father cut as he worked. I reached the door of the dungeon and was admitted by the guards. But when the Receivers General came to chain me to the wall, I jabbed my fingers into their eyes. I kicked them in the guts and shot streams of fire from my arms and knees simultaneously until they were burned to a black skeletal crisp. I managed to turn off the suit just a fraction of a second before I collapsed to the ground in exhaustion.

When my father found me in the morning he was beside himself, half with fury and half with worry. "Miranda, what have you done? The Business Suit is not for children." He pulled the pieces off me and carried me upstairs to bed. But when he reached my room, my mother was standing in the doorway, letters in hand. "What are these letters, Stewart?" she said. "Your daughter and I are not chattel to be exchanged without our consent."

Whatever else was said, I was far too delirious to catch it. I lay in bed for the rest of the day dreaming of razor disc birds and burnt Receivers General. When I finally came round, I learned we were broke and my father was out of a job. A tax collector was not supposed to give money back to the people. And to assault a Receiver General was an indictable offence punishable by death. It was worse than assaulting a police officer. In light of his years of service, however, Saturna elected merely to retire him, but would not press charges. There would be no gut-splitting, organ-rearranging surgery for me. There would be no separating the family. But neither would there be any more Serendipity.

"Never mind," said my mother. "It's high time for Dad to begin living a more restful life. We can move to the Unregulated Zone and open a produce store. If we sell durians everyone will think they are the source of that smell, which really isn't so bad anyway. And we will have money for our old age."

My father was inconsolable. "All my life I've worked for Saturna so that I could collect a modest pension and have a comfortable old age. I did nothing wrong. I don't understand how this could happen." He refused to blame me.

Needless to say, I felt terribly guilty. "I'll do all the ordering and stocking," I told them.

2. The Unregulated Zone

We sold our new sofa and the meticulously preserved dining set to Mr. Burke. My father's armchair went to a colleague who had staunchly though unsuccessfully defended him at the office. A few of my mother's old cabaret friends took the good dishes and some of the most recently purchased pieces of Tupperware. We sold the rest of the furniture in a garage sale, and packed away the small saleable items as start-up goods for the new store. The only item of furniture we kept was my mother's old vanity, which took up the bulk of space in the small trailer we attached to the back of my brother's ancient Honda, the one car remaining once we had cleared all our debts. The remainder of the space was taken up by two largish cartons full of dresses from my mother's cabaret years, which she refused to part with.

We found a little corner grocery store with living quarters attached in a residential area just outside the downtown core. It was well over a hundred years old and reeked of mildew and rot. We stocked the shelves with the remains of our old life, traded books for kale and arugula, pots for pumpkins, and furniture for bread. A few U.S. and Canadian dollars still circulated, although the national banks were so enfeebled and so at the mercy of corporate whim that few people trusted those currencies. Some people accepted Saturna, Soni, Monsanta or Nextcorp dollars, but the trade wars had given rise to conversion inconsistencies and technical problems, especially in the Unregulated Zone where none of them were, strictly speaking, legal. Most people preferred to barter. We made our profits in slight surpluses of goods.

Fortunately, my parents turned out to have good heads for business. My mother contacted the suppliers and growers and cheered them with her easy grace and sweet voice. My father took meticulous care of the books and watched the counter in the daytime. In the afternoons, my brother and I took turns at the till, although as his used auto parts business in the back grew, he worked in the grocery less and less. Which was fine by me. It was the one place where I could have a moment's respite from other people's uneasiness with my smell, the one place where, nestled among the freshest and plumpest durians the city had to offer, I could blend with my environment and those who passed through found the odour sweet and pleasant. People seemed more than happy to buy durians from us. In fact, we developed a bit of a reputation, so that we were seldom asked about the fruits, as people came to us with advance knowledge. Customers lined up outside our doors on Thursday and Saturday mornings when our shipments arrived, and snapped them up. But once a stranger passed through and asked me how they tasted. "Delicious," I said. But truth be told, not a morsel of the fruit ever passed my lips. The thought disgusted me.

When the shop wasn't busy, I swept the floors and mopped them down with bleach and water. I tidied the fruits and sprayed the vegetables with a fine mist of cool water to keep them from wilting. I straightened the dried goods on the shelves. Then I sat quietly behind the counter and applied myself diligently to my homework.

My mother was pleased, seeing this behaviour as evidence of an innately sweet and docile nature. She didn't have a clue how deeply motivated I was by guilt, and of course, I couldn't tell her. Not that there was much mischief a social pariah like me could get up to anyway. Three mornings a week, I attended a makeshift school in the basement of the St. James' United Church. But because of my smell, the other children shunned me, and so I studied my lessons alone in the corner, and rushed home without a word to anyone as soon as the session was over.

My brother's auto repair shop at the back of the store, which he called "Donna's" after his drowned wife, was at this time in our lives providing well over half the income the family made. When we had moved into this unregulated house, with the store on the ground level and the garage out back, my mother had begun a small garden in the backyard. My father encouraged her to grow vegetables for our own consumption and for sale at the back of the store, and so my mother planted a few rows of beans and lettuce, mostly in order to please him. "I'm worried that what I grow won't be safe to eat," she said, by way of excuse. "Nothing we buy is guaranteed any more," he said.

But she was really more interested in a pretty garden. She planted several bushes of white chrysanthemums in one corner to recall those my father had brought to her dressing room on their first meeting. She planted hydrangeas and rhododendrons along the walls and a thick hedge of raspberries to separate the garden from Aaron's messy work-yard. She planted local ferns, bleeding hearts and snowdrops, surrounded by unpatterned small-leafed hostas with their elegantly shaped leaves. These she interspersed with tall, crazy-looking hollyhocks in many different colours, which I loved. She laid in a rock garden, scattered with mosses and succulents, and a little pond with lilies and goldfish. I don't know where she found the money to do this, unless she drew from secret savings. But I suspected that it was more just that she had a very green thumb and a sweet, sociable disposition that invited others to help her, to give her rocks and plants and tips that made the garden thrive. So in some ways, what went on behind the store was more fruitful than what went on in front, but it didn't matter. Somehow we maintained our sanity and equilibrium and found daily joy in little things.

After the stock market crisis and the further devaluation of the dollar, after the number of cars on the street diminished to a dull roar, the number of reconstructed bicycles significantly increased. My brother developed a side business in bicycle parts and continued to thrive. He worked quickly and cheaply and when his clients couldn't pay cash, he accepted other things—fresh meat, clothes, radios, eggs. He even accepted a few ancient and battered televisions, which were enjoying a sort of renaissance here in the Unregulated Zone. Several pirate TV stations had started up on a low-intensity broadcast that could be picked up for several blocks around each station. And we continued to do reasonably, even as the big corporations, Saturna and Nextcorp among them, laid off workers and cut pensions to the point that my father began to think that perhaps his dismissal had been a blessing in disguise. Workers flooded out of the corporate compounds and into the Unregulated Zone. Many people, my father's ex-colleagues included, could not work out ways to make a living. The missions were full, and people died in droves beneath the bridges and in the open-air rooms of half-collapsed buildings.

It was then that stories of the dreaming disease began to circulate more widely. We heard from our customers of a girl who smelled of cooking oil, who remembered all the wars ever fought. She could recall and recount every death, every rape, every wound, every moment of suffering that had ever been inflicted by a member of her ancestral lineage. The only place she could find relief from this barrage of collective memory was in water. She moved into the family bathroom and spent most of her days and nights in the tub, but after a while, even that was not enough. The stories she told were terrible. She told her family she was going to drown herself. Already in deep despair over the content of her stories, her family did nothing to stop her. Her older brother, the only one left in the family with remotely steady nerves, went with her to the seaside. She walked into the ocean. A woman dived in after her, but her brother followed the woman and dragged her back. The girl kept walking under water, until the brother lost sight of the bubbles that trailed behind her. He waited patiently until high tide for her body to float to the surface and wash ashore. He waited for the next tide and the next. Word has it that he waits there still. Passersby bring him food and clothes. He has grown thin as a rake, and his beard sweeps the ground. Many others who have since acquired the disease have walked past him into the ocean, their bodies later beached by the tide. But his sister's doesn't return, and so he waits and waits and waits.

As for me, even though in some ways it seemed the world around me was collapsing, the fog of guilt lifted a little, and I felt lighter than I had in a long time. And as I grew bigger, the intensity of the durian stench that emanated from my person diminished gradually to a low hum, still quite pungent behind the ears as well as in the obvious places, but really no more offensive than anyone else's body odour.

I did not mean to kill my mother. My father said it was not my fault, that it was an unfortunate accident, that any one of us could momentarily have lost her or his grip, that I wasn't to blame. But though I never told him, I wasn't so sure. The moment unfolded slowly, each second unfurling like a long gauzy banner. The box seemed to fall in stop-frames, each following deliberately but inevitably from the previous as though it had been rehearsed for precision a thousand times over. So slowly that surely I could have reached out, snatched it from its fatal course or nudged it out of the way. Or shouted sooner and given her time to run. Instead, we both stood there, she and I, with our eyes wide and our mouths open as the box made its terrible journey from my hands to her heart. We did not watch the box, we watched each other, and just before the box hit her, shattering her rib cage and crushing her lungs, I thought I saw her mouth the word "goodbye," as though she knew this was her moment of departure. And then the terrible sound of bones snapping, of wood splintering and durians skidding absurdly across the store-room floor.

Let me catch my breath. What happened was this. I was sitting at the front counter when the durian man arrived. In the back, my mother received ten wooden crates. My father was asleep in his room and my brother was in the back, lying under an old Datsun 210 soldering a new exhaust system to its rusted underbelly. There were no customers in the store, so my mother asked me to come and help her put five of the boxes up on a shelf to make way for a shipment of vegetables that was coming later in the afternoon. And so I climbed up the stepladder and she handed the crates up to me one by one. They were heavy, those dark reptilian fruits in their wooden cages, and neither my mother nor I was a large person. We struggled a little, but we managed. I laid the crates in a neat row beside each other, one, two, three, four. In the fifth crate lay a particularly plump fruit with long sharp spikes that poked dangerously through the wooden slats. I didn't notice them until one jabbed sharply into the flat of my hand as I grasped the box. Startled, I tossed the box slightly upwards, meaning to adjust the position of that hand. That was when it fell away from me, heavy, determined and murderous, as though it had an appointment with fate.

I scrambled down the ladder yelling for my brother. My mother was still breathing when I reached her. The crate had shattered and several durians had split open on the floor, cheaply revealing the smooth, bloodless organs that lay inside their leather-hard shells. The room reeked. I heaved the remains of the shattered crate and several loose durians from my mother's chest. After that there was nothing to do but hold her hand and cry while my brother called the ambulance. They came quicker for us than they did for many because they knew my brother could afford to pay, but it didn't make any difference. My mother was dead before they arrived.

Only an experienced doctor present at the moment of impact could have saved her, they told me by way of consolation. Don't feel bad. There's nothing you could have done.

I felt more sick than sad. I had done this. I had killed my mother. It was a crime with no witnesses, and of course no one would ever suspect me, but I had done this. And there was no taking it back. I ran to the bathroom and vomited.

Ian snuck out of Serendipity to see me after my mother's death. It was the first time since our expulsion. I got him a Coke out of the refrigerator on the east wall and we went to sit on the back steps of the shop.

"Sorry to hear about your mother," he said, polite and strangely formal. He was still a small boy, but he wasn't as skinny as I remembered, and he was a little taller too. He seemed odd, as though he were not quite the same person, but an almost identical double.

"It's okay," I said flatly. Somehow I could not express to him the extent of my devastation. I pushed hair away from my face, self-consciously.

"I guess your dad got in trouble," he said, trying.

"Yeah," I said.

"It wasn't because of what you did, you know," he said.

I thought he was trying to console me. "Of course it was," I said.

"No. It was because of your disease. All the kids at school say so. I heard the Janitors whispering about it once too."

"You're a liar," I said. "Just like your parents."

In the garage my brother started the engine of a car with serious muffler and exhaust problems. The messy backyard, littered with rusted-out hunks of nondescript metal and shells of old cars my brother was using to supply spare parts, filled with noise and smoke. Suddenly I understood we had taken a step down in the world.

Ian took a big gulp of his Coke. "You'll be all right."

I glared at him.

He took another long drink and set the almost empty can down on the step. "Guess I'll get going then," he said. I didn't see him again for a long time.

My mother had willed all her money to my father, believing, I think, that the vast sums she had put away in her savings account had kept their value. My mother was not an investor; she couldn't stand the notion of risk of any kind. Nor would she trust my father to take care of her money, in spite of his financial expertise. Because she so seldom touched the account, thinking to save it for a truly rainy day, she didn't realize that the value of her once respectable holdings had diminished over the years to practically nothing. To my brother, she left all her jewellery because he was the one who loved shiny things as a child. Her will said she left it to him in hope that he would marry again. "Not likely," I muttered to myself, as our neighbour, who had once been a lawyer at Painted Horse, and was acting as one for us now, read that line. My mother had long since given up any hope that I might wear that outrageous stuff, and I was secretly relieved because I think I would have felt the pressure, even though she was gone. But what had she left me then? As the lawyer read my brother's share, I told myself that I didn't want anything, that it wouldn't matter what she left me, but of course it mattered. In those days, material things were still, for me, a measure of love. "And to my daughter, I bequeath the rights to all my songs, in addition to any hard copies, including originals, which I have left in a wooden box beneath my bed."

All my mother's beautiful torch songs, remnants of a long-ago glory I never really understood. The glory of another moment in the gold leaf and red velvet opulence of the New Kubla Khan, which I had never visited because children were not permitted to enter, and which was now forever closed to me since we had been exiled from Serendipity. She left me not only the rights, but also the original drafts, lyrics in her own fine hand, melodies in that of various admirers, but mostly in my father's hand, as it was he who wrote the music for her tuneless words, gave them that rich melty undertone that made her a small sensation in her day. My mother really loved me, bad smell and all.

For years after my mother's death I could not bear the presence of mirrors in any room. When I chanced on one by accident, I shuddered at the sight of my own reflection and wished with all my heart that I could simply erase it. Once, arriving at the home of a classmate for a party, I took off my shoes in the front hall and then looked up to be confronted by a large gilt-framed mirror with flower designs bevelled along the edges. In the centre my hateful face appeared. I picked up my shoe and threw it at the glass, shattering it. Needless to say, I didn't get invited back. It wasn't a desire for death, don't get me wrong. I wasn't suicidal. I just couldn't stand the sight of myself.

Later that night my father got the box out for me and placed it on the kitchen table. I opened the heavy teak lid. There the papers lay, in odd sizes, the edges of the larger sheets ragged and hanging over the edges of the smaller ones. I fingered the brown, crumpling paper of the first song, traced the letters of the lyrics. There was such an energy in the motion of the pen, the familiar motion of my mother's body, now just a trace of life, but not life itself. My eyes ran, silently.

There was a story in the papers. On the early leaves my mother's hand was always the same, but the melodies were written in many different hands and the tunes varied wildly. One hand lingered for a while then disappeared, to be replaced by another. You could tell something about the character of her admirers by the blackness of their quarter notes, the hollowness of their half and whole notes, the length of their quavers and semiquavers. Then there appeared the first melody in my father's hand carefully laid to the lyrics of my mother's first big hit.

Here's a song for Clara Cruise
A pretty girl who loved her shoes
Redder than a red red rose
The patent leather showed her toes
She fell in love with them on sight
The soles they made her feet so light

The pretty shoes of Clara Cruise
She danced in them throughout the night

Dancing whirling Clara Cruise
Danced to show she loved her shoes
Danced in them throughout the day
Tired though she wouldn't say
And when her feet began to ache
She tried to stop but couldn't shake
The pretty shoes of Clara Cruise
They danced her till her heart did break

They danced her till her feet gave out
Like horses on roundabout
They danced her till her love had passed
Until she breathed her gasping last
And then they danced her ragged bones
To the faint and haunting tones
Of lovers crying Clara Cruise
You should have loved us
Not your shoes

Shoes danced the bones till they were dust
A drifting heed to those who lust
For things that glitter in the dark
And seem they'll never leave a mark
Instead they take your breath away
So you can't love another day
The pretty shoes of Clara Cruise
Dance empty not so far away

They were a smashing combo from the beginning. I recognized all the songs from worn compact discs my mom always played, and some of the songs she sang while chopping vegetables in the kitchen, or mincing pork, or washing dishes. They were the tunes Aaron and I danced to around the kitchen table when I was four and Aaron was in his early thirties, and tunes admiring friends begged from my mother's withered lips when they came over for tea and cookies. Later, they were the tunes we sang as we stocked the shelves of our store, tunes we sprayed the vegetables to, tunes we hummed as we unloaded crates of durians. My father said that Serendipity had been built to the resplendent refrains of those songs. I dried my eyes on my dirty sleeve, so as not to ruin the papers.

I wasn't around when the songs were made, so for me they were always about nostalgia, but at this particular moment the feeling was heightened. I looked at my father. He was crying too. Through my tears, I grinned at him, and then he began to laugh. I began to laugh too. Aaron walked in and asked what we were laughing about, but we were laughing so hard we couldn't tell him. He thought we were ridiculously funny, and began to laugh himself. It was the first time we had done so since her death.

"Promise me that you'll never sell the rights," said my father. "Promise me that you'll always keep these songs in the family."

"I promise," I said.

The next day, my father moved my mother's vanity out of the bedroom and into the cold storage shed at the back of the house. He banged together a rough, makeshift closet with some half-rotted boards left by the previous owners and some bits of metal and wire from my brother's shop. He would have done better if he could, but building materials were sparse. He gave the thing a quick coat of red paint to make it cheerful and, when the paint was dry, hung my mother's dresses there. He covered the mirror with an old, dark brown tablecloth and put my mother's portrait—a glamour shot from the heyday of her fame—in front of it. On either side, he placed a tall red candle, and in the middle a Tupperware box, full of dirt from her garden. He produced three precious sticks of incense from goodness knows where and lit them reverently. Holding them in both hands, he bowed in front of the portrait the old-fashioned way, deeply and solemnly, and then stuck the sticks in the box of dirt. Then he made me and my brother do the same. "If you ever need your mother, Miranda," he said, "this is where she'll be."

I thought it was a load of bull, but I nodded gravely so as not to upset him. But in the middle of the night, I slipped out of bed and into the store. I selected the roundest, fattest durian on the shelf, placed it on the counter and split it open with the big meat cleaver we used on those rare occasions when a butcher or hunter supplied us with fresh meat. I arranged the reeking pieces on a pretty plastic tray and brought them to the shrine. When I placed them in front of her photograph, my mother's paper smile seemed to deepen.

What is the point of honour if it is always used against you? In his past life, my father would not have sold Saturna out for any price. He understood what we had. He understood the safety of the compound. He was not a greedy man. Our life was comfortable in a middle-class, suburban sort of way. It was not excessive. My father was content with that. He was proud of having fathered a child at such a late age. At seventy-five, he was proud that he was able to continue working for the company, that they valued his labour and his trust. That he could not afford to retire on the meagre pension offered did not bother him. My father was a stoic man. The only thing that marred his happy existence was my foul smell.

But now that we had been so cruelly cast out into the world, and now that his beloved wife, our mother, was dead, my father's sense of what constituted honour changed radically. What point was there in being loyal to Saturna when they were so clearly disloyal to him? What was the point of letting his children starve when he still possessed something worth selling? Hadn't he been there since Serendipity's beginning? He knew the tunnels beneath the city by heart. He knew the secrets of the Bank. He knew about the Game of tax collecting, how the Receiver General and razor disc birds connected to the more banal accounting softwares. He understood the narrative mechanisms of the Game that kept workers like himself hooked, in spite of real physical pain and suffering. Surely there would be people who would be willing to pay for these things. But as for me, I was too young to understand the great risks he undertook when he visited Saturna factories in the Unregulated Zone. I didn't understand why he went repeatedly to visit certain worker-prisoners there, nor did I know what they gave him in exchange for the information he shared. I knew even less of the secret organizing that went on behind those doors. Whatever our political beliefs, whatever our clandestine commitments, we didn't discuss them with family members, not wanting to endanger them. What I did know was that my father loved my mother. One day an expensive baby grand piano appeared in the back storeroom, casting its elegant shadow right over the spot where my mother had died. In the evenings, after a drink or two, my father would sit on its shiny black stool and hammer out her tunes, singing in his rough gravelly voice that didn't resemble hers in the least bit. But slowly, as the years passed, the tunes changed, took on melancholy minor tones, slipped from their cheerful, perky rhythms to complicated and irregular time schemes. He sang less. But late at night when he thought we were in bed, sometimes he would talk to an empty space beside him, though there was no one and nothing in the room but fruit, dried goods and tins. I began to worry about my father's mental health.

On the morning of my seventeenth birthday I told my father and brother it was time for me to go study. "I want to be a doctor," I said.

"It's too late to bring her back, silly," said my brother.

"Yes, but it's not too late to save you, or Dad."

My brother laughed. It wasn't that I was unrebellious, I was just very worried. My dreams galloped with disasters that might befall them.

"Which corporation do you think will take you in and send you to one of its campuses? No one will want the child of a known criminal," he said.

"But he was unjustly accused. . ."

"Can you prove it?"

I shook my head.

"Well, then."

I gave him my most baleful countenance.

3. Dr. Rudy Flowers

Just over a week later, on a rainy afternoon, my brother called me into the back. I had been minding the counter out front and working on my biology homework. When I entered the garage my brother was adjusting the seat of the old Volvo he had been working on for the last few days. A thin middle-aged man with lank brown hair and wire-framed glasses stood waiting. He was dressed badly in worn brown cords and a plaid cotton shirt, but there was something self-important and moneyed about his demeanour. I didn't like him.

"Miranda, this is Dr. Flowers," my brother said, "you know, of Painted Horse fame."

"Pleased to meet you," I said. I glanced sideways at Aaron.

"He's looking for an apprentice." My brother gave no indication of knowing that this was the man who had threatened to divide our family. I wondered if my parents had told him about their plans to send me to Flowers for treatment. I didn't know that Aaron, who was struggling to maintain an appearance of casual nonchalance, suspected that this man was his real father.

I nodded uneasily.

"I need someone to work in my blood lab," said the doctor. "I could teach you the odd thing or two on the in-between. Of course, no matter what I teach you, you can't practise officially. It's still against the law to practise medicine without a degree." But he winked, as if to say, who pays attention to federal law these days?

"Dr. Flowers is no longer with Painted Horse," said my brother. "He's been living in the Unregulated Zone for almost a year."

The doctor ran his private clinic on the top floor of an ancient crumbling office tower on a street of ancient crumbling office towers in one of the city's suburban satellites. I drove there in an old but well-kept Subaru station wagon my brother was repairing for a retired professor. In another century, this area had been used as overflow office space, cheaper than the more prestigious downtown addresses, but just as efficient, and more convenient for suburban-dwelling office workers to travel to. The buildings were almost empty now. The windows of the abandoned lower floors were broken and there were cracks in the concrete facade. In those cracks, mildew grew thickly and threaded away from the central tributaries in fine rivulets, giving the overall impression of a wall covered in green-black ferns. The upper floors were lit by recently reinstalled fluorescent lights salvaged from another age. From the ground you could see them flicker unsteadily, as though unable to maintain a steady hold on the current they were being supplied. The elevator, too, had been recently reactivated. I rode to the fifty-fourth floor—the top but two—and stepped through recently polished glass doors into a bright clean office, only slightly tasteless with its peach walls and posters of Impressionist paintings in bright orange frames.

Behind the reception desk sat a pale, sharp-featured young woman with masses of thick black hair that flowed down her back. "Hello," she said. "You must be Miranda." Her eyes travelled disdainfully up and down my badly dressed body. We weren't poor, you understand, but clothing was not one of my vanities. "Dr. Flowers was called away today, I'm afraid," she said, perfectly professional, "but Dr. Seto is expecting you. She's been involved in the project from the beginning and usually takes care of hiring."

She led me down a hallway that smelled too conspicuously of bleach, into an office where a roundish Asian woman sat, smiling in a neat white lab coat. The woman's hair was like the receptionist's in that it was thick and abundant, but it was streaked with white and wound neatly into a bun.

"Come in, come in. I've been expecting you," she said, smiling.

I stepped through the door. The receptionist closed it behind me.

The woman's face grew serious. "So you want to work for Flowers."

I nodded, though suddenly I was full of doubt.

"You know what you're getting yourself into, then."

I nodded again. I hadn't a clue what she was talking about.

"Flowers has told you about the disease?"

I shook my head.

"And well he shouldn't. I'm afraid I'll have to ask you to sign these before we proceed any further."

"What are they?"

"The conversation we're about to have must be held completely in confidence. The papers are to verify that. You're not obliged, if you don't want the job."

"I want the job," I said. I signed the papers.

"It's just a formality," she said. "There's no point starting unnecessary hysteria."

"Tell me about the disease."

"It hasn't got an official name. It hasn't got official anything. None of the corporations want to acknowledge it. But some call it the dreaming disease, or the drowning disease."

"I heard about a girl," I said. "She had to move into the bathroom because only water could stop her terrible dreams . . ."

"Case UZI, the first case outside Painted Horse."

I scratched my arm. It itched when I was nervous. "There have been more?"

"We're not sure how many. The symptoms are so peculiar, and so unlike any other known disease—foul odours of various sorts that follow the person without actually emanating from the body, psoriasis, sleep apnea, terrible dreams usually with historical content, and a compulsive drive to commit suicide by drowning. We don't even really know if it is a disease. We're still trying to isolate the virus. But yes, within the Painted Horse sphere a lot of people have been afflicted. But Aries William, the CEO, says there is no disease. He calls it mass hysteria. He won't allow research of any kind."

"So Flowers has moved into the Unregulated Zone."

"Exactly. And he needs technicians."

"I'm not afraid," I lied. "But I have no prior medical experience."

"We just need someone to take blood tests and skin samples," said Dr. Seto. "I can train you in a week."

"How does it spread?"

"On the streets of Painted Horse 3000, they say never to walk barefoot on the beaches where victims have walked into the sea and drowned. They say it spreads through the soles of the feet."

Dr. Seto taught me how to increase blood pressure in the arm by wrapping rubber tubing around it. She taught me how to plump a vein up and bring it closer to the surface of the skin by gently slapping the patient's arm. She taught me how to insert the needle without causing too much pain, and how to guide the blood into the sample plastic test tubes. She taught me how to take skin scrapings, and what different kinds of cells looked like under the microscope. It was easier than I thought. I'd spent so much time mucking with my toy microscope when I was younger.

Within a week I was seeing patients. After their visits with Flowers on the top floor, they came down to see me for blood tests and skin scrapings. I saw so much of the disease it was at times overwhelming. Not all of them told me their story, of course. They weren't obliged to. But many were eager to unload the weight of their terrible dreams on whomever they could. I met a man who smelled of milk and could remember all the famines that had ever been caused by war. I met a girl who smelled of stainless steel and could recite the lives of everyone who had ever died of tuberculosis. I met a woman who reeked of radishes. Hers were fabulous tales that involved the stealing of fruit and young women rescued from tall towers. Her tales were clearly not based in any sort of factual reality, and yet there was a resonance to them that I couldn't quite put my finger on. (Like mine . . . like mine . . . a whisper only.) I met a boy who smelled of oranges and could tell of such tragic romances that I wept as I drew his blood.

This strange disease was a great puzzle to me. Did I think I had been afflicted? If so, then I had been born with it. But Seto and Flowers seemed to think that it was something that could be caught, by walking barefoot on the sand, or on the earth, especially when it was barren and there was no grass or moss or leaves to protect the feet from open soil. They theorized it might be the product of mass industrial genetic alteration practices—that the modifications of agricultural products in recent years had contaminated the soil, that the microbes that lived in the earth were mutating and infecting humans. That humans could get diseases once only possible in plants, or that indeed, the new disease was a strange hybrid, combining those that affected plants and those that affected animals.

Once, when Flowers wasn't around, Seto suggested the disease had been intentionally manufactured, like the firefly disease created in 2010, which became a fad among hip urban youngsters. Since the late 1900s, scientists had been using luciferase genes from fireflies, jellyfish and algae to illuminate the actions of other genes. A young geneticist manufactured a virus containing sections of firefly DNA, which made its sufferers glow in the dark. Her boyfriend, a performance artist known as Lizardman, who until then had been making yearly visits to a plastic surgeon in order to make his body appear more reptilian, was the first to get the injection. While scientists had long suspected that fireflies lit up as a way of attracting mates, neither the young geneticist nor her colleagues anticipated the erotic side effects of their engineering. Lizardman changed his name to Lucifer and spent the three and a half weeks of his intentionally induced illness making the rounds of the local fuck clubs and passing the disease on to dozens eager to get infected in spite of the risk of other far less appealing diseases. "Although it isn't sexually transmitted, in many ways this dreaming disease is similar," said Seto. "People are catching a bug that gives them the memory structures of other animals—fish maybe, or elephants. I don't understand why it also affects the skin. If it weren't making people suicidal, I don't think either Flowers or I would be particularly interested in it."

Of this last disclosure, I was doubtful, but I just nodded politely. I wasn't at all certain of Flowers' or Seto's motives, though my personal history was sufficient to make me conveniently ambivalent. I didn't probe, and Seto offered no further information. She dropped in on me when she could, which wasn't that often, as she was busy working on a technique to capture her patients' various odours. I saw Flowers even less often, though I knew he was in the building by the handwriting on the bloodwork forms the patients brought, and by his car in the downstairs parking lot.

Sometimes I glimpsed myself in the patients and wondered. My durian stink in those days had diminished a great deal. My brother said he could still smell it, but only sometimes, and other people, Flowers and Seto included, did not seem to notice at all. I dreamt intensely on occasion, and some of those dreams were about drowning, but I chalked it up to residual anxieties over work, and did not let myself get overly concerned. Well, perhaps this is not quite true. Sometimes I thought about it. Sometimes I wondered if I too was afflicted with the dreaming disease, and might find myself one day walking down to the beach and not stopping at the water's edge. But as Dr. Seto said, they weren't even sure it could be classified as a disease and, as it stood, there was no cure. The only therapy was to take lots of baths, and in extreme cases to spend the better part of one's day in the tub. I didn't want to think about it. But then, I had not yet met Evie.

The first time I caught Seto looking at me funny, I thought it was because I had dirt on my face. As soon as there was a lull in the stream of patients coming in the door, I went to the bathroom to look. What looked back at me from the mirror was pale and a little sickly, but clean. Perhaps I had imagined Seto's stares.

But I caught her at it again the next day.

"Dr. Seto, is there something wrong with my face?"

"No, no, nothing, Miranda."

"Then why are you looking at me like that?"

"Like what?"

"Like . . . like I haven't combed my hair or something."

"You look fine," Seto said.

The smell is getting worse, I thought. When she left the room, I checked my breath and armpits. I leaned forwards in my chair and sniffed the backs of my knees. The durian smell was still there, but it wasn't overwhelming. A flicker of mistrust for Seto ran through me.

When Evie stepped into my lab, I didn't recognize her at first. Thin and wiry, she did not have the obvious beauty of her previous life. Her eyes glistened bright and keen, and she moved with a sharp, birdlike precision, nervous but also capable and confident. I had the distinct impression the past was leaking through into the present, though I could not have explained this.

She handed me a slip of paper. *Evie*, it said. There was no surname.

"I'm paying cash," she said. "I don't have to tell you my family name if I don't want to."

"I never asked," I replied, politely. "Sit here, please. Put your arm on the armrest with the palm facing up."

On that wiry arm, her vein wasn't hard to find. I slapped it gently anyway to plump it up. But it wasn't until I had sunk the needle in that I caught a whiff of a familiar fragrance, briny and sweet.

"It's you," I said.

"You're full of shit. How can you know anything?" she barked, but her voice trembled a little.

I snapped out of my reverie. "What?"

"Where do you recognize me from?"

"What are you talking about? I don't recognize you."

"You can't know. How could you know?" She yanked the needle from her arm, leapt out of the chair and fled.

Afterwards I wasn't sure what had happened. I had recognized something, but had no idea what. It felt as though something inside me was stretching, had always stretched to that moment of recognition, in the past, a stretching without knowing, a longing without certainty of the object, but in that moment when she rose from the chair, pulled the needle from her arm and ran out the door, I knew. Or rather, I had a glimpse of something. I could not name it, but I knew it mattered. This knowing without consciousness of what it was I must remember ate at me. I felt a terrible hunger inside, a hunger without a name. An ache that had always been there had suddenly become material.

In the afternoon the sky grew grey. Thick storm clouds gathered in the mountains and sank over the city, enveloping everything. The air was so thick with moisture that when it turned to liquid it didn't even seem like rain, but like an ocean materializing out of the air. I watched it from the relative safety of the blood lab, behind two strong panes of glass. The stream of patients, which had been steady all morning, dwindled down to nothing. It was probably a good thing. Evie's sudden absence sat with me. Torrents of water gushed down the battered streets and washed away even more of the already well-eroded asphalt.

With nothing to do and no one watching me (Seto was busy in her lab on the other side of the corridor) I plunked myself down in one of the patients' armchairs and turned my attention to the rain.

I don't know how long Flowers had been watching me before I turned and caught him. I jumped in my seat, startled. I scowled at him. Sure he owned the lab, but still, he could have knocked.

"How long have you had those?" he said, rubbing the soft flesh where the last outer whorl of his ear met the edge of his face. The mask edge.

I raised an eyebrow. My finger moved involuntarily to touch the corresponding spot beside my own right ear. I have a fistula there, and another in an identical position on the left side. An inheritance from my mother, something that, as a child, I had thought of as a regular part of human anatomy, a small hole that itches periodically and releases a thin stream of briny-smelling fluid when rubbed. My mother, I remember, was surprised the first time she noticed me pressing the fluid out of one. She laughed softly, as though it were some kind of genetic joke, a gift from ancestors long gone. "Poor child," she said, "you inherited a fistula from me."

"I have two," I said. "One on each side. What are they for?"

My mother said, "For?"

"You smell with your nose, you hear with your ears, you see with your eyes, you taste with your tongue. What are fistulas for?"

My mother paused for a long moment. Finally she said, "Cleaning."

"Cleaning?"

"Cleaning the bone marrow," said my mother. "The fistula is a tunnel through your head that goes all the way to the bone."

For some reason, I felt embarrassed to ever raise the topic again, but in secret, on my own, I developed a notion that the purpose of my fistulas was not just for cleaning the bone marrow, but that they served the function of memory, recalling a time when we were more closely related to fish, a time when the body glistened with scales and turned in the dark, muscled easily through water. This is why, when pressed, the liquid they release smells of the sea.

I had never spoken to anyone about them before, until now. It felt strangely intrusive. "I don't know," I said.

"Were you born with them?"

"I think so."

"You know anyone else that has them?"

"My mother, but she's dead."

"Anyone else?"

Now that I thought about it, that girl Evie had at least one. I noticed it as I was taking her blood. I told him so.

"Great," he said. "Where's the sample?"

"I didn't get one. She split before I could finish."

"But you have half a tube."

"I threw it out." I don't know what compelled me to lie.

"You shouldn't have done that," he said. "We could have done a check on her. The bank gives a reward for the capture of illegals. I'm sure you could have used the cash."

I looked at him blankly.

"I'll be straight with you, Miranda," said the doctor. "Dr. Seto and I believe that people with these strange fistulas are prime carriers for the drowning disease. We don't quite understand how it works, but it is our belief that there is a connection. If you would agree to take part in our experiments, that data we collect would be invaluable."

"You think I have it?" I asked, suddenly worried.

"We'd have to do a series of tests."

"What would it entail?"

"We'll up your salary, of course."

He volunteered no further information, but sat with an expression on his face that was at once officious and expectant. I'm sure it had worked on countless patients before.

"I'll think about it," I said.

The house smelled sweet that afternoon when I returned home. One of our suppliers had brought a particularly nice shipment of whipping cream. My father was making waffles and the house was cozily redolent of eggs and flour and sugar. Aaron was out back picking raspberries from our mother's now very fruitful bushes. Like the rest of her plants they grew like mad, scraggly and uncontained, still thriving amid all the mechanical junk that had drifted into her once sacred territory from the garage side of the raspberry hedge.

"Waffles!" I said. My father had always been good at sweet things, especially countertop sweet things, like waffles, crepes and omelettes.

He smiled, pleased that I was pleased. "Perhaps you could make some tea, Miranda," he said.

I filled the kettle with cold water and put it on the stove. I rummaged in the cupboard above the sink for tea and sugar, and the one below it for the teapot. I was filling it with hot water from the tap when Aaron came in with his deep round bowl of raspberries. In the doorway, he held it out to show us how many there were, and how ripe. Behind him light from the setting sun poured through the doorway, so that he appeared in silhouette. The bowl of berries he held out, beyond the effects of the backlighting, seemed all the brighter for Aaron's darkness. I smiled at him. He stood there. There was something frail about his dark shape. How old is Aaron? I wondered to myself. Almost fifty, almost an old man.

Aaron stood in the doorway too long. Because of the light behind him, it was hard to make out his face, so at first I didn't notice it grow pale, then twitch. Suddenly, still clutching his bowl of raspberries, Aaron collapsed to the floor. His body convulsed, once, twice, a third time, then lay still, while the berries rolled around him like fat droplets of blood. I was at his side at once, my hand on his heart, gently massaging. Please, God, don't let this happen to me again. But slowly his eyes opened and he took a deep breath. "What was that?" he said. He still looked terribly pale.

"Don't you dare leave us!" I said, relieved and indignant. "What happened?"

"It hurt so much, but now I feel fine," he said. "Very strange."

"What hurt? We'll phone Flowers immediately and ask him if he knows anything."

"Everything hurt. Like my whole body was on fire, and then I thought I had disappeared, like I was sucked up into a vacuum, into nothingness and then I was nothingness, I was gone. And then I was back, and fine. Weird." Aaron pushed himself to standing. On the floor, where he had been lying, was a shadow in the shape of his fallen body. It remained there for a second, then faded to nothing.

"I'm phoning Flowers," I said.

When I called the doctor, he said that he was almost certain I was suffering from the dreaming disease, and that I had probably passed it on to my brother. "As you know," he said, "there is no cure. Why not come in and take part in our experiment?"

Before Flowers took me to the experimental site he gave me a flimsy khaki-green patient's gown that tied at the back with three pairs of white laces, a housecoat and a pair of cheap plastic slippers. We went down the back escalator and into his personal car, the old but functional late-twentieth-century model Volvo that he had brought to my brother to repair on several occasions. He started the engine, threw the car into gear and we were off down the crumbling highway, away from the ugly skyscraping office tower. I felt unpleasantly vulnerable in my patient's uniform, as though our relationship had suddenly deeply changed. I suppose it had. We wound through the bombed-out sections of the Unregulated Zone, past rows of the jobless poor sitting in dilapidated doorways or standing on street corners fighting over drugs or empty Coke cans.

He had bought an old hotel in what was once down-town Vancouver, the first part to be abandoned after the earthquake of 2017 submerged several metres of the original waterfront of the city, including the Pan Pacific Hotel. The half-submerged building had stood unused and undemolished since that time. As was his habit, Flowers made no effort whatsoever to refurbish the exterior, but he had done a wonderful job of the interior. The foyer blossomed with an array of cut hothouse flowers and beautiful hand-knotted Persian rugs. We took the escalator downstairs and strolled through the old shopping arcade. Here the floors, walls and ceiling all still leaked and smelled unpleasantly of mildew and rodent droppings. In the distance, beyond the layers of leaking concrete, you could hear the dull roar of the sea. But one floor down it was sealed and dry. The walls had been newly replastered and painted a soothing mustard yellow. The floors had been retiled, the door frames reinforced and the doors replaced. Or at least some of them had—the doors to the rooms with ocean views. On the other side of the corridor, there were no doors. They had been plastered and painted over.

"Welcome to my lab," said Flowers. "I hope you'll be comfortable here." He pulled a jangling set of keys from his trouser pocket and unlocked the door marked 113. "Reserved specially for you," he said. He pushed the door open. The sound of the ocean was deafening. The room was small and carpeted. It contained a spartan white bed, a table and a chair. But the most remarkable thing was that the far wall was made completely of some kind of sturdy Plexiglas, and outside it, the ocean pressed, full and furious at being shut out of this territory, which clearly belonged, by natural rights, to it and not to us. It whipped furiously against the glass, clamouring to get in. It slammed things against it—seaweed, old bottles, frayed rope, scrap metal, swaying schools of fish—whatever it could conjure up from its polluted floor.

"I'll go mad in here," I said.

"Don't worry, the glass is double-reinforced," said Flowers. "It won't break." He nudged me gently but firmly into the room.

"I don't know. . ." I said, glancing furtively at the door, which still stood open.

"Only for a few hours," he said. "Then we'll come get you. I'll give you something for your nerves." He produced a small box of pills from his bag and a bottle of water. "Now there's just one more thing," he said. "If you can sit with your back to me."

I felt helpless in my green gown. I sat down on the edge of the bed and swivelled away from him. He placed his fat hand on my neck. It was flabby and cold like a rubber glove filled with water. He massaged my neck coaxingly. I suppressed a shudder. Suddenly there was the sharp, searing slice of a knife. "What are you doing?" I cried.

"Shhhh," he said. "It will be over in a minute." He continued to massage the wound. It hurt. I could feel my own blood trickle warmly down my back. Then suddenly he squeezed the wound open and popped something cool, round and powdery into it as though it were a mouth opening to accept a holy wafer.

"No!" I said. "Get that fucking thing out of me."

"Shhhh," he said again. "In a few moments it will have dissolved and then you won't have a thing to worry about. We need to be able to measure your brainwaves."

He smoothed the wound over with a bit of antiseptic-smelling cream. It felt icy cold. "This will make it heal faster," he said.

"I've changed my mind," I said, making for the door.

Something sharp jabbed my calf. I collapsed. I felt myself being lifted onto the bed, and a calm, disembodied voice said, "Just for a few hours." Then everything went black. In the darkness I dreamt myself very small. Small, and long, like an earthworm travelling tremendous distances in the dark, unhindered by the stink of earth, the sleeping vegetative matter that cluttered my path. I dreamt I hit water, a deep well, and fell down deep into a cool wet darkness.

Nu Wa

South China, early 1900s

THE ISLAND OF MIST
AND FORGETFULNESS

1. Crossroads

We didn't quarrel all the time. We needed each other. Canton was an endless maze of alleyways that twisted in on themselves and unravelled in ways you would least expect. Toothless old women leaned out of doorways selling toys and flowers and candy. Young girls leaned out of doorways selling things infinitely less innocent. I tried to find work in one of the many small silk factories that we stumbled across, but no one was hiring. We picked among the great garbage heaps behind restaurants for food and slept in alleys while our clothes grew more and more tattered, lessening our chances of finding respectable work as each day passed.

There are people who grow grey and hideous as hunger takes its toll. And then there are people whose slender good looks turn to a gaunt, apocalyptic kind of beauty the thinner and more desperate they become. I was one of the former, the Salt Fish Girl most decidedly one of the latter. Of course, the kind of men who accosted breathing grey bundles in doorways couldn't tell the difference and bothered us both with equal regularity. Mostly they were drunk. We pushed them over, held them down, emptied their pockets and ran away.

Once in the afternoon when I was making my rounds of the silk factories and tailor shops, a man in a Western suit approached the Salt Fish Girl. She was sleeping in the back of an abandoned truck, dreaming of fish ball noodles. He woke her up by pinning her roughly against the rusty floor of the truck. She woke to find his heavy paw on her chest and his thick breath, reeking of alcohol and insufficiently cooked meat, in her face. In a panic, her hand flew to the fish-cleaning knife she had thrust beneath her skirts the night we escaped. She angled it towards his flabby underside. Before he knew what hit him, she had slit his belly open and spilled his guts untidily all over herself and the truck floor. He gasped once and collapsed. Quickly, she emptied his pockets and then hurried to the river to wash.

That night as we were settling down in a doorway, we heard a hawker passing by one street over, moving away from us rather than towards. "Sweet potatoes!" he cried. "Sticky rice packets! Hard-boiled eggs!" The Salt Fish Girl was hungry. She handed me a few coins from her recent heist, and I hurried round the corner after the sweet voice calling the names of late-night snacks. She huddled in the doorway waiting for me.

It took me a long time to catch up to the hawker. The street was quiet. People were clearly minding their own business, and had no time for a lone hawker lugging a too-heavy basket of rapidly cooling wares. The hawker sensed this and walked quickly. I could have shouted at him to slow down, but I didn't want to draw attention to myself. By the time I caught up with him I had walked six blocks from where we had been sleeping.

When I returned with warm pockets filled with steaming treats, there was no sign of the Salt Fish Girl, although our blankets were there and still felt warm to the touch. I opened my mouth to call out her name, and then thought better of it. I wandered the streets looking for her while the potatoes grew heavy and cold in my pockets. I entered the factory district in full moonlight. The first alley, like all other alleys in the city, was long and narrow, but somehow the brick buildings seemed greyer and more dilapidated without the cheery tilework and frescoes that decorated even the poorest residences of the city. And unlike the windows of ordinary inhabitants' sleepy domiciles, the factory windows burned with the low, unnatural light of nocturnal labour. I peered into one of them. Inside, seated on the grey stone tile floor, a dozen or so men and women were busy organizing large heaps of unwoven rattan into neat bundles.

I walked on, down the empty alley, my footsteps clipping too loudly against the cobblestones. I paused frequently, peering into every lighted window. Inside I saw women and men, young and old, all crowded together assembling rattan brooms, or building rattan chairs, coffee tables, birdcages.

The next alley dealt in paper products—lanterns, stationery, brightly dyed cutouts of opera masks, palace ladies, luscious flowers and exotic animals. Older women stamped bright dyes onto the paper. Younger women, their eyes still sharp, worked with tiny scissors under the low light, snipping away at the paper so that each figurine emerged in lacy detail beneath their hands. I did not linger long enough to notice their eyes growing dimmer, or notice the older women, nearly blind, wasting away in the dark corners of the factory mixing the colours and wheezing in reaction to the bright, powdery, dry chemical form of the dyes. I said to myself that this might not be bad work, at least for a while, till I saved enough money for the Salt Fish Girl and myself to start a business of our own.

The whole night I searched, window after window, until I had a strange sense of bodilessness, of gazing in on too many lives, to the point where I disappeared into the act of watching, fell into my own shadow and vanished beneath it. The only reason I knew this was not the case was that my legs began to grow stiff, and a twinge developed in my left knee. Just before sunrise, I paused beneath a particularly poorly lit window, and looked in. There she sat in the dim light, bleary-eyed and leaning over a scrambled mess of tin animal arms and legs, trying to nudge a spring into place with a pair of tweezers. As soon as she saw me, she waved me away, her lips mouthing the word "run."

The panic in her face clearly came from concern for me. Of course, I couldn't leave her. I scuttled into the nearest alleyway and hid behind a heap of garbage. I was shocked. The romance of all those other windows had evaporated in the instant of seeing her. Shortly afterwards a long line of young women dressed in identical tan-coloured uniforms with military-style pockets filed out the factory door. The very last of them was the Salt Fish Girl.

I beckoned to her from my hiding place and we moved to a doorstep a few streets away. We sat down and ate the cold sweet potatoes and rice together and she told me what had happened. The factory foreman was short of workers. He had seen her running away from the corpse of the man in the Western business suit and threatened to tell the police if she didn't agree to come work for him. The wages were pitiful, barely enough to buy dinner for the evening, if she did not eat too much for lunch.

"We'll go north," I said. "He won't come after you. Canton is full of girls looking for a job."

"It's not that bad," she said. "At least it's work."

I was incredulous. "You're being blackmailed."

"But my hands are cleaner than they have been in a long time," she said. "It's bad enough that we've abandoned our families. Why fall further than necessary?"

"Why?" My voice trembled. I didn't want to shout. Something of my decent upbringing remained with me in spite of everything. "Why? Because. Because the falling's been done. There is no further."

"I don't agree," she said flatly. There was instability in her defiance. Her eyes weren't steady and so I knew I could push her if I wanted to. Now, I wish I had. Instead, I responded to the part of her that was stubborn. I glared back, feeling humiliated, unappreciated and hateful.

Our partnership took on a different tenor. No longer did we roll drunks together and gloat over the loot at night. She spent all the hours of daylight, and often many of darkness too, crouched under the dim lights of the factory, straining through a magnifying glass to attach tin torsos, wings, arms, beaks, legs, guns and bicycles to their springs and wind-ups with precise mechanical accuracy.

She brought home enough money to feed us at the end of the day, but I didn't want to rely on her charity. I could have gone back to the paper factory and asked the foreman for work, but truth be told I did not want it. Though I could not say so, even to myself, I despised and pitied the Salt Fish Girl for having given up her freedom in exchange for so little. I did not want to make the same mistake.

I stopped luring men into quiet corners, being too afraid for my own safety. Instead, I picked pockets daily on the busy streets. My favourites were Western tourists and business-men, who were too busy and in too much awe of the things they saw as quaint—cages of chickens on the backs of bicy-cles, or firecrackers going off for good luck above the door-ways of new shops.

Then, one day, an unfortunate thing happened. I was hang-ing out at the beggars' market, two blocks from the factory where the Salt Fish Girl worked, trying to sell the silver Rolex I had lifted from a German businessman that after-noon, as well as a couple of fountain pens I had picked from the pockets of two dazed young Jesuit priests. I was just in the middle of negotiations with a man I knew to be an opium seller. I didn't care. I just wanted to unload the watch and get some money so I could start dinner before the Salt Fish Girl came home from work. Just as we were closing the deal and he was handing me money, she stepped into view. She had gotten off work early and was on her way to the little room above a live chicken shop that we had begun to rent earlier that month.

"Why do you have to associate with those kinds of people?" she said. "I've got an honest job now, I can support us."

"Look how much I made today," I said, showing her. In truth, I was beginning to enjoy pickpocketing. I liked the thrill of it, the intimacy of slipping your hands unnoticed into a stranger's pockets, the danger of getting caught.

"I thought you were looking for a real job."

"There aren't any. Unless you want me to work in some stupid wind-up toy factory," I sulked.

"Don't you dare insult me! I'm working myself blind so we can live an honest life and you insist on being a cheat and a thief!"

It was true about her blindness. Her eyesight had deteriorated rapidly. She now wore a pair of much-too-large black-rimmed spectacles that had been discarded by some rich but charitable person in America. Behind them, her eyes looked impossibly small. The glasses made her look like a big bug.

"Don't yell at me. I left a perfectly good and loving family to be with you."

"You killed my father."

"We could have gone back. You were the one that didn't want to."

We didn't quarrel again for a long time after that. She did what she needed to keep us eating and to pay the rent on the room.

In the daytime, I left her to her own devices, and she left me to mine. At night, we still huddled together as in the doorways of our first nights, but more out of habit now than love. She didn't mention her father's death again. If we had nightmares about blood and drowning, neither of us mentioned it to the other.

One day, by a fountain at a crossroad where six narrow roads converged, I saw a woman feeding pigeons. She was a foreigner, and an outlandish-looking one at that, dressed in white from top to toe, with long unpinned hair the colour of sunlight and eyes so pale they seemed to be gazing inward instead of out. When she saw me looking, she waved me over. She scattered a handful of grain at my feet and the pigeons gathered around me in an eager, friendly circle. I smiled at her. She smiled back and glanced over her shoulder in the direction of the dark alleyway from which she had come. Then she turned and was gone.

That night the Salt Fish Girl came back looking exhausted and dishevelled. A Malaysian girl who worked at her factory had been stricken with hysteria, had gone to the toilet and begun screaming and tearing at her hair. She had been working at the factory for nearly three years and was half blind and bored out of her wits with the tedious repetitiveness

of the work. Her hysteria had provoked others, until half
the women in the factory were screaming and howling and
throwing themselves against the walls in sheer frustration
with the dreariness of their toil and the damage it was exact-
ing from their once young bodies and once bright faces.

The Salt Fish Girl did not look at all well. She was thinner
than ever. Her face was deathly pale and there were bruises
on her legs and shoulders that suggested she had not been
entirely passive in the goings-on at the factory.

She asked me to buy her medicine in the morning and I
promised I would. Before we went to sleep, she gave me a
big coin that she had been saving for such emergencies, and
asked me not to disturb her when I woke.

On my way to the herbalist's, I had to pass through the
same crossroad where I had seen the foreign woman feeding
pigeons the day before. She was there again, only this time it
was crows at her feet, dark as the night sky. She motioned
me over and scattered her last handful of grain at my feet.
The crows gathered around me and pecked greedily. Their
feathers were black and shiny, and beside them the foreign
woman looked paler than ever. Her pallor wasn't the sickly
kind that plagued the Salt Fish Girl. Rather, her skin was so
healthy it was almost translucent. You could see an immense
vitality behind it.

When the birds had finished, she took me by the hand
and we ran down an alleyway and then turned down another
and another, until I lost all sense of direction.

"Where are you taking me?" I asked. "Someone I love is
very sick and I have to bring her medicine."

She just laughed and continued to hold my hand and urge me forward. Her eyes sparkled like two big, dry stars. She was taller than me, but slender. Surely, I could have wrenched myself free of her grasp and turned around if I had truly wanted to do it. Surely.

But I could not have wanted to very much, because I followed her along a winding path at the edge of the cliff, into mist so thick that in a short time I could not see her at all, although she continued to grasp my hand tightly. I could not see my own feet either, but the ground felt reasonably solid beneath them. Or at least, it did for a while, although imperceptibly, bit by bit, it grew soft and springy. My footsteps fell lighter and faster. When our heads emerged from the clouds, I was shocked to see the land so far below.

"Where are we?" I asked, or tried to. The words came out in a gargly burble I didn't understand.

"Are you asking where we are?" she said, her language plain as day. "I'm taking you to my home, the city of Hope on the Island of Mist and Forgetfulness."

"What's that?"

"You know how sometimes when you look at clouds over the ocean? The long flat greyish kind?"

"Yes."

"You know how your eyes can play tricks on you, how sometimes you can't be sure if they are clouds in the sky or islands in the water?"

"I think so."

"Well some of them truly are islands, and we are going to one of them. It's not much farther."

"But my friend at home . . ." I protested, weakly and without any true feeling. The Salt Fish Girl's coin weighed heavily in my pocket.

When you own nothing, it's hard to believe you have anything to lose. I can't say what it was that made me follow this strange woman, except that it took more weakness than strength.

2. The City of Hope

We walked through the fog. The ground was spongy, like moss. I felt increasingly sleepy. Then my heel clicked against solid wood, which snapped me awake. The fog thinned and through the drifting wisps I could see we had stepped onto a long pier. Water surged gently against the sides. We followed the pier towards land and stepped finally onto a dock. Above us towered an astonishing city, glinting pink and gold. We walked through an archway with strange characters at the peak of the arch. I must have been mesmerized by them because the bird-woman leaned close. "It says 'Progress,'" she said. "This is the east gate of the City of Hope. The inscription over the west gate says 'Democracy.'" On either side of the arch, standing out of strange grey stone that looked as though it had been poured in moulds and then solidified, was a geometrically stylized, low-relief image of a woman holding a large sheaf of grain, not rice, but wheat perhaps. As we entered the city my eyes bugged wide and I clenched the bird-woman's hand. All of the buildings were huge and

pressed tightly against one another, but without ever breaking their carefully planned geometry.

"My name is Edwina," said the no-longer-foreign woman.
"Welcome to my hometown."

I rolled the syllables of her name over my tongue.

She took me into one of the glossy buildings, which turned
out to be a hotel, sat me down in the lobby and ordered me a
drink. "To loosen your tongue," she said. "Otherwise no one
will understand a word you're saying."

While we waited for our drinks, I practised her name.

She laughed. "All right. Don't wear it out."

Our drinks took a long time to arrive. "They're terribly
short-staffed," she said. "But I imagine it's only temporary."

It didn't occur to me to ask why she should think about
the hotel's staffing problems at all. I sipped my drink. It
tasted odd—bitter and herbal at the start, but then it slipped
down my throat sweetly and made my cheeks flush and my
head spin. As I drank, my breathing became deep and cold, in
a camphorish, eucalyptus-y sort of way. With each breath
I felt a new language enter me. With each sip of the drink,
I lost grasp of the old one. It was a tall glass. My bladder
swelled. I went to the bathroom to pee. As the hot liquid
rushed out from between my legs, I felt my old language
gushing away from me, liquid, yellow and irretrievable. I did
not feel sad. I felt light, and terribly giddy. I pulled the flush
cord and watched it swirl away.

I returned to the table. My old glass had been taken away
and a new one stood in its place. I sat down and sipped at it
gladly. If there was something inside me that resisted, some-

thing that doubted the healthfulness of the drink, I ignored it, and gulped with abandon.

"I thought perhaps you might like to stay here for the evening," said Edwina. Her words were clear and sharp. They sounded brand new to my ears, and also deeply meaningful because of their freshness. This drink is making me smarter than I was before, I thought.

"That would be delightful," I said, pronouncing each word carefully, but with a practised smoothness that had not been there before.

She smiled at me. "I think you're going to do just fine here on the Island of Mist and Forgetfulness. Come on, I'll help you book a room."

For the first time the name of the place troubled me, but I didn't want to let trouble in, and so I shrugged it off. A name is just a name. It doesn't have to mean anything.

Edwina booked me a room for the night, showed me how to order room service and softly kissed my cheek by way of good night. She smelled of expensive face powder and the kind of cologne that comes in crystal bottles.

She didn't come to see me the next day. Or the day after that. I didn't understand why she had abandoned me until the front desk attendant handed me my first bill. I had no means of paying it, nor did I have any means of contacting Edwina.

"My friend said she would help me," I told the attendant. As I said the words, I realized they weren't true. I had just assumed she would help me; she had never said so. Still, there was nothing to do but continue. "Only problem is, I've misplaced her phone number. You wouldn't happen to have it? Her name is Edwina."

"Edwina what?" said the desk attendant.

"That's all I know," I said. "Should there be more?"

"Look, I don't know who brought you here, or why they prepared you so poorly for whatever it was, but you can't go around racking up hotel bills that you can't pay," the attendant said. "I'm sorry, but I'll have to call the general manager."

The general manager was six feet tall and balding. He smelled of sour milk. He took my hand and enclosed it in his. I think he was trying to be friendly. His palms were smooth and cool, but I didn't like the feel of them. "Come with me to my office," he said, "and we'll have a little talk."

He took me into the elevator, grasping my hand the whole time. We came out on the eleventh floor. He took me into a shiny office. I sat down on his white leather couch. He sat beside me, still holding my hand, and gazing into my eyes in a too-meaningful sort of way. It was extremely unnerving.

"You don't have any papers, do you?"

"What papers?"

"How did you get here?"

"Edwina walked me here, through the clouds."

He shook his head. "You know I can get you deported back to China, or Spool Island, or wherever it is you come from, at the drop of a hat. I don't want to do that. But I need you to co-operate."

I nodded, even though in that moment I would have been happy to return to China.

"I'll give you a job in the hotel. It won't be much, but you're not educated, are you?"

I shook my head.

"So you won't know the difference."

He gave me a job as a toilet scrubber and bedsheet changer for the hotel. "If you don't like it, there is other work that pays better," he said. "But I won't offend you by suggesting it. You just come look for me again if you decide you're interested."

I scowled at him. "I won't be interested."

You wouldn't believe it if I told you all the things people do in rented rooms. How badly they can make the sheets stink after one night's use. The liquids they leave in the sinks and toilets, the bugs, the bloodstains. You wouldn't believe the things they leave behind by mistake—wedding rings and diaries, drugs and incriminating letters. Once I found a fingertip. I didn't want to speculate how it ended up there.

But I couldn't avoid finding out. Its owner turned up on the television news that night, wriggling a very plastic-looking finger at the camera and insisting that it was the one he was born with. He didn't realize how the sharp studio lights emphasized the seam and the distinction between the colour of his flesh and the colour of the plastic tip. But what was more disturbing to me was his remarkable resemblance to Edwina—the smooth brow, the high cheekbones and the clean angle of his nose. When he smiled, insincerely, his thin lips curled in the same slightly irregular line.

He owned the hotel. In fact, he owned a whole chain of hotels of the same name. He denied that the removal of his fingertip signified his allegiance to any secret society and he denied sanctioning the sale of heroin in any of his hotels in spite of the fact that the number of known junkies living in any one of them was well above average.

"Why don't you credit me with helping the victims of predators," he said, "if there are so many of them in my hotels. You'll find, I'm sure, that there is not a single dealer among them."

Later that night, I awoke to the smell of smoke. I sat up in bed. Smoke was pouring in through all four of the vents in the ceiling. I leapt up, pulled on some clothes, and dashed out into the hallway. Many of the girls who stayed on this floor were already out, in their satiny gowns and robes, hurrying down the hallway towards the exit. Junkies slunk out of their rooms more slowly, their pale faces too languid to register the shock. One of them muttered something about a spilled ashtray on the third floor.

I scuttled down the smoke-filled hallway towards the nearest exit. Against the wall, just a few feet from my room, lay a young woman. I couldn't tell whether smoke inhalation or some prior activity had left her in this state. Her eyes were closed, and her breath slow and laboured. I reached underneath her body and tried to pull her up by her armpits, but she weighed into me like a sack of rocks. The hallway was dense with smoke. I pulled her a few feet, and then I started to cough, and couldn't stop. Smoke filled my mouth and eyes. I couldn't breathe, and my eyes smarted and ran with tears. I could pull her no further. I left her in the hallway and ran howling out the exit at the end of the hall and into the safety of darkness. As I ran, I could hear the roar of the fire, and the screams of the men and women trapped on the upper floors. When I was far enough away that there was little danger of being hit by falling debris, I turned to watch. Just as I turned, a woman in flowing blue robes jumped from the twelfth storey. She fell like an angel, blue against the orange light. But the flames licked at her until the gauzy stuff of her nightgown caught fire about halfway down. She tumbled to the ground flaming.

Several minutes later, the entire third floor collapsed, and all of the building above it leaned towards the city and crashed to earth.

All night I wandered the City of Hope. Except for the occasional twin-propeller plane that breezed between different levels of walkways above, it was dark and quiet, and sharp with the cold bite of the sea. I climbed up and down the narrow hilly streets, lined with clapboard row houses in bright colours, although all hues dulled to grey in the dark and fog. Most of the houses were quiet, and the only noises that escaped to the street were those of late-night lovemaking, and quarrelling in the singsong brogue of the working class. I strolled by the dark shape of the Roman Catholic Basilica, a great beast hulking in the mist. If its stone exterior had not been so cold and the building so imposing, I might have dared a side door entranceway for shelter. But the building frightened me, and I moved on. I took myself downtown, found a doorway to a woollen goods shop that seemed inviting and settled into it. I did doze off, but the night was thick with ghosts and drunken pub-crawlers. One of them kicked me and threw beer in my face, then ran off down the street laughing. I suppose I should have been thankful it was beer and not urine. I picked myself up and continued to wander. I went down to the docks to watch the big steel freighters and breathe in the fishy smell of the sea. I wondered if there were other ways home besides the way Edwina had brought me. Some of the ships smelled enticingly of fish, but none of them had Chinese names. I watched the waves lap up against them and toss them gently against the dock. Above them, seagulls circled and screamed.

At dawn I saw a sign on a telephone pole that intrigued me. It said, "Got the gift of the gab? Earn up to twenty dollars an hour just for talking." Underneath was an address as well as a phone number, which was good because I didn't have even a dime for a phone call. The one gift I did have, albeit at the expense of my native tongue, was the gift of speech. I walked halfway across town to the address on the page, and presented myself as soon as the office opened.

There were two men working behind the counter, a Forgetfullian and a Chinese, the first I had seen since my arrival. They introduced themselves as Mr. Jow and Mr. Pettigrew.

"We're a telemarketing firm," Mr. Jow explained.

"Part of a new federal government initiative," said Mr. Pettigrew. "We have start-up money from a special job creation fund."

"The business is new, and so still very fragile," said Mr. Jow. "We need people we can trust."

Mr. Pettigrew nodded meaningfully.

"You can trust me," I said.

They gave me a job as a telemarketer selling big chances to win at the state lottery of China. The old folks I called believed me because of my accent. I told them I had an insider's tips on the horse races, which, as you may have guessed, are almost always rigged. That was my trick. I brought them in on a conspiracy. That way, if they ever realized the scam, they would have to incriminate themselves in order to get me.

I accepted their cheques and money orders. I accepted cash in the mail. I maxed out credit cards, from the cheap plastic to the kind truly made of gold and studded with diamonds. I bought them a few token tickets in some offshore lottery. In the meantime, I acquired a charm and a proficiency in Forgetfullian that I had never had in my own language. I lied like a dog.

One afternoon, towards the end of my shift, when my silver tongue was just a little less slippery, when my guilty conscience was just beginning to seep into my daily thoughts, I got a little old lady with a slight lilt to her voice.

"An insider, eh?" she said. "I wonder if my daughter knows him. She's half Chinese, you know. She's teaching there now."

"China is a big place, ma'am. I suppose your daughter might know him, but I'm not free to divulge his name, not for the good rate I'm giving you here. Don't want to take any risks, you know. We're very cautious about security. Protects us, protects you too. Otherwise I couldn't give you any guarantees, could I?"

"Just the same, I think my daughter might know him."

I wasn't sure what she was driving at. Maybe I should just let her go. "That may very well be, ma'am," I said. "But I doubt your daughter could offer you guaranteed winnings, could she? Now what's your credit card number?"

"I don't know," said the little old lady. There was a strange hissing sound on the line.

"What's that noise?"

She hung up.

The following day, the newspaper headlines ran "Asian Gambling Racket Fleeces Pensioners." They played my voice on the news. I should have smelled it coming but I didn't. I cursed the day I had ever followed Edwina to this godforsaken place, where there wasn't a respectable job to be had for love or money, where everyone was either a scam artist or the victim of one, or sometimes both at once, and where not a day passed without a scandal erupting and outraged reports appearing in tabloids and broadsheets alike all over the country.

I didn't bother to collect my final paycheque. Across town, I found a room in another, dingier hotel where there were lots of sex trade workers and immigrants, but no thick men in business garb. I grew depressed. I missed the Salt Fish Girl.

One night, I was lying in my narrow bed, drinking tequila straight from the bottle and listening to a radio play about aliens invading earth. The mattress was thin and the bedsprings dug into my back. There was a knock on the door. It was Edwina. She was dressed from top to toe in soft cream-coloured leather, but her eyes were manic and her hair dishevelled. "I'm so glad I found you," she said. "My father lost a hotel chain in a buy-out. He's been drunk for five days and won't leave my apartment. I think he might have done something terrible to my mother. Can I come in?"

There was a drama and a tragedy to her grief that seemed very genuine to me. My anger took a sidestep. I opened the door and let her in.

"I'm so glad you're not angry with me for not checking up on you sooner," she said.

"I'm not angry," I lied, gazing into her eyes. I did not mean the gaze shrewdly. I did not mean it to make the lie more convincing. I gazed into the watery blueness because I could not believe she was here. I gazed trying to grasp a sense of her materiality, trying to understand whether or not she was real, trying to look into her and see what lay beneath the pale shimmer.

"Can I spend the night here? If you let me, tomorrow I'll take you to Spool Island. We can go shopping. We can get our nails done. It will be way more fun than lying around being depressed and hiding from my dad."

"I don't know," I said, dubiously.

"Don't be like that," she said. Her eyes grew round and amazingly damp.

"We'll talk about it tomorrow," I said.

She went to her bed and I went to mine. I did not understand where I was, or how I had come to this place. In my home village I had heard stories of men who invented South Sea islands, and sold gullible dreamers citizenships in places that did not exist, for outrageous sums. Perhaps the wanting of so many desperate and hopeful people had made one of those islands real. But then why was it like this, so cold and damp, and where were the others like me? A thick mist wafted through the window.

I woke to find that she had made coffee and pancakes. All the sorrow and despair that weighed her down the previous night had vanished, and I felt proud, as though I had done something to effect this.

"The weather is brilliant," she said. "It's going to be a fabulous trip. Pack your bathing suit."

I could still have refused to go, but it seemed terribly surly. I ate the pancakes and drank the coffee. I packed a bag.

The sun was still low in the sky when we reached the marina, but it was already warm and the fog that hung perpetually over the land was thinner than usual. She steered us out of the haze that surrounded the Island of Mist and Forgetfulness and out onto the brilliant sea.

She had not said anything about being met on the other side, so I was surprised when we were greeted by two men at the dock. They were handsome and friendly. Edwina seemed to know them, and to be glad to see them, so I pretended I was too. They were not locals but Forgetfullians like us.

Their names were Sam and McDonell. They took us for a fancy seafood lunch in a cozy restaurant on the ground floor of a colonial-style hotel. Sam sat beside Edwina. He talked about the new self-contained underwater breathing apparatus that was the latest craze on Spool Island, and rubbed her knee. Edwina listened intently to his every word, nodded and smiled while his over-large hand kneaded her thigh.

I jabbed at my plate of garlic and lime grilled scallops and scowled at him.

"Those were old friends of mine," said Edwina as soon as they were gone. "Why did you have to be so rude?"

"Because they were irritating," I said crossly.

She shook her head and brushed her hand against my cheek. "Have you ever had a pedicure?"

"I haven't."

"It's the most wonderful thing, and the women of Spool Island are better at it than anyone anywhere else in the world."

Her enthusiasm and the promise of a luxurious pleasure were overwhelming. I forgot that she had abandoned me at the hotel. I would have trusted her with anything.

She took me down an ancient cobblestone street and through a very modern set of glass doors into a little salon with terra cotta–tiled floor and glass shelves loaded with jars of pretty coloured liquids.

The proprietor, a soft, honey-coloured woman with dark hair and eyes like mine, led us into the back and seated us on a green brocade sofa strewn with pillows. At each end was a deep brown ceramic basin full of steamy, sweet-smelling water, atop which floated pink and white flower petals as though some graceful tree had just shaken its branches over a steaming pool. Two breastless and hipless young women dressed in flowing whites came to attend to us. They washed our feet, dried them, and massaged them with lemon-scented lotion. They clipped and filed our nails, then polished them with pretty glazes that made our nails look like the insides of seashells. The whole time, I fidgeted in my seat, feeling scruffy in my ill-fitting dress. Edwina, however, reclined serenely on the soft multicoloured cushions, blissful and elegant.

Afterwards, we took a leisurely stroll to the beach and lay in the sun until the air began to cool. We meandered lazily back to the boat, reluctant to return to the Island of Mist and Forgetfulness.

It was dark when the Coast Guard pulled us over and boarded our little speedboat.

"Where have you been, ladies?" asked the inspector.

"To Spool Island," said Edwina, much too sweetly.

"For what purpose?"

Edwina lifted her skirt just high enough to reveal her beautiful feet.

"What else did you do while you were there?"

"We had lunch, and went to the beach."

"Did you meet anyone or speak to any of the locals?"

"Just the women in the salon."

I opened my mouth to say something about Sam and McDonell, but Edwina shot me a cold, hard look.

The inspector waved up to another man on the Coast Guard boat. A large German shepherd jumped down into our speedboat. It sniffed around and began to bark excitedly somewhere near the motor.

"If you ladies wouldn't mind coming with me," said the inspector.

We rode back to the Island of Mist and Forgetfulness in silence. I wanted to ask what was going on, but the way

Edwina looked at me I dared not make a sound. I began, in fact, to feel vaguely guilty, although I had no idea what it was that I might have done.

She spoke not a word to me or the Coast Guard people for the entire length of the journey.

They handcuffed us and put us in separate police cars, long and black. There were two policemen in the car I rode, one to drive and one to keep an eye on me. I didn't move. He said they were taking us to Ville Despair, the administrative centre of Island of Mist and Forgetfulness.

Ville Despair had once upon a time been settled by the French, who named it Ville d'Espoir. Ever competitive, the English had named their settlement, on the other side of the Sighing River, "Hope." As the English took over the island, years before it became unmoored from history, lost its connection with the past or the future and floated into the sky, the name had slowly slipped from the original to Ville Despair, the name that went down in all the books from the moment the British won the Battle of Heart's Delight and took legal and administrative control. The two cities had since grown considerably, so that they now bled into one another. The Sighing River had been dammed in four places and was criss-crossed by eleven bridges.

The car I rode in came to a halt. Farther ahead, Edwina's car pulled up in front of another entrance. I saw her step out of the car in her cream-coloured leather suit, her head still held high. She did not turn to look at me, though I think she knew my eyes were locked on her. She did not turn until she was almost through the swinging glass doors in front of her and then she cast a brief glance my way and I thought her eyes showed pity. Then they hauled me, a policeman at one arm and a Coast Guard officer at the other, through my own set of double swinging glass doors. I was greeted by a long blue hallway with a wicket to one side near the entrance. They guided me up to the window where I gave my name, birthdate, occupation and permanent address. They asked me to name a next of kin, but I could give none. Two police-men led me through the iron gate and down a blue corridor. There were steel doors on either side at regular intervals. The doors had tiny windows at eye level and a slot near the bottom through which food could be pushed. They unlocked one of these doors and shoved me inside.

"Please," I said to the one that had been with me since Edwina and I disembarked from the boat, "tell me why I'm here."

"Don't get smart with me, missy."

The other policeman, however, read to me from a card. I was under arrest for illegal immigration, and for smuggling thirty-six kilos of brown heroin into the Island of Mist and Forgetfulness.

"I don't know what you're talking about," I protested.

The cops looked at one another and shook their heads. The steel door slammed behind me.

The cell contained a narrow mattress with a coarse grey blanket thrown over sheets that reeked of bleach, a sink, a toilet and a camera with a beady red eye high in the far corner. I suppose I should have been thankful for the cleanliness and the lack of blood on the walls, but somehow the sterility of the place frightened me more than anything. Except for a slight sag at the centre of the mattress, there was no evidence of any previous presence in this cell. No evidence of beatings, or pain, no trace of the invasion of subdued bodies, and yet somehow those things were all present in the reek of the bleach and the gleam of the walls. I sat on the mattress with my head in my hands and waited, because that was all there was to do.

I was still sitting like that when they came to get me in the morning. The Chief Interrogator, a tall, broad, once-handsome man with wise grey eyes and a thick beard, said Edwina had confessed everything. On her evidence they would have no trouble convicting me of drug smuggling and of the intention to immigrate illegally. She had shown them my forged papers—papers I had never seen—and explained to them how it was done.

"At first she said you were innocent, but we made it worth her while to tell us the truth," the Chief Interrogator said.

"You tortured her?"

"No need for such crude tactics. We merely promised her reduced charges and a shortened sentence. She was, after all, only the accomplice."

Why shed blood when people can be bought and sold so easily?

They locked me up in a prison for women. Most of my companions were either drug offenders like me or had maimed or killed their abusive husbands.

We sat and rotted in the dark.

After six months, I asked for and received permission to study. They like prisoners to keep busy because it keeps them out of trouble. The discipline I chose was probability. I hoped that when I got out I could get a dull but respectable job as a statistician. I calculated the likelihood of all kinds of unlikely things, such as the chances of having seven sons in a row, or the chances of getting a daughter on the eighth try if you already have seven sons, or the chances of getting a decent job in a town where people can only imagine you as a powermonger, a criminal or a charity case. I read books on population and demographics. I followed the stock markets. I avoided the abuses of the guards as much as possible until they started hiding cockroaches in our mashed potatoes. Angry, humiliated and provoked, we yelled and rattled the bars. In the night, we all set fire to our beds at the same time with one match each from a package the newest inmate had smuggled in with her. We planned to riot when they took us out of our cells, but they never did. They hosed us and our beds down with cold water, turned out the lights and left us in the wet cold dark for three days.

There was a young woman who was there because she shot her husband the week after he pressed her face to a hot element. She caught the flu and passed it on to her neighbours. It moved down the line until every woman in the place was coughing and vomiting. The guards turned down the heat. Years later, when the prison finally came under government scrutiny, the guards denied active malice, although they admitted they at times might have been neglectful, which was only to be expected given the extent of the prison's overcrowding.

I pinned the pages of my books to the bars to dry them and studied by candlelight until they put the lights back on.

I was released two years early for good behaviour. They gave me back the ill-fitting dress I'd been wearing the day I was arrested. Unwashed for five years, it smelled of old seaweed and rancid sweat. On the hem was a small pink stain, the brilliant nail polish from the pedicure I'd had that long-ago morning. I walked out into the city that had once seemed so shiny to me. It looked a lot dingier than I remembered. The glass and concrete didn't wear well in the rain. I asked for and received directions to the nearest employment centre, and there I discovered that in order to work in a statistics office you had to join the Statisticians' Guild. And if you were foreign-born, you had to have five years of experience as a statistician on the Island of Mist and Forgetfulness before you could join. It was illogical of course, but the Guild secretary told me it was up to me, not her, to figure it out.

I blamed Edwina for taking me away from my home and from the natural course of my life, no matter how troubled and impoverished it had been. I blamed her for my endless string of failures. And then I blamed myself because it was I, after all, who had decided to follow her, against my own better judgment.

One day, in the middle of the afternoon, I had a dream about the Salt Fish Girl. We were standing together beside a river, having just caught a fish the size of a human being. We gutted and flayed it, cut its flesh into strips, sprinkled it with salt and laid it on bamboo racks to dry. I took some of the fish before it was quite ready and placed it in my mouth. It tasted like my own tongue. Its human taste shocked and horrified me. The realization that I had swallowed some before noting the taste made me sick to my stomach. I leaned over, retching and spitting. A gold coin tumbled out of my mouth and rolled with a clink onto the rocks and into the river.

I woke up sweating and crying. The sun had just set, leaving a thin band of pink along the horizon. I got up, bathed, dressed and went out into the streets. There was a slight breeze, which kicked up quickly into a strong wind that whirled and eddied and tossed about garbage and dead leaves that had collected in gutters and dead-end streets.

I found myself in the doorway of the same bar that Edwina had last taken me to. I went in and took the elevator up. Surprisingly, no one questioned me in the foyer. I left my coat at the coat check and went in.

The place smelled strongly of cigarette smoke, expensive perfume and hard liquor. A large cage stood in the centre of the room—a rattan cage with many little domes and turrets, a shuttered door, a little swing. Inside, a slender young man wrapped in diaphanous scarves danced. His face was concealed by a beaked and bespectacled mask.

The table where Edwina and I had sat last time was empty, so I returned to it, ordered a beer, lit a cigarette and sat watching the dancer for quite some time.

He gazed at me for an attenuated moment and then, behind the mask, his eyes moved sharply to indicate a small dark archway painted onto a fresco depicting a garden scene, which covered the entire far wall. The painted archway was framed by a tall hedge. If you looked closely you could see that there was in fact an opening there, covered with a thin screen of black gauze. Under the dancer's intent gaze, or perhaps compelled by it, I crossed the painted garden and moved towards the opening. I pushed aside the gauze screen and stepped into the space. It was pitch dark. I could smell something sweet and smoky, but nothing more. But after a few moments, my eyes adjusted and I realized it wasn't entirely dark after all. I was standing in a little room with a Persian carpet on the floor, a dark wood desk in one corner, and an overstuffed leather chair in the other. On the chair sat a man, apparently unconscious, with a pipe, still smoking, in his hand. Against the wall was a flat, wide, bed-like couch, covered with a black-fringed, flowery spread. Edwina lay on the couch, on her side, smoking from a silver water pipe that sat beside her. Her pupils were so wide and dark that her corneas were reduced to narrow rings. In the dull light, her long pale hair looked white.

I stepped up to the couch and lay down facing her.

"I want to go home," I said.

"After all you've invested?"

"Yes."

"You will never remember your old language." She said this not as a mere statement, but more like a curse.

"I want to go."

"You don't know the meaning of perseverance," she said. I got angry. "Who are you to judge me?"

"I'm not keeping you," she said. "You are free to go."

She offered me no help, and it hurt my pride to ask. "I don't know the way," I said.

"You need a map. It will cost you. Not much though. Just one gold coin."

The only gold coin I had was the one the Salt Fish Girl had given me. Reluctantly, I drew it from my pocket and dropped it into her outstretched hand. From the folds of her skirt, she drew a tattered brown map and handed it to me. "Go then," she said.

I hated her. She gazed at me with such an assured sense of her own superiority that I bit my tongue in fury and felt hot blood gush into my mouth. Before I knew what I was doing, I had pulled the fish-gutting knife from my side and pressed it into her belly. Her blood spilled out over the bed like water, flowed towards me and seeped into my clothes, without staining them. There was no heat in it. I stared at her in horror. She did not look away, nor did her serene facial expression waver until the last minute, when a brief blaze of anger flashed through her eyes. I remained in the grip of her gaze until at last her eyelids blinkered shut.

In the leather chair, the unconscious man's head lolled to the other side and he let out a long sigh.

Clutching the map in my hand, I hurried out into the club, through its heavy oak entrance doors and down the stairs, not stopping to look at the birdcage dancer or to get my coat.

Miranda

**Unregulated Zone
and Serendipity, 2062**

A SONG FOR CLARA CRUISE

When I woke it was evening, and I'm fairly sure it was still the same day. There was no sign of the doctor. I was not lying on a bed in that strange hotel room, with the ocean crashing against the far wall, but rather sitting in one of the high-backed chairs I routinely seated patients in while I took blood samples from them. I didn't know who had moved me, or whether I had in fact imagined the trip to the Pan Pacific Hotel. Seto wasn't around either. I checked my file to see whether I had done any blood-work that day. I hadn't. I put my hand to the back of my neck. I felt a shallow circular depression, and an incision recently closed and still crusted with dried blood. No one tried to stop me as I went out through the double doors and made for the elevators. No one stopped me on the grounds either.

I climbed on my bike and headed back towards town. My brother was busy that week with an extraordinary number of cars and so I had been cycling to and from work. It was a long way from Flowers' suburban clinic to the edge of town.

Just short of the halfway point sat a grey concrete compound in the middle of a field, surrounded by a chain-link fence. There was a small plastic sign clipped to the fence that said "Zodiac Industries" in neat lettering. I passed the compound every day on my way to work, but it was the kind of thing that is just grey and there. You don't think about it.

But on this day, a bunch of ragtag political types were blockading the road that ran beside the compound. A wall of riot police in brown uniforms moved towards them in even columns, the heels of their high black boots clicking in unison against the concrete. Automobile traffic was backed up for miles on either side of the wall of people, who stood silently, calm and orderly but refusing to budge. I pedalled through the mass of held-up cars towards the back of the motionless crowd. There were perhaps twenty or thirty other cyclists also waiting there.

Suddenly, without warning, the riot police pulled masks over their faces and from the back of their ranks a large cannon fired a cloud of thin mist into the air. Cars honked, people rushed back away from the direction of town, away from the road. But I hardly noticed. My eyes and nostrils burned and the urge to cough rose in my lungs. I turned my bike around and tried to pedal back the way I had come, but it wasn't long before I found myself lying at the side of the road hacking and wheezing. Without warning a great spurt of blood shot from my nose. The burning sensation intensified. I tried to pinch my nostrils shut, but blood oozed rapidly through the pinched closure and flowed over my fingers. I tried to scream, but my throat burned dry. And then there was somebody carrying me away into the green field. I closed my eyes, felt my own blood gush over my mouth and down my chin, and through the sharp burning sensation smelled the iron stink of it. I didn't know who was carrying me or where, but I was too confused and disoriented to fight.

Whoever it was put me down in the tall grass, poured a thin stream of cool water over my face from a small plastic canteen, and wiped away the blood with a torn piece of T-shirt. My nostrils were clamped shut and my head held forward until a clot formed. I looked up. In the distance, I could make out the grey shape of the concrete compound and the swirl of red police lights flashing. I turned to inspect the face of the person who had helped me. She wore a tattered brown nylon jacket over a greyish undershirt that had probably once been white. Her face was long and thin. She wore a cheap cardboard party mask, spray-painted silver, over her eyes. The paper was crumpled and the edges worn, but the mask was held very firmly in place with a thick piece of elastic that had been stapled on to replace the flimsy stringy one provided by the mask company.

"What was that?" I asked.

"B324—the latest in crowd-control technology. It's some kind of supertoxic chemical irritant."

"How come you're not affected?"

"I dunno. Used to it, I guess. What were you doing there? You don't seem to be the type to be involved with the factory workers' movement."

"No."

"Didn't think so."

"I was just on my way home from work."

"Well," she said, irritated, "you'd better just run along then."

I didn't understand her rudeness. "Okay, I'm going. Thanks for everything." I had not intended a sarcastic tone of voice, but there it was. I pulled myself to standing, but as I did so, my head grew light and my field of vision narrowed. My knees went soft and I sank back to the ground.

"A bit feeble, aren't you?" she said, derisive.

I felt a trickle of blood run over my lip, but did not move to wipe it. She leaned close with that dangerously rank scrap of T-shirt. But somehow, beneath its dirty human scent and through the iron stench of my own blood, I caught a whiff of something subtler, and infinitely sweeter.

"It's you," I said.

"You don't know what you're talking about." But she sounded frightened. And I myself was shocked by this odd glimpse of clarity, this moment of knowing, sharp as a sea breeze, and passing just as quickly.

"It's okay," I said. "I won't take off on you this time."

"Excuse me, but I think it was me that ran away from you." She raised her hand and pushed the paper mask from her face. "At the clinic this morning."

I smiled.

"If you're spying on me, all I can say is they picked a really stupid-looking spy."

"Thanks a lot. No, I'm not spying on you. I just feel something. I can't explain it."

"Well," she said, belligerent. "I don't recognize you. And I recognize everyone from the factory."

"Factory?"

She had a knife at my throat so fast I didn't know what it was until its clean edge pressed against my skin. "Who are you working for? What did you do with the blood you took?"

"I'm not working for anyone," I squeaked. "The blood is in my pocket."

Without withdrawing her gaze from mine, she reached forward and dipped her hand into my pocket. She produced a thin vial, less than half full of her own dark blood. As she reached, the salt fish smell emanating from her pores intensified. My eyes watered with sudden sorrow. She pressed the blade closer.

"What are you crying about?"

"If you only knew," I said.

She must have known something because she pulled the knife away, held the vial up to catch the last light of the darkening sky.

"You're fucking crazy," she said.

I sniffed back snot and tears. "You should talk," I said. The tears dried as quickly as they'd arrived. I felt very confused. However familiar she had seemed, she suddenly didn't. She now appeared alien and very dirty.

I got up and ran.

She made no attempt to come after me. When I got closer to the road, I saw the police were still there, questioning people and gathering up abandoned property, including my bike, and shoving it into a van. No doubt it would appear for sale at the next monthly police auction on the main floor of what used to be the public library.

I didn't get home until nearly midnight. My brother and father were furious, and all the more so because I had lost my bike. "You think they grow on trees?" my father said.

My brother said, "I'm not driving you tomorrow. You better get up early so you can take the bus."

I hated the bus. In the urban part of its route it was rank and crowded, all those bodies that could not afford anything better pressed up against one another, too intimately close. If there was anything to be picked out of one's pockets, it was invariably picked. If you weren't careful, other more personal pockets might also be violated, which was not nice at all, unless you were into that kind of thing, and there was a subculture of people who were.

In the suburban parts of the route, the crowd thinned to a breathable density, but the route wound without end through every mildewing subdivision. It took hours to get anywhere. If your lungs could withstand the grey smog that hung perpetually over the land, walking would have been faster, but very few had that kind of lungs.

I made sure my pockets were empty and my person sealed as tightly as possible inside my clothes before setting out the following morning. The ride was relatively uneventful except for a young pickpocket making a futile search of my jacket pockets and a couple of teenagers hucking orange peels at a humpbacked man with barrettes in his hair. The bus driver told them to smarten up and they backed off.

The sun was round and high through the haze when I stepped off the bus just across the road from Flowers' clinic.

Evie was waiting for me at the edge of the parking lot, a heavy canvas knapsack slung over one shoulder. She wore the same grungy clothes as yesterday, including the tattered silver cardboard mask.

"I've seen your face before, remember?" I said.

"It's not you I'm hiding from." She held a brand-new mask in sparkly iridescent green towards me, still in its thin cellophane package.

"What's this for?"

"Would you recognize Flowers' car?"

"I guess so." It wasn't hard, since my brother worked on it all the time. Besides, there was only a handful of cars in the lot to choose from.

I pointed to a slate-grey Volvo with leather seats. Evie set her knapsack down beside the car. From its gaping mouth she produced a blanket, a crowbar and a screwdriver. She laid the blanket over the driver's-side window to muffle the sound, and then launched vigorously into it with the crowbar. The glass shattered silently.

Horrified, I asked, "What are you doing?"

"I thought you might enjoy a little jaunt through the mountains."

I clutched the cellophane package, unable to respond.

She unlocked the door, brushed the glass from the driver's seat, sat down and began bashing into the steering column. I winced. Did she know how hard Volvo steering columns were to come by in this day and age? "This is Flowers' car. He knows who I am."

"You have to decide which side you're on, baby girl."

"I'm on my side. This job is my education. I need it."

"Then run upstairs and get on with it."

I stood there.

She jammed the screwdriver into the ignition. The engine roared to life. Nonchalantly, she leaned over and unlocked the passenger-side door. "Coming?" she asked, without even glancing at me.

I hesitated for a moment and then climbed in. As Evie dropped the handbrake, I took the shimmery cardboard mask from its package and pulled it over my face. She stepped on the gas and we tore out of the parking lot, aimed straight for the mountains. The wind rushed through the broken window. Our hair flew back and the cheap cardboard masks rattled against our faces. The car wound up into trees and quiet. After an interminable amount of time, she turned into a side road blocked by a gate. She had to stop the car and get out to open it, drive through, and then get out again to shut it. As we drove down the dirt road, rocks and pebbles flew up in front of us, battering the hood. We came to a halt somewhere in the mountains, in a small parking lot beside a glistening lake.

"When was the last time you went into the forest?" she asked.

"A long time ago."

"Shall we?"

"I think I'm hungry."

She opened her knapsack and pulled out a paper bag full of steamed buns which she must have purchased earlier at some roadside stand.

"Cha siew bow?" she said. "Or gai bow?"

"You're crazy."

She laughed gleefully and passed me a bun.

When we stepped into the woods her bravado softened. Her eyes grew quiet and contemplative behind the paper mask. A cool fresh smell blew off the lake and blended with the green scent of cedar and pine, and the rotten smell of dead needles and branches underfoot. The lake lapped quietly at the shore, and above our heads a slight wind hissed through the trees. She walked slowly, kicking at the ground. The brown, humusy scent of earth rushed up at us.

I munched quietly on my bun. I worried about the devastating blow I had delivered to my career. It was very likely we would get caught and very unlikely that Flowers would give me another chance. I tried to tell myself that I didn't care, that these were merely the vicissitudes of life and that there were much larger situations and more important goals than what an individual might or might not make of oneself in a lifetime. I tried to tell myself that Flowers was corrupt and self-serving, and my brother's and father's hopes provincial, but it didn't help. I didn't know how I would face them.

Evie's eyes had completely changed. What had glittered with mischief and defiance the whole length of the journey now deepened into something calm and dark.

"It's like a church in here," she said. "Not like a church, but like how a church should be."

"You went to church?"

She smiled. "Never had a chance. Always wanted to. I think I'm a closet Catholic." She grinned and her yellow teeth flashed.

"If you wanted to, why didn't you just go? Religion is still free."

"Not for everybody."

"Yes, for everybody. It's in the Pacific Economic Union's mission statement."

"Not everybody. Only those defined as persons."

I looked at her blankly.

Exasperated, she quickly shed her dirty hemp jacket, turned her back to me and pulled up her T-shirt. At the base of her spine was a series of numbers, which looked at a distance like they had been tattooed on, but if you looked more closely, the digits were raised ridges filled with some kind of powdered black metal. They could be read by touch, Braille beneath the skin. She raised her T-shirt higher, revealing something infinitely more horrific. A scar along the valley of the spine, a shiny red hollow, and across the shoulder blades bumpy red ridges as though wires had been ripped from beneath the skin. And between the ridges was an odd scalloped pattern, giving the distinct impression of feathers. I reached out and ran my fingers over them, without stopping to think whether it might be rude.

"What an amazing scar."

"You've never seen one of these before, have you?"

"No."

"Do you never take the bus, or what?" She pulled her T-shirt back down and turned to face me.

"I don't, except today. I usually ride my bike. Or some-times my brother drives me."

She shook her head. "You have to ride the bus or you never find out what's going on. I suppose you read the papers and believe what they say." I nodded. "The papers are still independent."

"They aren't. They belong to Aries William, who is a major shareholder in the Central Bank."

"But there are laws about freedom of expression."

"Yeah, they don't gas bus riders for talking on the bus, yet. Though it wouldn't surprise me."

"I don't understand what this has to do with your . . . wings."

"You ever hear of a firm called Johnny Angel?"

"Sure. They're seed designers."

She sighed and leaned back on her elbows. "Designers. Okay. You ever hear of a shoe company called Pallas?"

"Of course, everyone that can afford them owns a pair of Pallas shoes."

"And they both belong to Aries William of Nextcorp fame. They've been making people for years."

"Making people?"

"Why do you think their labour costs are so low?"

"But the shoes are expensive."

"Well, why do you think some people are so stinking rich? Especially the PR types."

"I don't know."

"That's what they bank on. Excuse the pun."

"You're telling me you're a clone."

"You don't need to be so crass."

"But that's illegal."

"Being one, yes, just about. But not making them."

"I've never heard of it being legalized. There was an article in the papers last week about the ethics of it. I remember because a lot of the produce we sell is affected. Animals and plants are allowed, but not humans."

"I'm not human."

I recoiled slightly.

"My genes are point zero three per cent *Cyprinus carpio* —freshwater carp. I'm a patented new fucking life form."

I stared, speechless. Finally I said, "That's an enormous loophole. There must be laws governing human biomaterial."

"There was until about twenty-five years ago. That's when they figured out how to grow certain organs in the lab. Livers and kidneys, I think. I ought to know. It's my own personal history. But the education of Workers is not something either Pallas or Nextcorp concern themselves with overly."

She creeped me out. I may not be the most natural creature that ever walked the face of the earth, but there was something sordid about her origins.

"Are there a lot of you out there?"

"Lots of me, yeah, at least a hundred thousand with identical material."

"Oh, God, that's not what I meant."

Those yellow teeth again. "I know."

I still felt stupid, but now I felt kind of freaked out as well.

"You wanted to know if they let very many of us go."

I nodded.

"They don't. I got out the same way I got that car. Because I wanted to. We're not designed for wits or willpower, but I was an early model. They couldn't control for everything. Maybe the fish was the unstable factor." Behind the mask, her eyes burned with bravado.

"So you're the only one?"

She pushed the mask over her face. The bravado was gone and she suddenly seemed small and young and frightened. "At my factory there was the rumour of a secret house where other escapees are living together and planning to sabotage Pallas. I don't know if it's true, but I'm looking."

"And the scar?"

"My Guardian Angel."

"I don't understand."

"It's a device they use to keep track of us. Johnny invented it himself. Or at least that's the story. We're taught to respect our Guardian Angels. The GA looks after us, monitors our body temperature, notes the presence of disease, helps rescuers find us if we get lost. . ."

"Or if you escape."

"You're a swift one, aren't you? I scraped the central disc out on a jagged bit of broken concrete wall, and pulled until the wiring came free."

"It must have been incredibly painful."

"I could hear them coming with their dogs and guns and chains as I worked the thing out of my back. I had no choice. I had to rip it. I flung myself over the razor-wire fence. Lucky I'm athletic. Blood everywhere. I crossed a glacier to throw them off the scent. Just like Frankenstein, you ever read that one? I spent a night on the glacier and came out of the mountains in the morning."

"Free."

"Alone. It wasn't easy to leave, you know, when you are used to being surrounded all the time by your sisters, and have been raised to believe you are being benevolently watched from above."

"Do you know who your . . . source was?" I asked softly.

"Some of the others talk about a woman called Ai, a Chinese woman who married a Japanese man and was interned in the Rockies during the Second World War. She died of cancer right after the war ended. He died of grief. The bodies were sold to science. They say she collected fossils near the Burgess Shale. But it's all rumour. For all I know one of my co-workers made it up." She smiled bravely, showing the edges of her sharp teeth. "Pallas tries to keep it quiet. A nice myth of origins after all, would be a perfect focus for revolt, don't you think?"

"I don't know."

"I do know that Nextcorp bought out the Diverse Genome Project around the same time as I was born."

"Diverse Genome Project?"

"It focused on the peoples of the so-called Third World, Aboriginal peoples, and peoples in danger of extinction."

"And so all the Workers in the factories . . ."

"Brown eyes and black hair, every single one."

"Stuff like that is not supposed to happen any more."

"Stuff like that never stopped."

"But the newspapers say . . ."

"Shhhh . . ." she leaned over and stroked my hair, tucked the loose strands neatly behind my ears. "It's all there right in front of you. All you need to do is look. There are thousands of compounds all over the PEU. Don't you ever wonder about them?"

"I was raised to respect private property."

She shook her head. "Is everyone in this town as out of it as you? I don't get it. It's not like you have this comfortable life to protect."

"I'm not out of it," I snapped. But my stomach wavered. My world had suddenly become something quite different from what it had been mere moments ago.

She just laughed. Then she did an odd thing. She leaned over and kissed me. Her mouth was soft and full of a strange warmth heightened by contrast with the chill that blew off the lake. The razor edge of those yellow teeth brushed pearly and dangerous against my upper lip. The tremor in my belly changed to something else. She pulled away and gazed at me from a distance of a few inches, crooked teeth grinning.

"That wasn't very Catholic," I said. I took her cold hand and pulled it under my T-shirt, pressed my nose and mouth to the soft space behind her ear. The smell of salt fish was unmistakable.

There was something that moved and breathed inside Evie that was cold and sharp and electric, more alive that anything of this earth. The fishiness of her drew me, but I tried not to think about the strangeness of her conception. Her fingers moved over my skin, cool and tingly as ice water. I wanted to turn into water myself, fall into her the way rain falls into the ocean. I moved through the cool dark with her, my body a single silver muscle slipping against hers, flailing for oxygen in a fast underwater current, shivering slippery cool wet and tumbling through dark towards a blue point of light in the distance, teeth, lip, nipple, the steel taste of blood, gills gaping open and closed, open and closed, mouth, breath, cool water running suddenly piss hot against velvet inner thighs and the quick shudder silver flash of fish turning above the ice-blue surface of the lake.

Afterwards her body burned, ember red in the blue dark woods. I lay beside her on the rot stink of decaying leaves and needles, not speaking, just listening to the lapping and whispering of the dark as it surrounded us. Perhaps it was at this moment that the child took root.

But soon it grew cold. We dressed quickly, not looking at one another.

"Why did you come to the doctor's in the first place?" I asked.

She turned to me and pulled her hair back, revealing the curve of her ear. I couldn't see much in the dark. I reached into my pocket and was pleased to find the book of matches I sometimes carried in case of power outages. I struck one and held it close. Beside her ear pulsed a huge boil, red and ripe with pus. Further up where the last whorl of the outer ear should have given way to smooth flesh, there was a small fistula which tunnelled into her head. Instinctively, I reached up to touch my own. I remember that once the right one got blocked with a bit of dust, and that a huge boil developed below it, full of the fluid that otherwise leaked, briny and fetid, from the hole when rubbed. My mother, who also had a fistula, though beside her left ear only, lanced the boil with a sharp sterile needle, and the pus ran out, hot as blood, down the side of my face.

"Do you have a needle?" I asked. "Or a pin?"

As luck would have it, she had used two safety pins to hold together a torn section of her T-shirt. She unfastened one and handed it to me.

I struck another match and held the point in the flame to sterilize it, and then waved its blackened tip about in the cool night air until its temperature dropped back to normal.

"Hold still." I eased the sharp point into the fattest part of the boil with the expert hand of one who had administered many needles. A thin stream of pus reeking of fish and ocean water shot out at me. For a moment I thought I felt something shift inside me that remembered another longer, leaner shape. I pressed the flesh around the hole, encouraging the pus to drain.

Evie produced a half-mickey of vodka from her knapsack, took a swig and passed it to me. With a scrap of napkin left from some long ago lunch, I swabbed the small wound down.

"You get these infections often?"

"We all do. It's one of the defects. Flowers used to help me with mine sometimes."

It took a running push to jump-start the car when Evie and I emerged from the woods later that night. Finally something my brother had taught me was coming in handy. We wound slowly back through the Fraser Valley in the dark, abandoned the car in a suburb reasonably far from Flowers' clinic and hurried quickly towards the nearest bus stop.

The bus was empty except for a young Asian woman with long hair sitting in one of the long row of seats installed in a long row with their backs to the windows just after the rear doors. Evie sauntered to the very back and plonked herself down. I slipped in beside her.

"What are you going to do now?" she asked.

"About what?"

"About your fall from grace."

"You mean about my job."

She nodded.

So she did think about my world the way I thought about it. "I don't know," I said. "Flowers is conducting this experiment. He wants us both to take part. He was asking after you."

"Don't you dare ever tell him about me."

"Why?"

"And don't ever let him touch your feet."

"I don't understand."

"Don't you know? That's how it spreads. It comes up through the soil. Not everywhere but in certain areas, close to where they've grown GE potatoes. It comes up through the skin of your feet and gets into your bloodstream. Makes your skin all funny."

"Funny?"

"Shiny, scaly, sometimes a little bioluminescent."

"Evie?"

"Yes?"

"I think both of us have some of the symptoms. How do you know we're not already carrying the disease?"

"Do you feel unwell?"

"No."

"Then what's the problem?"

We didn't finish the conversation, because at that moment two young white men stepped onto the bus. They were tall and clean-cut, smugly good-looking. One had sandy blond hair and a little goatee, the other was dark-haired and wore a pair of small, wire-rimmed glasses that made him look fashionably intellectual. They gave the bus driver a used pair of runners in lieu of fare and strode towards us. Abruptly, they turned and plopped themselves down on either side of the long-haired girl. She instantly blushed red.

"Hi," said the blond man. "You're pretty."

"Hi," she said, so nervously it came out a scratchy whisper.

"What's your name?" said the glasses. He snuggled against her, too intimately close.

"Jane," she breathed.

"Where are you from?" said the blond.

"Painted Horse."

"Are you studying here?" Glasses.

"Yes."

"Where?"

"Langara."

"Are ya studying business?"

She nodded and seemed to relax a little. I wondered if she could detect the deadpan mockery in their voices. I wondered if, yesterday, I could have. I grew suddenly aware that I was watching and listening in a way I had not known how to before. I glanced at Evie. She was seething. She pushed past me as though I weren't there, but then she grabbed me by the hand and dragged me along behind her. She sat down beside the blond man. It was the last seat in the row, so I moved up the aisle and deposited myself onto the seat beside Glasses.

"Hi," said Evie to Blondie, snidely. "You're pretty. Where are you from?"

"From here, what does it look like?" said Blondie, annoyed and indignant.

"I mean, where are your parents from?" Evie, determined to embarrass him.

"Why don't you just fuck off?"

"Just trying to be friendly."

"We were having a nice conversation until you came along, weren't we, Jane?"

Jane glanced uncertainly at Evie. The dirty clothes, the spiky hair.

"Were you?" Evie said to Jane, her eyes too full of challenge.

Jane lowered her head and shook it no.

"So why don't you just get off the bus?" said Evie to Blondie.

"Actually," said Jane, her eyes full of panic, "this is my stop." She reached up and rang the bell.

There were a few moments of awkward silence until the bus pulled up to the corner. Jane rose and stepped out through the double doors and onto the dark street. The bus was just about to pull away when Blondie jumped up and scrambled out the doors. Glasses dashed out behind him, turning just once to say, "It's our stop too."

Evie rose to follow them, but the bus had already re-entered traffic.

"Shit," said Evie. She reached up and rang the bell furiously, but the bus kept moving. Evie kept ringing. "I don't think so, lady," the bus driver yelled from up front. "You feminists were just trying to give those boys a hard time."

"They're going to hurt that girl," Evie howled, still ringing the bell. I looked out the back window and could make out two tall shapes on either side of a shorter one, heads angled intently downward.

"They were just being friendly," said the bus driver. "Besides, she is a grown-up."

"Okay, just let us out at the next stop," said Evie.

But he wouldn't. Nor at the stop after that, or even the one after. It was only a coincidence that some people were waiting to get on at a stop not too far from my family's shop, and he was forced to let us out.

It was raining. We hovered a block away from the shop, me feeling distressed and wondering if Flowers had already spoken to my brother or my father. I didn't fear punishment so much as the pain I might inflict on others, especially those I loved.

"The doctor has no idea you were in the car with me," said Evie. "Any evidence he has is entirely circumstantial."

"For all you know he was leaning out the window taking photographs."

"He wasn't. I would have felt it. Besides, any grief you've already caused your family has already been caused, no? Unless you are afraid of punishment."

We didn't talk any further about the illness, although I could not push it from my mind either. It was true, I did not feel unwell. Through all the years of my strange durian odour, it never occurred to me to tell anyone that nothing hurt. And as for the dreams of water, if the truth must be told, they comforted me. I dreamt often of the sea, but not of drowning. I only worried because I felt I should. Every now and then, small flashes of Flowers' basement room returned to me, but never with any clarity. I didn't feel any different from before those events had taken place. Perhaps Flowers was more benign than I thought. Not that it mattered one way or another now.

"Well," she said, pushing a stringy wet lock from her face, "I'm going to go."

"Where do you go?"

"I have a place!" she said, a bit defiantly.

"Why don't you come to the shop for a Coke?" I said.

"Maybe another time," Evie said.

Before I could say anything further, she turned down a narrow alleyway and vanished in the failing light.

I could have rushed after her, but I had the odd feeling that she actually had disappeared, that no matter how fast I ran in the direction I had last seen her go, I wouldn't find her. Feeling terribly alone, I walked as quickly as I could towards the family store.

Nu Wa

South China, early 1900s

DROWNING

I felt no remorse for Edwina's murder, but I did fear punishment. I rushed out onto the street. Briefly, I paused over the folded map. The paper was smooth and oily. It flapped in the wind. I unfolded it. There was nothing on it but a picture of the Sighing River with a line beside it. I had parted with the Salt Fish Girl's coin for this? Even in my fury, it occurred to me I could still retrieve it from Edwina's clenched hand upstairs. But the thought of touching that cold flesh one last time made my skin crawl. I did not go upstairs to get it.

I found the river by the train tracks, downtown. I followed the path into the clouds.

It was dark when I got my first sighting of Canton. It appeared below me like a little island of green and orange light that pulsed as though the city were a large animal breathing. I descended into the light, let it swallow me whole.

Although I was tired, I was determined to find the Salt Fish Girl that night. I checked all the doorways as I passed them for grey, breathing heaps. I disturbed an old man with long flowing hair, and a couple of street urchins huddled together for warmth. But there was no sign of the Salt Fish Girl. I searched until I myself collapsed into one of the dark doorways and fell asleep.

I was disturbed early the next morning by a short-tempered baker who gave me an unceremonious shove with his smelly brown leather boot. I begged a stale bun off him, which he gave most ungraciously, and then I hurried off to continue my search.

I stopped an old man to ask if he had seen her, but he merely shrugged and rushed away as though I might bite him. I asked a young boy. He gave me a terrified glare and ran off. I asked an old woman. She put a finger to her lips and said, "You'd be better off not asking such questions. You don't want that evil woman to find you, do you?"

As the sun began to sink behind the mountain, splattering the sky red as a butcher's apron, I passed a house with a telltale odour. It was dark and shabby. I knocked on the door.

"Who's there?" Yes, I was sure it was her voice.

"It's me," I said.

An eye darkened the peephole in the centre of the door. There was a gasp of surprise. The door swung open.

It was her all right, but her face was wrinkled as a dried mushroom and her hair flowed down her shoulders, white as a funeral robe.

"I only let you in because you remind me of someone," she said. She grabbed my arm and pulled me in quickly. The door slammed shut behind me.

"I am that someone," I said.

"Speak Cantonese. I don't understand that foreign tongue."

I understood her perfectly and I tried in vain to get my mouth to form the familiar words. My throat could not push them out. The language of the Island of Mist and Forgetfulness rolled off my tongue in rapid-fire explanation, but she only scowled at me. I said her name—that much I could manage—and she nodded and asked how I knew her. I said my own name and vigorously jabbed my chest with my index finger, but she shook her head.

"How can that be?" she said. "You're young enough to be my daughter."

I nodded and thumped my chest insistently, feeling stupid and desperate and alien.

"If you are who you claim," she said, "you should look as old and grey as I. You should speak your own language. And you should begin by explaining where you've been these past fifty years and what you did with that coin I gave you."

Fifty years? I had heard crazy old storytellers in the market tell such stories when I was a girl. Or I thought I had. I had always listened surreptitiously because the old madmen berated and tormented their listeners into paying once the tale was told, and of course I had no extra money to spend on such frivolous things. If I had known it would happen to me, perhaps I might have been more generous, given them the candy money my mother sometimes gave me when she was feeling sentimental.

I sputtered helplessly.

"You should at least make an effort," she said. "Cantonese used to be your mother tongue."

"I'm trying," I said, weeping in frustration and disappointment. I had been aching to see her for such a long time.

"I haven't forgotten how you abandoned me," she said. "I haven't forgotten who you left me for either. And now you speak only her language and have forgotten ours."

I gazed at the floor in shame and remorse. How easily we abandon those who have suffered the same persecutions as we have. How quickly we grow impatient with their inability to transcend the conditions of our lives. I had taken the easy way out. She knew my shame and she didn't forgive me.

I got defensive. I said, "If it weren't for you we could have lived happily in the village. I gave up a perfectly good and loving family for you. I committed unspeakable crimes for you, so I could be with you. You have no right to accuse me of anything!"

She might not have understood my words, but she understood their sentiment. "You killed my father," she said. "When I was sick and asked you to get medicine, you took the money and ran off with some paleface witch. Now I'm an old woman and you are still so strangely young. Why did you bother coming back, except to make fun of me?"

"I can explain," I said. "I know I've made some terrible mistakes, but I'm here now and I want to make it up to you."

Uncomprehending, she scowled at me. "I don't understand a word you're saying," she said. "Go away and come back when you've learned to talk."

I burst into tears. I could not shake Edwina's terrible curse. The language would not come. She pushed me unceremoniously out the door.

People on the street outside stared and whispered among themselves. One came up to me and said, "You went into the unnatural one's house and you weren't killed. How did you do it?"

Blinded by tears, I pushed past them and ran as far as I could without having a clue where I was going.

I found myself beside the river. It rushed by under the darkening sky, cold and indifferent as a snake.

A worn path ran beside it. I followed it aimlessly, or perhaps more accurately, I followed it out of habit, out of the memory that resided in my feet, recalling our earlier euphoric, if desperate, journey to the city. In three days, I arrived back in my home village. I left the river. I crossed the mulberry fields. I passed the fish ponds. I found the alleyway I had played in as a child and followed it to the door of my parents' house. My mother sat in the doorway, bald and toothless, smoking a cigarette. Age had shrunk her to half her original size. When she saw me, her eyes nearly popped out of her head.

"I know you," she said. "Are you my husband?"

"Your daughter, Ma," I said.

She stared at me. "Why do you talk so funny?"

My brother appeared in the doorway behind her, himself an old man. A memory of carrying him on my back to the market flashed through my mind. "Who are you talking to, Ma?"

Then he noticed me, dusty, tired and travel-worn in my tattered clothes.

"Move on, beggar," he said. "We've nothing to spare for you here."

"Don't you recognize me?" I protested in my strange language.

"Your father," said my mother, pointing. People have always said I look more like my father than my mother, so she wasn't wrong to see the resemblance.

My brother came close and peered at me. "What is your name? Are you my lost sister's daughter?"

He didn't understand my answer, but he took me by the arm and guided me into the house.

His daughter, who looked not a day younger than I, greeted me with a glass of tea. In a few minutes, she had also warmed some leftovers for me and laid them out neatly on the table. Her steamed fish tasted so much like my mother's I could barely tell the difference. My mother grinned tooth-lessly at me while I ate. It broke my heart to see her so worn and lacking in mental capacity. I began to weep. My tears spilled into the fish, salting it.

My mother reached out and touched my cheek fondly as though there were a part of her beyond her loss of memory that recognized exactly who I was and loved me in spite of all the pain I had caused.

My niece, watching from the kitchen doorway, said to my brother, "She looks like me, Ba."

It was true. In appearance, we could have been sisters.

"It's too bad she talks so funny," said my brother. "Maybe she is related to us, but how are we going to find out for sure?"

I jumped at the possibility to show him. I got up from the table, grabbed his hand and led him to the back room where I used to sleep with my sister. When we were young, my brother, my sister and I had hidden a dirty book we had bought from a foreign trader behind a loose brick. I moved the brick to show I at least knew the hiding place. To my delight, the book tumbled out along with a heap of ancient fish bones. The glue of the spine had long since given up its hold on the pages, and so now quaintly archaic drawings of naked men and women caught in compromising positions and thoroughly ridden with wormholes fluttered to the ground.

My brother laughed.

"My sister?" he said. "But how can it be? You haven't aged since you left us."

To give the true reason for my foreign tongue and tender years to other villagers would draw unnecessary attention to the family. It would also have destroyed my prospects for marriage, which didn't bother me in and of itself, but only concerned me insofar as I couldn't bear the thought of hurting my family again as I had hurt them before. How many people are as lucky as I was in getting a second chance to do the right thing? I'd do what they wanted me to do this time, I thought. My brother adopted me officially as his daughter to avoid gossip that would have pegged our family as abnormal.

But because of my likeness to both my niece and my brother, the neighbours suspected I was the product of an extra-marital affair. Although this was unexpected, my brother had reasons for wanting people to believe this rather than the truth. To begin with, it harmed his reputation less. Admittedly, it harmed his wife's more, but he didn't let that bother him much.

The timing of my arrival, as it turned out, was the worst possible. To explain why, let me take you back to the long-ago past day of my supposed murder. My father, with whom I had always been close, had been stricken with grief and fury. He insisted that the full extent of the law be applied against the salt fish merchant, who as someone from another district was already at a disadvantage. My brother was right behind my father, gathering evidence.

My father's show of grief and outrage, combined with the butcher's flawless testimony, was sufficient not only to send the salt fish merchant to his death, but also to require his family to pay indemnities. These were the dying days of Imperial rule, and magistrates were eager to show their sympathy with the people.

Our family began to receive compensation money from the salt fish merchant's brother, a tobacco importer. Because he was away in Gold Mountain, across the wide Pacific Ocean, it was some years before my brother met him—our father had passed on by that time. When they finally did meet, my brother was instantly charmed. In spite of his foreign sympathies, the salt fish merchant's brother was a traditionally minded man who believed in social debt. He was appalled at the events that had taken place in the village and felt terribly guilty. He went to great lengths to make it up to my family, at the same time feeling he never really could. He supplied them every year with as much tobacco as they could smoke, as well as other interesting imported goods including cheese, wool and the occasional little black ball of opium.

My father never forgave the salt fish merchant or his family and went to his grave early with a heart full of hatred. But after my father died, my brother's instinctive liking for the old tobacco merchant grew into a sincere fondness. The old man, whose hands were always full of strange and wonderful gifts, began to fill the place which my father's early death had left empty.

When my brother reached the age of twenty-one, the old man gave him fifty per cent of the tobacco business. The other fifty he gave to his own son, and suggested that, if they wished, they could leave the business intact and become partners. Like his father, the tobacco merchant's son felt a great unpayable debt towards our family and in addition, being some years younger, looked up to my brother who bossed and bullied him with impunity. Despite the grave inequalities in their relationship, a true affection grew between them, so that by the time the old man made this proposition, both were prepared to accept it.

Ten years later, unable to make money in China's flagging economy, they decided to expand the business to include a Gold Mountain base. The tobacco merchant's son set sail and opened a grocery, not in British Columbia as many overseas

Chinese chose to do, but in Toronto. There he met a logging cook, fell in love and pursued her all the way back to the rainy shores of Newfoundland, the island of her birth. On that cold grey rock, he opened a little grocery store and called it Hap's for Happenstance. And there he lived, more or less contented, selling dry goods sent regularly by my brother to the local restaurateurs and curious locals, and Brookfield ice cream, baloney and Wonderbread to everyone else. He ate fish 'n' brewis when invited, and if occasionally his wife scowled at him for ordering salt fish from China, he shrugged his shoulders and said, "What does Newcastle really know about coal if all they ever burn is their own?"

Now, some fifty years later, wife and father buried in the soils of their respective birthplaces, Hap was coming back to the comfortable China home of his old business partner and friend, my brother.

God forbid that in meeting me he should discover my true identity and in discovering it realize that it was our family who owed his family a grand apology and lifelong debt, and not the other way around! My brother didn't even want to contemplate it.

"All my life I've been the injured party, and he has been the injurer. Our love for one another is entirely based on that fact. Now, just as we're about to settle down as comfortable old friends enjoying the last years of our lives together, here you come, having long since abandoned us to upset what we have worked all our lives to create!"

"Perhaps I shouldn't have come," I said. But of course, he didn't understand. My niece plopped a bowl of congee with lean pork and two kinds of preserved egg in front of me and I slurped it back, feeling guilty.

I was halfway through the bowl when my brother's face lit up with an idea. "I could return a life for a life if you married him, and he need never know who you are. If I deliver you back into that family's hands, the debt would be repaid. And at the same time, we would be connected through marriage and you would have Canadian citizenship and could go back to Gold Mountain and start sending us remittances. What do you say?"

"If he knew who I really was, surely he wouldn't want me," I said.

"If he knew who you really were . . ." my brother said, reading my mind. "But no, he's an idiot. He'll never guess."

If Hap was surprised at my brother's offer of marriage to his own daughter, he was too polite to say so. The fact of the matter was that he was as uninterested as I was, but never having said no to my brother in his life, he couldn't start now. The arranged marriage of such an old man to such a young woman was considered very old-fashioned. These days, people married for love.

As I beheld my frail and withered husband in the bridal chamber that night, I chuckled to think that my birthdate actually pegged me a full nine years older than he. He made no attempt to touch me.

"Are you happy to be here?" he asked.

"No more unhappy than anyplace else," I said, still thinking longingly of the Salt Fish Girl.

"I am happy to keep you in my house more as a sister than a wife," he said, though he hadn't understood a word I had said.

All would have been well, or at least, bearable, if my brother had not started pestering for a grandson. "Hey, son-in-law," he shouted, "you got any more fish swimming around in those stagnant ponds of yours? When are you going to make me a grandfather?"

I shot him a dirty look. Did he think flaunting the lie would make it go away?

Hap looked hurt.

At first these humiliations took place only within the walls of my brother's house or ours. Then one day, as some government officials from the north were examining our mulberry bushes, my brother poked Hap in the ribs and whispered, "Any silkworm action lately? I don't see any cocoons in sight . . ."

Hap came home looking desperate. As I leaned over a counter cutting vegetables, I felt something cold and bird-like clutch my arm. I looked up. There was a desperate determination in his eyes as Hap gripped me meaningfully in his bony claws. I tore away from him, pushed him up against the counter and held the vegetable knife to his throat. "Try that again and I'll kill you," I said.

He did not skulk away as I had expected, but continued to look me in the eye with a wounded sort of ferocity. "Find someone else then," he said. "Pay him if you want. I'll give you the money."

I found a fisherman by the banks of the river. He had just pulled in his net. In its threads, perhaps twenty fish were trapped and wriggled furiously—silver, slippery, and bright as stars. I indicated plainly what I wanted, which shocked him less than I had expected. Times change a lot in fifty years. He said he would do as I asked if I helped him untangle the fish and drop them into the large rattan basket that he kept for the purpose. Resolutely, I gripped a firm hand around the first one, and began to tug at the twine with the fingers of my other hand. The fish squirmed with the full force of its long silver muscle. Its eyes bulged and its gills opened and closed helplessly, gasping for water. It sparkled in the sun as it writhed, beautiful in spite of, or perhaps because of its desperation. I dropped it twice. The fisherman glanced up at me and laughed.

The fisherman's hands were rough but warm. His body was heavy and smelled of tobacco, fish and woodsmoke. There was nothing wonderful about him, but there was nothing unpleasant about him either. But later that month, when the moon rose full and white, my blood gushed out after it, like a dog chasing a fox. So I had to go back to the fisherman. Again, no luck.

The third time I went to visit him, I had no inkling that anyone was following me. It was not until we had finished that my niece, or my sister, depending on whom you ask, rose up from a hiding place among the river reeds, shrieking as she ran straight to my brother's house with the news.

The whole village had heard by the time my brother came looking for me at Hap's house. Had they not, would he have spared me? Who knows? As it was, too much face had been lost. It was Hap's mother, a frail tender-hearted woman, who had to order the drowning.

A group of village men came for me in the middle of the night. My husband answered the door dressed in nothing but shorts and a singlet, tears streaming from his eyes. His grief made him look thinner and older than he was, but the villagers took no notice. They pushed past him and stormed into his neatly kept house. (Not a stitch of housework did I. He kept the place swept and scrubbed, kept the rosewood chairs brightly polished and meals on the table. I usually threshed the rice, caught the fish, fixed broken doors, and chopped firewood when we ran out of straw.) They turned the place upside down, scratched the smooth arms of his grandfather's chairs and knocked his precious American-made radio to the floor.

They found me in the bedroom closet, huddled in a heap of dirty clothes trying to make myself as small as possible. Two big men grabbed me by the arms, but I broke out of their grasp by using a few quick manoeuvres I had learned long ago in the streets of Canton and polished to an art in the streets of Hope. I made for the window, climbed out and scaled down quickly. They were too scared to follow me, and so lost time by having to find their way back to the front door. By then, I had already noticed the pig basket meant to cage me waiting in the alleyway.

I knew I couldn't evade them forever. I had spent the day in the mulberry fields and was already exhausted when they arrived. In no time, my pace began to slow and I could hear them behind me, yelling. Soon I saw the light of their torches skittering through the dark like angry fireflies. In the jerky light, I could make out the lines of the pig basket, which one of them carried above his head. I pushed myself to run harder. By the time I got to the riverbank, I was winded and gasping for breath. And there wasn't a skiff in sight for me to steal. The lights and yells moved ever closer.

I looked into the almost still black-green water. By the light of the moon, I saw my own reflection gazing calmly back at me from the depths. The slow motion of the river distorted the reflection slightly so that I imagined I saw, not myself, but the Salt Fish Girl staring sadly back at me. She was safe down there. I reached my hand to the surface, as though to touch her face. Dark human shapes appeared behind her. I looked over my shoulder once and then leaned into the water, merging with my reflection and obliterating it at the same time.

This is what it's like to drown: You take a last look at the sky, a last breath, slowly. Air goes into your lungs and then you are under water. You let the air out molecule by molecule, realizing for the first time how precious it is, this thing that feels like so much nothing, neither liquid nor solid. Your eyes are open wide. The world goes cool and green and you keep falling. There are shapes in the darkness, fronds of river weed waving, dark indescribable things that float and then sink with you. You never knew you were so heavy. The density of your flesh has never been of such prime importance. The air leaks out of you in spite of your mightiest attempts to hold it. You need more but there is none. Leafy things flail.

The water's coolness is no longer soothing. You gasp. Water rushes into your lungs and floods them. Your eyes stare wider. You thrash. You want more than anything to live, to be able to rise again, but you keep falling. The river is bottomless. It pushes you along in the direction of its current like an impatient auntie, but it won't let you to the surface. Your eyes are wide open, but slowly everything goes black. You begin to float beneath the surface. You are conscious of the coolness again, of how green everything is. You move with the water and through it. You have left your body far behind. The river has become a part of you.

Miranda

The Unregulated Zone, 2062

THE NEW KUBLA KHAN

The store was closed. I went around to the back and let myself in to the kitchen. My father was cooking. The house smelled pleasantly of rice and garlic and pork.

"How was work?" he asked.

I couldn't think of anything smart to say. "Fine."

I didn't see how I could go back to Flowers, having done what I had done. I knew that not to go back was tacit admission of guilt, but I also didn't see how I could possibly face him. I knew it wouldn't be long before my family began to miss the small cheque I brought in every month.

I clopped upstairs to my room, which sat directly above the store, overlooking the street. Sat down and opened my journal, an oversized red and black book with lined paper inside, which my mother had given me just a week before her death.

"Everything is getting worse," I wrote. Downstairs, I could hear my father dolefully rolling the chords of "Clara Cruise." I pulled the paper mask out of my pocket, inserted it between the pages, shut the book, lay down and went to sleep.

Seems to me that it was after that day that the first little slips of the past returned, memories of a muddy river and of a body wide as a road and just as thick arcing through the cool dark and burning with a messy, generative fury.

In the following weeks, I spent the early hours of the morning sitting at my narrow child's desk and looking out onto the dimly lit street. From downstairs, sometimes, I would hear my father's sad renditions of my mother's old songs. It struck me that we had never had a piano in the Serendipity house, at least, not since my birth. Nor had I ever heard them make music together. Sorrow made people a bit crazy, I thought.

I began to draw pictures of a woman with my mother's face, and then, where the neck should start, a slender coiled body, green and delicate, covered in millions of tiny, luminescent scales. After a while I grew dissatisfied with these, made her face rounder, her body human to the hips. Drew her hair long and streaming in the wind. Gave her a belly big enough to swim in. And then, just where the legs should divide, a thick rope of tail descended, covered in scales glittering silver and white. It made me think of Christian Andersen's Little Mermaid, her tail's fatal bifurcation, the agonizing pain of every footstep, which, he said, felt like walking on broken glass.

When my father saw the drawings, he told me the story of Nu Wa and Fu Xi, the snake-bodied brother and sister who were supposed to have created the first people.

"But that's incest," I said.

My father said, "It's just a story."

After that I drew the two of them, tails interlocked, lying in the mud beneath the pouring rain. I drew them as twins, faces androgynous and almost identical. I drew Nu Wa staring into a still pool at her own reflection. I drew her fashioning the first people out of mud and setting them down on the riverbank. I drew them laughing, though whether it was a laugh of genuine cheer or merely a brave attempt to mask searing agony I couldn't say. I drew them with divided legs, no snaky tail and no innocent garden either. Perhaps they were having a chuckle over a dirty joke. I drew them having an orgy on the riverbank and howling with demonic glee.

I drew a series of images of Nu Wa under water with her mouth open. The first people swam out from her throat like words. I drew a series in which Nu Wa was transparent like a long cell beneath a microscope. The first people grew in her belly and pressed out through her skin. I drew Fu Xi as a woman, emerging from the glossy surface of the lake to embrace Nu Wa while she knelt to examine her reflection in the water.

One evening, as I sat in the rock garden, now strewn with used car and bicycle parts, Ian Chestnut's head appeared over the tops of the overgrown, fruitless raspberry bushes. I had just got home from "work" which for the last eleven days had consisted mostly of hanging out in a dark eastside basement with a bunch of raggedy-looking students Evie had introduced me to. We ran off anti-Saturna and anti-Pallas flyers using an ancient printing press revived from some long-ago age before the advent of computers. We laid the type in with tweezers and cranked out the flyers by hand. Those of us not in immediate danger of arrest spent our afternoons handing them out on street corners, though who read them I have no idea. I heard that some artsy types were collecting them as bits of pseudo-retro kitsch, which really wasn't particularly helpful. The sun was setting slowly over the back fence now, splashing the sky with a stunning array of colours. I knew their brilliance was a product of pollution, but it was nonetheless a lovely and calming sight. All I really wanted to do was make a bouquet from my mother's overgrown poppies and daisies, watch the sky change and not think about too much.

So when Ian Chestnut appeared and called me by name, I was quite taken aback. In his early twenties now, he had gracefully morphed from a pale fragile child to a slim golden young man, casually dressed in a white T-shirt, expensive, well-cut jeans and a pair of Pallas runners in deep navy with thin silver strips along the sides.

"What do you want?" I said. His loveliness annoyed me.

"No need to be so welcoming," he said. "I'm here to do you a favour."

I eyed him dubiously, aware as I did so that my capacity to trust was not what it had been. In his presence I felt dirty and ragged. "I'm not a charity case," I said.

"Well, then you can do me a favour in return," he said. "What's wrong with you? It isn't my fault you were kicked out, you know." He made a cross face that reminded me of the innocent boy I once knew. "I thought you'd be happy to see me," he said. "I just wanted to invite you to a party. There's someone who wants to meet you. But if you don't want to meet him, then that's okay. Just come for the party." He handed me a flyer on cheap, khaki-green paper. It had a ticket clipped to it at the top. Then he ducked back down below the wall and vanished. The paper said:

SATURNALIA

SERENDIPITY IS FALLING.
FOR THE FIRST TIME IN 50 YEARS
PARTY INSIDE THE WALLED CITY!
EMBRACE THE CONTAGION.
48-HOUR CARNIVAL AT THE NEW KUBLA KHAN
2200 Friday, May 24, 2062

Creatures dressed in the uniforms of various corporate security forces danced around the borders of the text. One had a goat's head, another that of a fish, yet another that of a fox. I don't know if I would have been less tempted had another venue been offered, but as it was I couldn't conceive of not going. I wished I'd been nicer to Ian. As it was I'd make it by midnight if I left right at that moment. But because I didn't want to tell my father or my brother where I was going, I would have to wait until they were asleep.

In the meantime though, while my father minded the counter, I snuck out to my mother's shrine at the back of the cold storage. Guiltily I placed the half-complete bouquet in front of her photograph. It was the wrong thing, but it was better than nothing. Then I began to rummage through her closet. I didn't entirely expect to find the dress. After all, we'd had to leave many things behind in Serendipity, and I knew she hadn't brought everything. So I was delighted when my fingers ran over a sequinned fabric hanging on a second pole behind the first. I pulled it from the hanger and hauled it out. There it was, that red sequinned cheongsam from the first time I had spied on her watching an ancient CD-ROM of an even more ancient cabaret performance, the night the bubble of my parents' love had popped. *Fan Tan Fanny was leaving her man,* I hummed. I pulled back the brown tablecloth that covered her vanity mirror and held the dress up in front of my lanky body. I wouldn't fill it the way she did, but its length and width were about right. I folded it carefully and put it in my knapsack along with Evie's tattered mask.

When midnight rolled around I got out of bed and tip-toed down the hall. I put my ear to my father's door and was gratified by the low rumble of snoring. If I was quiet, it wouldn't matter if my brother was awake downstairs. I slipped out the back door, and, since I'd lost mine, took my father's bike from the garage and started down the road towards Serendipity. The sky had flushed pink along the eastern horizon by the time I arrived at the front gates. There was a coil of razor wire blocking it, and beyond that an ominous brown military hut with two big, hawk-eyed guards staring out through the glass. I veered away from the entrance and looked at my invite again. South End, it said, in small print. I followed the wall towards the opposite end of the city. It looked strong and sturdy until I reached Teacher's Corner. There the wall had been blasted away in huge chunks. Stray hunks of concrete were scattered around the outside. I stepped through one of the gaps in the wall. A double layer of chain-link fence and razor wire separated the part of Serendipity that was still under corporate control from the part that wasn't any longer. I wouldn't dare to cross into the green field beyond the fence. I wandered the main street of South End towards the New Kubla Khan. It wasn't familiar to me. Our house had been deep in the suburbs of North Side, and as a child I'd never had a reason to come this far out. But I recognized the New Kubla Khan from my mother's CD-ROMs. It wasn't nearly as glossy as I remembered though. Its red brick facade was crumbling and riddled with bullet holes.

I ducked into an alley, shimmied out of my cycling clothes, and, sweaty and rank-smelling, slipped into the red sequinned dress. As best I could, I slicked my hair off my face, braided it and wound the coil round my head like a crown. I pulled Evie's tattered mask over my eyes and waltzed in the front door.

It was dark inside and smelled of dope and vomit. I gave my ticket to the doorman, checked my bag and went inside. The chairs and tables of my mother's era had all been put away, except for down in the pit. People danced in the tiered auditorium and on the stage to a bizarre booming music I recognized vaguely from the portable orchestras some kids who hung out near Flowers' offices had. The lush velvet curtains were still there, pulled back and tied with the frayed gold cord. They had been so eaten by moths that I could make out the holes even from where I was standing. I scanned the faces of the strangely attired revellers as I stomped through in my clumsy boots, aware of how dirty and different I looked. It took me a full fifteen minutes to realize that Ian was sitting in the pit, surrounded by friends, all of them strangers to me. He was dressed from head to toe in chain mail made of some light, sturdy alloy that gleamed in the club's flickering light. I pushed my mask up onto my forehead and went to meet him. Before I had even sat down, the bearded man beside him said, "Splitting image, Ian, Holy Jesus. She looks just like her mother." I grinned at him, conscious of how unbrushed my teeth felt.

"Come on, Miranda, sit down," Ian said kindly. "This is my friend Adrian Withers. What would you like to drink?"

Remembering how rude I'd been earlier that evening, I was very relieved. "Champagne cocktail," I said, thinking of my mother relaxing after her number in this very room, or perhaps in one of the dressing rooms in the back.

"Unbelievable," the man was saying. "Could be her twin."

Suddenly the music stopped. "The sun has risen," an authoritative voice boomed over the loudspeaker. "Praise the Second Midnight! It's time for the Cabaret of the Diseased." The way he pronounced it I wasn't sure whether he had said "diseased" or "deceased"—perhaps he meant both at once. Revellers descended from the stage and the moth-eaten curtains swung shut.

The unpleasant scent of artificial bananas rose in the room, just moments before the curtains slowly pulled open again. A woman in a long white dress lay on an operating table. Above her craned a large surgical lamp pouring its stark white light over her body. Downstage sat a little trolley. It was draped with a clean white cloth, and on top of the cloth was laid a variety of peculiarly shaped instruments, some very sharp, some oddly curved. A doctor entered from the left dressed not in hospital greens, but in a white shirt, waistcoat and tails. Over one eye he sported a thick monocle that glinted in the brilliant stage lights. The woman sighed deeply when he pressed the scalpel into her chest. A red stain spread through the white fabric. He began at the clavicle and moved downwards, humming a discordant little tune as he did so. The white dress grew horribly bloody. When he reached the pubic bone, he stopped and wiped his fingers absently on her skirt. A nervous laugh stuttered through the audience. With a blunt tool, he appeared to prise the ribs apart. With a curved one, he dipped into the cavity. The woman groaned. Squelching sounds came over the loudspeakers. I covered my eyes with my hands.

"Look, she's getting up," Ian said.

I peeked. Moving as though in a trance, the woman swung her legs to the floor and stood up. She reached into her own body cavity and one by one drew out a heart, a liver, a kidney. She threw the heart into the air. In a moment, she was dexterously juggling the three, grinning demonically the whole time. It was only then that I recognized the fakery. I breathed a sigh of relief. The audience hooted and clapped. The doctor left the stage ahead of her. The woman followed him, stage left, still juggling.

If ice can be said to have a smell, that was the scent that filled the room when a small Chinese boy took the stage. He was thin as a stick and wore thick spectacles. The room grew palpably colder as he sat down at the enormous grand piano workmen had wheeled onto the stage. "Oh no, not another child prodigy," Withers groaned. But the child's fingers did not plunge into an accelerated and complex show of dexterity and rhythm. Instead, he had the lightest touch, the most patient hand. The piece was a simple one, not at all technically demanding. But the tones that hit our ears were full of such wrenching sorrow that audience members burst into uncontrollable tears within the first twelve measures. Ian graciously passed his handkerchief to a young man in tight go-go shorts. I would have laughed, but the sorrow had filled my heart too.

But it was the third act that unnerved me the most. A beautiful woman ascended the stage in tie and tails, not unlike the suit worn by the doctor of the surgery act. There was something familiar about her, but I couldn't put my finger on it. Behind her, tap water ran into an elegant white porcelain tub with feet in the shape of lion's paws. Someone had poured in a generous amount of bubble bath, and as the tub filled you could see the froth rising. A raunchy stripping tune boomed over the loudspeakers. She doffed her top hat. A sumptuous mass of black hair cascaded down her back. She took off the jacket, the tie. Slowly and teasingly, off came the shirt and trousers. Underneath, she wore a leopard-spotted bra and underpants. With the elegant grace of an old-fashioned stripper, she removed them with her back to us as she stood behind the now brimming tub. She slipped beneath the bubbles. I thought that would be the end of the number, but instead a little orchestral interlude struck up. The woman opened her mouth and began to sing a song about a crane woman who bathes in a rocky pool while an unscrupulous young student peeps through some bushes. She waits for him to leave so she can get out of the water, but he steals her feathered dress. She yells into the forest, begging him to bring it back, but the only response she gets is the wind sighing through the trees. The stripper pulled the plug from the tub, and we heard the amplified sound of water rushing down the drain. When she stood, her entire body was covered in small shiny white feathers from which droplets of water slicked as though off a duck's back. It was only then that I realized how much like Evie's her face was. The audience hooted and screamed and clapped. I stared, my mouth gaping wide.

I was still staring when a daringly attired MC mounted the stage, spray-painted gold from top to toe and sporting a marvellously realistic-looking pair of downy angel's wings on his back. "Ladies and gentlemen," he said, "we've reached that point in the evening when we turn the microphone over to celebrities in our midst. Is that Ian Chestnut I spy down there in the pit? Who has he brought with him this evening? My goodness, she's looking a little rough around the edges, but I'd say that girl is the splitting image of Miss Aimee Ling, the long-ago doyenne of the New Kubla Khan. Can she sing, Ian?"

To my horror, Ian nodded his head.

"No!" I said.

"Come on," Ian whispered, "I've heard you a hundred times at your kitchen table. You can do this."

"You are crazy. I should have socked your head the minute I saw it this afternoon."

Ian smiled. Adrian Withers pushed a bill with a lot of zeroes on it across the table. American dollars. Still good in the Unregulated Zone. It would buy back the time I'd lost skiving off work, and then some. The golden MC came towards our table holding the mike towards me. I snatched Withers' bill off the table and stuffed it down the front of my dress. Graciously took the mike, ascended the stairs and in a wavery voice began: "Here's a song for Clara Cruise . . ." I don't know how I did it, but somehow I held them. The audience listened raptly. As I sang, I felt a presence at the pit of my belly that could be no one but her. My long-lost mother. I felt a sense of comfort that I had not felt in a very long time. My voice poured like honey. I watched the audience, watched Ian beaming from the pit. Watched the strange, shifting face of Adrian Withers. And then, further back . . . oh no, could it be? Farther back, in a white suit with a pink carnation poked through the lapel buttonhole, stood the doctor, Rudy Flowers, smiling grimly as he clutched the hand of Dr. Seto and swayed to the music. I finished the song and descended quickly from the stage, well before the applause died down. It was rude, but I couldn't just stand there and look at them.

"That was great," Ian said, as I sat down. "Didn't I tell you she'd be great, Adrian?"

"Fantastic!" Adrian said. "Really fantastic. You look like her, you sound like her. It really is amazing."

"Glad you thought so," I said brusquely. "Listen, I have to get going now. Gotta work today."

"You won't make it before lunch on your bike," Ian said. "Why not let Adrian drive you?"

"Naw, I have to go." I glanced nervously over my shoulder. I couldn't see Flowers at all. I prayed he wasn't working his way through the crowd towards me.

Withers said, "What kind of shoes do you wear, Miranda?"

"Shoes? I don't know. Whatever shoes my brother gets from his customers." I slung my bag over my shoulder and headed towards the door. To my alarm, Withers got up to follow me. Maybe it was good. At least I wouldn't be alone when Flowers caught up with me. In the pit, someone began to play the piano. The tune was "Dim Sum Daydreams," another of my mother's old songs. Later, I thought the interpretation reminiscent of my father's, but my memory plays tricks on me, I'm sure. At the time, all I could really think of was running.

"Ever own a pair of Pallases?" Withers was saying.

"No. Can't afford it," I said.

"But you like the way they look. You've tried them on and you can feel the support they provide your feet."

"I like the way they look. But we get things third-hand and ten years old where I live. They don't provide much support." From the foyer, I could see Flowers pushing through the crowd.

"Let me be straight with you," Withers said. "I work for a small agency that does ads for Pallas. I'd like to buy your mother's shoe song. It's only the first verse I'm interested in really, but of course I'll pay for the whole thing."

"I don't think so."

He followed me out into the bright sunlight. I was annoyed. I wanted to change before hopping on my bike, but at this rate it wouldn't be possible, even if there was enough time. I unlocked it from the post I'd chained it to and hopped on. He ran beside me. I angled down a back alley so that Flowers wouldn't immediately see me if he stood on the main street. "A hundred thousand dollars," Withers said. "A hundred and fifty if you'll appear in the ads yourself. You could buy your way back into Serendipity."

"Serendipity is collapsing, in case you haven't noticed," I said.

"I can do things you can't even begin to imagine," Withers said. "What do you want?"

I ducked into a small alcove so I could catch my breath. "What do I want? A respectable, anonymous job. Immunity from the law."

"Immunity from the law? You kill someone?"

"No."

"Blow anything up?"

"No."

"Perhaps I can help you then. But first the song." He held a paper towards me.

"How do I know you can do anything for me at all? And how do I know I can trust you?"

"Because I don't have to do this. It's only because I believe in doing the right thing."

He took a wad of cash from inside his jacket pocket and placed it in my hands. I counted it. A cool hundred thousand. I held one of the notes up to the sun. The grain was right, and the holograph of Salmon P. Chase's face seemed to have the appropriate depth, though, never having seen an American ten-thousand dollar bill before, I wasn't much of a judge. I counted the bills. My family and I could go anywhere we wanted. A car screeched around a corner not too far away.

"Do you have wheels?" I said.

"Sure," said Withers. "A ten-minute walk from here. I can drive you anywhere you want. Sign here and we'll go."

I thought about my promise to my father. "No," I said. I thrust the money back at him.

Withers said, "You ungrateful little minx. I could just take your song, you know. I'm still somebody in Serendipity. You couldn't sue me. You aren't even a citizen."

A black sedan whipped around the corner ahead of us and came barrelling in our direction. I snatched the wad of cash and stowed it securely inside the tight front of my dress with the bill I had accepted earlier. I grabbed his pen and signed my name. Then I jumped on my bike and fled.

It wasn't easy, cycling in that red sequinned dress. My knees got caught up in its draping skirt. It hugged just a bit too tight around the lungs, making it hard to breathe. As I turned a corner down a narrow lane, the hem got caught in the chain. I was desperately trying to ease it out without damaging the precious dress when Flowers and Seto pulled up beside me in an ancient but smoothly purring Ford Mercury. There were two sturdy young men in the back whom I didn't recognize. They wore smartly cut uniforms the colour of hospital gowns.

"Want a lift, Miranda?" Flowers said.

I shook my head and continued to tug at my hem.

"Don't play stupid with me," said Flowers. The young men got out of the car. "You know I know what you girls did to my old car. I could arrange things so you never see the light of day again. You're just lucky I'm interested in you."

"Well, I'm not interested in you," I said. The young men were at my side. One of them bent down and ripped my hem from the bike chain. My mother's beautiful dress. The other tossed my father's bike to the side of the road and pushed me towards the car's open door.

Flowers said, "That doesn't matter. If I were you, I'd just come quietly. Come back to the lab with me and finish the experiment. Then I'll forget about the car."

I struggled, but the young men were twice my size, and there were two of them. They shoved me mercilessly into the back and then took a seat on either side of me.

"It's a good deal I'm offering you," Flowers said. "You should be grateful."

Unceremoniously they delivered me to the clinic in the basement of the Pan Pacific Hotel. The front foyer had been redone in roses and its walls painted a lush, saturated rose pink. The carpet on the floor was knotted with elaborate pink and yellow blooms. On an ornate table with thorny legs a large vase held a spray of at least a hundred blood-red buds. The air was filled with their sweet scent.

The young guards on either side of me each gripped an arm and propelled me to the escalator. Flowers and Seto followed behind. Somehow, Flowers was making money. The hallways were now clean and smartly sterile.

"We've improved our technology," Flowers said. He opened one of many doors that lined the hallway and led me, this time, into a narrow hall with an elevator at the end. He pressed a button. The door opened. It was not a conventional elevator, but a narrow column that seemed to be made of glass. But when I stepped in, it was soft and gel-like. Silicone maybe. It puckered at the bottom like a plastic bag filled with air and twisted shut. The guards pushed me in. The door closed. "No!" I screamed. Outside the bubble was blackness. I felt very claustrophobic. The bubble began to descend. The blackness slipped away above me and I was under water. The ocean pulsed against the walls of the bubble. Down we went. I could see something way below me. It looked like an old-fashioned rattan birdcage with a domed top that drew to a point at the tip like a minaret. The bubble fell towards the point. When the centre of the pucker at the bottom of the bubble came in contact with the minaret tip of the cage, both opened. The bubble began to squeeze in at the top and I was pressed out of the narrow opening like toothpaste from a tube. I crashed to the floor of the cage. It was made of the same sturdy Plexiglas as the single wall of the room I had last visited, but now it surrounded me on all sides. The point closed before a drop of water could leak in. The bubble expanded again and floated back up.

There were amplifiers in the floor so that the sound of the ocean outside roared and crashed in my ears. There was a bathtub in the corner of the room, not unlike the one I had seen the bird lady bathe in mere hours earlier, except that this one was dry as a bone. On its lip, by the faucet, a razor blade balanced. In another corner sat a dozen cans of Aunt Dinah's Liquid Nutrition. Otherwise the room was empty. Outside, a school of tiny fish swirled. In the distance I could see a forest of white anemones clinging to a distant rock and waving their frilly arms. "I will not use the razor blade," I thought. "I will not go mad." I lay back on the cool Plexiglas floor. The scar at the base of my neck felt strangely cold. My eyelids ached to close, to give in to the lure of another kind of dreaming. I resisted the drowsiness, forced myself to replay the events of the recent past—my abduction by Flowers, and before that the sale of "Clara Cruise" to Withers. How could I have sold my mother's greatest hit to that shark? And in the service of shoe sales? It wasn't as though I didn't understand where the shoes came from. Evie had described to me in lurid detail the mad, dark factories, the greed that drove pay ever lower as contractors moved their factories to more and more desperate places. Evie, I thought, would be furious. The fat wad of cash burned against my chest. What the hell, I thought. I didn't personally do anything to those factory women, did I? What harm could it do for my mother's song to have a second life? It would bring the memory of her to millions, introduce her genius to a new generation who hadn't heard it the first time around. It would put a bit of real glamour into the lives of the women who bought the shoes—bored suburban housewives for whom an evening aerobics class or a morning run through the park was the only time of day they did something for themselves. It would bring a moment of beauty to women who were scared of growing old, women who had worked hard all their lives, women who deserved the beauty they worked for even as time took its toll, loosened their once tight clutch on immortality. My mother's song about the dangers of glamour would on its second pass deliver what in its first incarnation it had refused. This time the immortal shoes would make their wearers, in their multitudes, truly immortal. My imprisonment, I thought, was a kind of martyrdom. I closed my eyes.

Nu Wa

South China, early 1900s

A SEED

1. Sinking

I fell into my reflection. I became river water moving through river water. And then in the next moment there was something about me that was heavier than before. The speed of the river increased, and as I was washed out to sea I also began to sink. Out the mouth of the Pearl River to the South China Sea and down. Deep down. What was this weighty water I was becoming? Almost flesh. As I sank, the water around me sank. It too was changing substance as we fell into the cold dark. In the dark and in the cold under the great pressure of the sea above. Ice could not form, but ice did. No, not ice. Glass. I whipped an almost solid tail against it and found I could not penetrate to the other side. Trapped again in a glass cage, and sinking slowly. And slowly transmuting from a thing of water to a thing of flesh. It ached, this coming back into being. A coming back that took a long time, too long, two hundred and fifty years to be exact. I lay on the floor of the glass cage and moaned, a deep rumbling, mumbling moan that reverberated against the glass and travelled through the miles of water above, up to the surface and back up the river, against the direction of the current, right up to the gates of the house in the city, where the Salt Fish Girl sat against the window combing her long white hair. She heard it, I am sure.

2. The Durian

A pearl in the mouth. Smooth knot of promise glistening pink and pulsing so imperceptibly one must hold it in the mouth to tell. It had been there, sitting at the back of my throat, ever since I could remember, warm and smooth, a tiny planet that guaranteed my immortality.

Who knew what human being dreamt my secret first? It's a funeral ritual now. When someone dies, they place a stone in the mouth—jade, a pearl, something cool and precious to lay in the cavity from which speech comes. The dark and empty rooting place of language. A pearl, a seed, how little space it takes to record all that is essential to know about life.

I sat in my nasty little glass cage and ached with longing for the fat sea that lolled beyond the glass. I held the pearl in my mouth, smooth and round, harder than the hardest gem.

I brooded. I worked the pearl around in my mouth as though it were a peach pit to which some idea might cling like a last succulent morsel of fruit. I brooded and I schemed, trying to push the obvious solution from my mind. Surely I could find another way, and I would find it if only I had the patience, if only I could empty my mind and wait for the quiet arrival of a plan. None came.

And then I saw her, saw that perfect form of my own invention, a dark silhouette against the surface of the water. A wide torso, a head, two arms, two legs. I doubt that I could ever dream such a form again. My mother swam on her back, the water a pillow beneath her, looking at the sky hanging blue and gold above. Where does normal air end and the sky begin? She watched the clouds and stretched her arms behind her into the future. She wasn't looking where she was going, but I could feel her sense of hope, even through all that water, and the thickness of the glass. I tongued the pearl, one last caress of that life-sustaining smoothness. What is the point of eternity behind a glass wall?

I took a deep breath and spat the pearl hard against the transparent surface. Pearl and glass shattered and the shards shot out at me, slashing my face, my chest, my arms. Blood spurted as the ocean smashed through the hole in the glass and the fluids mixed, but I wasn't paying attention. I shot into the water and up up up towards the swimming figure. I moved fast, but it didn't matter. By the time I got to the top, she was gone.

I wasn't daunted. I took a deep breath. The exhilaration of being free after all those years of boredom and longing gave me a sense of patience quite supernatural in its tenacity. I knew I was far from being defeated, pearl or no pearl.

Languorously, I furled and unfurled my long body in the water, myself again, or at least, one of my selves.

There was a tree growing beside the water. It stretched roots into both the land and sea, drew water and salt up into its thick, convoluted trunk. It was a durian tree in full flower, and its yellow buds were already sending out that strange and marvellous odour that might be crudely described as cat piss blended with unadulterated euphoria. I made myself as small as a worm, crawled through the tiny aperture of a barely opened bud, and coiled myself round and round its small black heart. I closed my eyes and went to sleep. In my sleep, I dreamt the flower opening, dreamt it drinking sunlight and warming my belly with the heat. Its petals dropped half onto the ground and half into the ocean. I coiled more tightly than ever around the heart. Slowly, a shell grew over me, leather-hard and spiky on the outside, but on the inside smooth, veined and sticky moist. Around me seeds grew thick, and over them a dense yellow-white flesh. As the meat grew plump, that terrible and heavenly cat-piss smell intensified to an almost unbearable degree. Sometimes I felt disgusted by it, but sometimes it comforted me. I stretched a little, readjusted my coils around the fattest seed. She knew I was coming.

The day my mother visited the ocean, she didn't see me, but she saw the durian tree in full flower. "Oh," she said to my dad, who waited patiently for her on the beach, "how I would love to have one of those fruits when they are ripe."

"It's not a good idea, Aimee. Please don't ask me for things I cannot give."

"This durian tree doesn't belong to anyone. The fruits are going to go to waste. I don't see what the big deal is."

"We're in the Unregulated Zone. The fruits aren't patented. They might not be safe. Don't you think it's strange that a durian tree is growing here? This is hardly the tropics."

"So the world has warmed up since we were young," she pouted. "I haven't eaten durian since I was a child. How can you be so stingy?"

I relaxed my grip on the seed momentarily and then squeezed it more tightly than ever in the firm grip of my winding coils. The yellow flesh sweated, effused scent. In my tight grip, something inside the seed seemed to stir. I felt a slight, momentary vibration. Though I held the heart of the fruit, the fruit held me. Its strange acids worked at my flesh in a way that discomfited me. I found a small hole in the seed. I scaled down further and crawled inside. I became the seed and the seed became me. Whatever grows from it will be mine.

Unregulated Zone, 2062

WATER ON ROCK

1. Wind-up Toys

The dreams were too much. They were more than I wanted. Outside the cage, the ocean crashed. I went to the wall and slammed my fists against it. I kicked it. It was too sturdy. It repelled my blows as though with volition. I hurled my entire body at it and saw the embedded wires vibrate ever so slightly as I fell to the floor. I got up and climbed into the tub. More than anything, I wanted to forget. My body felt heavy, as though the contents of each cell had been replaced with iron. I knew the faucets wouldn't work, but I turned them anyway, furious and cursing. I lay in the dry tub and sang the song I no longer owned, sang it as though it were water that could engulf me. I picked up the razor blade. If memory could not be washed away, perhaps it could be cut. I tested its sharp edge against my thumb and was surprised to see a fat drop of blood swell where the blade had brushed. It didn't hurt very much, but it was just enough pain to jolt me back to my senses. I stood up in the tub and shook my fists at the space above me, at the pointed tip of the cage. "Let me out, you bastard!" I yelled. The high-pitched fury of my voice made the cage vibrate. To my surprise, a single drop of water fell from the minaret tip and landed on the floor. I got out of the tub and pushed it to the exact centre of the room. Another drop plonked, this time onto the white porcelain. I can be patient, I thought. I can weather this. I climbed into the tub and let the drops fall slowly, one by one. I stood up. I sang my mother's cabaret songs as loud as I could and with as much fury as my parched throat could muster. The drops fell faster. I lolled in the tub, greatly relieved. After three days, the tub began to overflow. In a week, water filled the cage, and I floated slowly to the top. In the last metre of air, I took a deep breath and then pushed through the pointed tip. It was designed to give to pressure exerted from the outside. I forced it with my foot, and took a last gulp of air before the ocean rushed in. As I shot up, the front of my dress gave a little and Withers' money floated away. My boots loosened from my ankles and sank. With a tankful of air I could have chased them, but I had to be economical with my single lungful. I kicked up as fluidly as I could. I popped gasping to the surface.

In the late afternoon light I swam for the dock. As I did so, memory did not rush away from me, though it did diminish in intensity. I swam under a small industrial pier and crawled up onto the pebble beach. I collapsed and dozed until the air grew cold.

It was dark when I awoke, and my skin itched. I brushed my arm. There was something covering my skin that was smooth and hard and slippery. When I brushed in the opposite direction it was rough. My arms were covered in scales. I brushed more firmly against their grain and they fell away. I brushed my legs, and again felt scales loosen and come off in my hand. They were so naturally embedded in my skin I couldn't imagine they hadn't always grown there. I brushed every exposed inch of my body and then I brushed under the tattered red dress until my skin was smooth again. The intensity of my recent ordeal made the real world seem suddenly very strange and very banal at the same time. I could go home, I thought. I could tell my father and brother everything, make a clean bone of it, and hope that they would take me back. Though as Flowers was one of my brother's regular clients, I wondered how long it would be feasible. But even if I couldn't live with them any more, surely my family would help me. Besides, the only alternative was Evie, and I didn't even know where to find her. In bare feet, clinging to the remains of my mother's poor dress, I walked through town in the direction of the family home.

Half a block away, I could hear the old piano. Intermittently, little snatches of my mother's cabaret tunes were audible, but otherwise it was a strange discordant music that rumbled out into the night air. At the door to the storeroom, I could hear my father muttering, though the content of his speech was inaudible. I walked round to the back door of the residential part of the house, fished under the doormat for the spare key, and let myself in. I turned on the hallway light, went straight to my bedroom and wearily opened the door. Light from the hallway flooded in and I heard my brother yell. He was lying in a double bed beside—it couldn't be—Evie. Beside her, my brother looked like an old man. The entire room had been refurnished and redecorated.

My father's macabre music crescendoed and diminished. I shivered.

It was Evie, wasn't it? The woman looked like her, but her eyes were all wrong. Everything about her was wrong—her hair, not, of course, that she couldn't have changed the style, but its texture, the way it caught the light was different and there was an emptiness in my nose and mouth when I looked at her. She had no odour. She was an empty vessel. I don't know how long the three of us remained like that, they in their bed, naked beneath the sheets, and I in the doorway, a dark shadow lit from behind. We stared at one another in shocked silence, not knowing what to say. We breathed names, correct and not. "Miranda?" "Evie?" "Aaron?"

"Yes."

"No."

"Who is Evie?" my brother said.

I realized I was swaying, that I'd gripped the door frame to maintain my balance.

"Evie," I said, looking at the woman in bed beside him, waiting for those empty eyes to flood with recognition. Instead something pale—was it fear?—flickered through them. I felt irrationally angry.

My brother said, "Miranda?" There was a slight quake in his voice as though he were unsure of whom he addressed. He turned on his bedside lamp. The sudden brightness made me squint.

"It's me," I said. "Asshole."

Aaron said, "My God, Miranda. We thought you'd had it. Flowers told us he'd seen your body laid out in the gym at St. Edward's."

"Trawling for raw material was he?"

"He's a scientist, Miranda."

I said, "He's evil. Why didn't you go look for me?"

"We did, but without luck," said Aaron. "We've been worried. This is a great relief."

I looked at him. Something was wrong.

He said, "Dad thinks you're dead. It might be better if it stayed that way." Again the music swelled. I knew my father was not well.

"What are you talking about?" I said.

"Don't you dare play innocent," said Aaron. "Mom's face has been on every billboard in the Zone. Every time we turn on the radio 'Clara Cruise' is selling Pallas gear. It even comes on some of the pirate TV stations. They've got this woman who looks just like her. Your father never leaves that God cursed piano. The grief is killing him."

I didn't know what to say. I looked at the Evie lookalike in his bed, regarded the walls of what had once been my room with hollow-bellied dismay. How had things gotten this out of control? I didn't feel the extent of my father's grief the way I knew I ought to. Not after Flowers' strange cage, or the presence of this most perturbing woman in my brother's bed. I whispered again to her, "Evie?"

"Who is Evie?" said my brother. "This is Karen, my new wife, okay? I don't know what goes on in that little head of yours that makes you do the things you do, but it really disturbs the peace for the decent people in this house."

It was only at that moment that I recalled what Evie had told me that long ago day in the mountains. Somehow I didn't believe that there could really be thousands, or even hundreds of thousands of women in the world who looked just like her, who were locked up in grey compounds like the one I used to cycle by every day on my way to Flowers' office. I couldn't make sense of Evie's unlimited capacity for resistance and rebellion in the face of this Karen's docility. I wondered what the other clones were like, if they were as different from one another as Karen was from Evie. I couldn't imagine how I would react if I were ever permitted into one of the factories and saw them working side by side. Or to one of the clandestine meetings where Evie and other escapees worked out plans for public campaigns or covert sabotage. The uneasy creeped-out feeling that had come upon me on the first day I met Evie returned with an intensity I had not experienced before. I didn't know how I could face her again.

As for my father, I couldn't believe that he wouldn't want to know I was alive. But I wasn't sure what my return would mean to him. I was a fugitive from Flowers now. His strange scar still marked the back of my neck, and I had no idea what the effect of the dissolving disc had been.

I worried for my father's health. I didn't want to reappear only to disappear again. But I was angry at my brother for his arrogance.

"Where did you meet this new wife of yours?" I asked. "Maybe you should know where she came from before you get on your high horse."

"You burned the doctor too," said my brother. "Karen knows about that. He was kind to her. Helped her get her picture into *New World Brides* magazine when she was starving to death in the ruins of Painted Horse. We're happy. Don't spoil it."

"This is my room," I said.

Aaron said, "Not any more. You can use my old room if you really have to stay." He reached across Karen to a pair of trousers draped over a chair beside the bed, and pulled them under the covers. My stomach lurched.

"I can find my own way," I said. I pulled the bedroom door shut. I tiptoed back along the hallway, downstairs to the basement and my brother's old room. I threw open the door and turned on the light. The naked bulb glowed an ambient purple red. Every inch of the wall was covered with images of his first wife, Donna, who had drowned before I was born—photographs of their life together, hand drawings, sculptures of her embedded in frames, like statues of Guan Yin or the Virgin Mary, painted gaudy colours and surrounded by stars. But in some of the drawings and sculptures she wasn't human. A scaly fish tail descended from her hips. In another, the tail was long and snaky. Memories from the ocean room rushed at me. My father's eerie piano noise rumbled directly above. I turned towards the door and fled out onto the streets of the Unregulated Zone. Others lived there. I could too. That night I found myself a bed at a small Christian mission. At suppertime, I helped them with chopping and washing, and in that way kept myself near the head of the queue for a bed the following night.

The first time I took something, I wasn't conscious of reasoning, only the thrill of illicit behaviour for the pure joy of it. It was a wind-up toy I took, a duck on a tricycle with a whirligig atop its foolish flap-mouthed head, a nineteenth-century European fantasy of eccentricity and madness, made on the eastern rim of the PEU in what used to be China. It was an awkward shape and rattled loudly, but I had lots of space beneath my overcoat and a very steady, quiet foot.

I sold the toys to the kids who wore plastic bags instead of socks. Sometimes they gave me money and sometimes food. A considerable array of wind-up toys passed through my hands—a plastic goose that ducked its head as it moved and scooped its neck down, then up and forward as it came to a halt, a wind-up frog that jumped helter-skelter across the park bench I retreated to afterwards, a small-scale replica of the *Hindenberg*, an elephant that twirled around and balanced a beach ball on its nose, an alligator that snapped its jaws as it scooted forwards and a panda bear that marched and beat a drum to keep the time. At the beginning, I promised myself I would never visit the same toy store twice, but my passion for these quaint, odd toys got the better of me. And there was a shopkeeper who had better taste than anyone else, who brought in wind-up fish and butterflies, grasshoppers and spiders. The precision of their movement, their lifelikeness, was more accurate than that of the toys anywhere else and they delighted me. Later, when I looked at the price tags, I realized that I was costing him a pretty penny. At some level I must have known he suspected me, but by then I couldn't help myself. The adrenalin rush that accompanied the thrill of rebellion had become an addiction I couldn't shake. A wiser thief would have diversified and made a much better living, but I was not a wiser thief.

One particular Friday, he had a green wind-up snake that slithered across the floor on its belly with such accuracy I had a shudder of recognition. I loitered until he disappeared for a moment, I thought, into the storeroom, and then I snatched the thing up and dropped it into my overcoat pocket. He had me by the scruff of my collar before I had a clue what hit me. How he could have gotten there that fast I have no idea.

"Get your greasy fingers off me, you ugly bugger!" I yelled. But I didn't have to say much more because suddenly there was a small explosion like a pop can bursting right beside the cash register, and then flames spreading rapidly up the walls and over the counters. He dropped me like a rock and ran to save his cash box. And then Evie was there. She grabbed my hand and we ran out the door laughing like idiots. In the distance, I could already hear sirens wailing. Evie pulled me into a dark narrow alley and we ran. We ran and we kept turning corners until I completely lost my sense of direction. Having been raised to believe that it was far too dangerous to walk in the city, I had no idea about these alleyways, no idea that the city was connected by them, that it had this whole other internal logic, an organizing principle beyond its noisy, commercially active facade.

We tumbled out of the maze onto a dilapidated street in which many houses were abandoned. The walls of some had crumbled, leaving steel and concrete beams exposed and rusting. Others were hopelessly covered in a black fuzzy mildew that seemed to thrive on cheap aging stucco. A few were occupied. There was no electricity. Torches and candles burned in the windows. Evidently, there was no running water or functional sanitation system either. The street reeked of raw sewage. Numerous scrawny cats and the odd stray dog also roamed the boulevard and in the gutters rats fat as small footballs scampered, sleek and foul, their yellow eyes gleaming.

"Better stay with me until the dust settles," Evie said.

I scrutinized her face, her yellow teeth. A faint whiff of salt fish rose from her warm skin. It was a great relief. I said, "My brother and father . . ." I didn't know where to begin. I wondered if she'd seen the Clara Cruise commercials on pirate TV. She must have seen the billboards. They were unavoidable. I wanted to ask her about Karen, but I didn't want to push my luck. In the meantime, staying at the mission was wearing on me. I knew the police would find me there easily. I needed somewhere to go.

I knew which house it was because of the tree, even before we got to the end of the block. It wasn't tall—barely the height of the house. The tree sloped in a little towards the porch, so that it protected and obscured the house at the same time. Its branches were knotted, growing away from the trunk in acrobatic contortions. Its leaves were dark and fluttered a little in the evening breeze, revealing their slightly paler undersides and the faint red of their veins as though blood flowed from the trunk, down the gnarled branches and into the veins of the leaves. As we approached closer, I saw the first fruit, nestled in the dark foliage—greenish-gold bodies covered in spikes, distinctly lizard-like. Different from the durians that had passed, over the years, through our family store, these ones flushed pink at the ends of their spikes. It was as though blood flowed from the inside to the pointed tips, as it appeared to in the leaves, or as though some giant hand had tried unsuccessfully to crush each one and had left the bloody trace of the attempt on each incisor-sharp point. But the thing that most shocked and astonished and at the same time oddly comforted me was the odour that poured from the fruits, wafted off the leaves and seeped from the bark. It was the same heavenly cat-piss-and-pepper odour that had been the bane of my childhood existence, the odour that still trailed me around like a stray dog.

I felt the tree pulling at me, as though I were a small moon caught in the gravitational field of a heavy planet. I moved towards it and Evie followed, stood with me under a low branch that sank beneath the weight of the fruit. She reached up with both hands, picked the fattest one and held it towards me. I took it. It was heavy in my hands, like a small corpse.

She guided me away from the tree, down a wood-plank walkway that led to the rear of the house.

On the back porch sat an old woman in a rocking chair, smoking a pipe and reading by the light of a single candle. There was something oddly familiar about her face, although I was quite sure I had never met her before.

"My eldest sister, Sonia 14," said Evie.

"Nice to meet you," I said to the old woman. She lowered her pipe and nodded at me politely.

We stepped in through the screen door. The kitchen was lit by four torches, one on each wall. In the corner by the stove was a large heap of cabbages and a small basket of pretty radishes, round and red. Before the kitchen table, on long wooden benches, sat six other women, all in their late teens or early twenties. They were chatting rapidly in a language I could not quite get a hold on, though I thought I recognized a smattering of Chinese, a few words of Spanish, some French, some English. Four of them were busy wrapping a seasoned mixture of pork, bamboo shoots and black fungus into won ton wrappers. Two held young infants in their arms—girls, if their ragged baby dresses were any indication. Along the benches were four makeshift cradles made from old fruit crates, in which four children slept, quiet and peaceful in spite of the chatter and raucous laughter. But the uncanny thing was that, except for pimples, scars and wrinkles, all six of the women's faces were identical to Evie's.

"Sonias 116, 121, 148, 161, 211 and 287."

"Your sisters?"

"Yes."

I nodded hello, but my stomach churned. A gaunt cat rubbed up against my right leg, another came up along my left.

"Just kick them away," said Evie. "The place is crawling with them."

One of the Sonias came and took the durian from me.

"How come you're not also called Sonia?" I asked Evie.

"I am. I'm Sonia 113. I changed my name when I escaped. It's weird though, never quite comfortable."

I didn't know how to respond, so I said nothing.

"You hungry?"

"A little."

She moved towards a little pot-bellied stove that sat in the corner and lifted the lid of the pot that sat on top. Whatever was in there, there wasn't much left. She scraped some out and spooned it into a bowl. Sticky rice with lap cheung, ha mai and dong gwu. It was still warm, though a bit dry.

I sat down at the table and dug in.

"You're lucky it's dark out," she said. "In the daytime we eat out of cans because we can't risk anyone seeing our smoke."

I wondered about the eight of them and their children, living in such secrecy so far from the inhabited parts of the Unregulated Zone. Did Pallas send security people out to look for them? Who were the fathers of these quiet children?

As I was finishing my rice, the Sonia who had taken the fruit from me rose to get a knife. She put the durian on the table and split it neatly in two. That delirious smell rushed into the air. The yellow pieces glistened like fresh organ meat.

Evie took a few pieces and put them on a plate. She laid a pretty spoon beside them, and handed it to me. Had it been any one but Evie offering me this delicacy, and had it been any moment but this, I think I would have refused. I had always thought there was something cannibalistic about eating it, and so I never had. But this time an overwhelming sense of wonder compelled me. I scooped the creamy yellow flesh into my mouth, felt its taste and odour merge with my own. It gave me a very peculiar sensation, as though I'd bitten my own tongue. And yet it was delicious. I gobbled it down and held the plate out for more.

When I was finished, Evie picked up a half-burnt candle that sat in an old brass candle holder beside the defunct electric stove stacked with chipped bowls and plates. Put a match to it and headed down the hall towards the stairs. As she walked, the salt fish scent she left in her wake was subtle but unmistakable. No wonder cats followed her. I followed her too.

There was a hallway at the top of the stairs, and at the end of the hallway, another door, which opened into a narrow stairway to the attic. The steps creaked under our feet as we climbed.

"Who helps you?" I asked.

"We help ourselves," she said. "Wherever Pallas goes, there are pods of Sonias hiding out just beyond the walls of Pallas's cities."

"How come Pallas security doesn't track them down?"

"You already know more than you ought to," Evie said.

The ceilings were low and slanted in the little attic room. The floor was strewn with books and papers. In the corner slumped a stained, beat-up old futon, without sheets, and with the stuffing poking out of the holes. A ratty synthetic quilt and a couple of limp grey pillows without cases lay haphazardly tossed on top.

"You can trust me," I said. And then I paused because I knew it wasn't true.

She sensed my hesitation. "That so?"

"No," I said. "You're right. It isn't." Quietly I began to recount the events of the last few days. But she barely gave me a chance. When I told her about the sale of my mother's song, her eyes narrowed and darkened. I could see something bitter rise in her chest. "How could you?" she sputtered.

"I don't know," I said defiantly. "It just happened."

Her fury frightened me. I thought of the ancient Sonia sitting outside in her rocking chair, the four younger ones downstairs making sui gow. How many were there working in Pallas's dark factories and what did they have in them that gave them the wherewithal to escape? I wondered if their backs were drawn with scars in the shape of wings, like Evie's.

Evie ranted. Playing right into the hands of the enemy. Not to mention massacring your own talent. How could you? But her hand reached out and touched my face. Her fingers burned against my cheek. When she kissed me it was like both eating and drinking at the same time. The stench that poured from our bodies was overwhelming—something between rotting garbage and heavenly stew. We rode the hiss and fizzle of salt fish and durian, minor notes of sour plum, fermented tofu, boiled dong quai—all those things buried and forgotten in the years of corporate homogenization. Steam rose from us like water splashed on a hot pan of garlic greens.

Afterwards she fell asleep, warm breath on my neck, not a deep sleep, but a light doze, affectionate and almost domestic. She snoozed and my mind raced. I could not stop thinking about shoes. Shoes worn by middle-class, middle-aged suburban women scared of growing old, uninterested in the world they live in, except insofar as it can provide them with beautiful things to reward them for their long treacherous days in office towers pumped full of fake air, or at home, organizing groceries and menus, vacuuming, trying to make something they can call their own from what comes in cardboard boxes and plastic wrappers from the megastore strip mall. I thought about their shoes, about the freedom they longed for, their brief moments of peace on the road or at the gym or, if they were lucky, in the still-wooded pathways behind their subdivision houses. The freedom, the seemingly immortal beauty that, having gotten them this far, had now begun to fade. How they fought its fading, pushed the bodies they knew wouldn't last to extremes of exhaustion as though this pushing would hold off the inevitable. Certainly scientific studies published in glossy magazines said it would, and these, of course, were women who believed in science. I didn't suppose Adrian Withers really intended to land me a job in an advertising agency. I didn't want to think about how to sell shoes to people who were afraid of dying. Winged sandals, thousand-league boots— supernatural shoes have been around for a long time. Shoes these days were like cologne, holding the mysterious promise of life eternal. I closed my eyes and dreamt of shoes—Puss-in-Boots pussyfooting into the most promising bedrooms for the sake of his rakish master, Dorothy's red shoes, click, click, send me back to China, twelve dancing princesses who waft nightly out their windows and dance until their soles are worn skin-thin. I had recently heard a rumour that Pallas intentionally made its shoes out of shoddy materials so that they would wear out faster. The twelve dancing princesses would have been good customers.

Ironic really that my life this time around should revolve so intimately around shoes, having finally, after hundreds of years of tradition, evaded the threat of foot-binding. Crushed foot bones bandaged tight, their equation with grace—what a close call I've had. Narrow escape of only a hundred and fifty years. It occurred to me that it was women's hands that did the breaking. How could a mother do such a thing to her daughter? Even if it was an assurance of the child's social status later on. Not that I would know, being a motherless child myself.

I dreamt of shoes and inside me something turned. Something without feet. Something as yet without arms or legs, something long and coiled. I dreamt that it spoke. *This is the best hour of the day, right now, as I hang here in your womb as though asleep in some ancient garden. My body has not yet sprouted limbs, not yet become definably human. Here I hang, long and coiled with large bright eyes that can sense more than they can see. Serpentine. It's one of the oldest forms going, and I'm not ashamed to say I find it comfortable.* And then the thing slept, and I kept dreaming. I dreamt I was drowning, arms flailing under water, reaching, grasping at weeds that seemed closer than they actually were, my fingers never closing over anything solid.

I awoke when Evie rolled away from me, stretched to a more comfortable position. She pushed her pillow further up the ratty mattress towards the wall. Something cold and hard slipped out from underneath, glided in to nestle beneath her chin, against her neck, small and silver and sleek. A gun—at first I thought it was just a plastic toy, another of Evie's props that she might use to stage one of her minor heists. But when I looked closely at it, I could tell that the metal was solid, that its mechanics were precise and meant to work. I coiled away from her, suddenly frightened again of her strange origins, her odd sisters now shuffling through the dark to their own cold beds.

I did not think I had fallen asleep again, but I must have, because when I opened my eyes there was sunlight streaming in through ancient ugly polyester curtains. Evie was gone, and so was the gun. Could I have imagined it? I stretched stiffly and sat up, pulled the dusty curtain aside and looked out the window. Out on the back porch sat old Sonia 14, smoking her pipe and rocking in her rocking chair. At her feet sat Evie, puffing on a cigarette, eyes turned intently up towards Sonia 14, listening and nodding. Beyond them was a vegetable patch, consisting of neat rows of cabbages in several varieties, green and purple, and a few rows of tender green leaves that I assumed to be the tops of radishes like the ones I had seen yesterday in the kitchen.

My eyes turned back to Evie and Sonia 14. I watched them for a long time. I did not feel half so creeped out as I did envious. To have access to oneself as an old woman. Was it like that for them? Did Sonia 14, having lived them, share Evie's foibles? Had she come to an understanding of them? Did she see Evie's life as an extension of her own, as a second shot at those things that had failed the first time?

Evie spoke rapidly, her sharp face animated. Sonia 14 inhaled deeply from her pipe and nodded gravely. I watched them for a long time.

Finally, I pulled on my clothes and trundled downstairs. The three younger Sonias sat at the kitchen table drinking coffee and eating sweet cereal in atrocious pinks and greens. Dubiously, I accepted a generously loaded bowl and stepped out onto the porch.

"Sonia 14 thinks it's safe for you to go home," said Evie. "As long as you stay home and don't hang out downtown any more."

"She does? But yesterday you said . . ." I still hadn't told Evie about my brother and Karen. I dreaded my brother's wrath to a certain extent, but the thing that I wished to avoid at all costs was facing my father's disappointment and grief.

Evie said, "I wasn't thinking straight. It's anyone's guess how safe this house really is."

I nodded, thinking of the gun. "I can't go home. I can't face them."

"Of course you can," she said. "They're your family. They'll forgive you."

"I've disappointed them too often."

"You did what you needed to."

I got angry. I said, "I did what you needed."

"That isn't fair," she said.

"Girls," said Sonia 14 in a tone that indicated she expected obedience. I felt childish and stupid.

"Sonia 14 wants you to take this," said Evie. She handed me a knapsack. Rudely, I pulled back the zipper and looked inside. "Breakfast cereal?"

"I know it's a weird present," said Evie. "She says it was wrong of me to make you lose your job, and so she feels responsible."

"I don't need your charity."

"Just take it. She'll be insulted if you don't. Besides, the stuff tastes awful."

"I guess we could try to sell it in the store."

She led me on a circuitous route that avoided downtown, brought me as far as a field several kilometres west of the Zodiac compound where we had been gassed mere months ago. She kissed my cheek, but in a distant sort of way, as though to let me know she was still unimpressed with my actions of the recent past. Stubborn as ever, I kissed her back, in the same cursory sort of way.

2. Darling Tom

I walked the last few kilometres to the shop alone. On an abandoned street corner, where long ago there had a stood a bank and a barber shop, a group of urban youngsters loitered, wearing plastic bags inside their shoes. The edges of the bags hung outside the cuffs of their pants like crazy transparent socks. Today the sight of them made me think of the doctors, Seto and Flowers, and what Seto had told me about how some believed the dreaming disease was caught through the soles of the feet.

In this part of the Unregulated Zone, where the barefoot terminally unemployed lived, many now roamed the streets with glazed eyes and scaly skin, or sat on street corners spewing memories of genocide and smallpox, smart bombs and slow starvation. The odours that accompanied these memories—of steel and blood and shit and old potatoes—mingled with the smell of uncollected garbage and open sewers. The destitute wandered shoeless and hungry and dreaming with an intensity that only the destitute can dream. On the side of a concrete building some ten blocks from my parents' shop, beneath a billboard of my mother's look-alike dressed in an old-fashioned Chinese suit with cloth buttons up the side and a pair of Pallas runners, someone had graffitied step-by-step instructions on how to seal one's feet inside plastic bags effectively, so that no leaking would occur.

I didn't expect my brother to be kind, but the thought of facing him was still much easier than the thought of facing my father. So instead of walking into the shop, I went around back to the garage. I saw my brother's boots sticking out from beneath the body of a rusted-out old sedan. I prodded his foot with my own and he wheeled himself out.

"Miranda?" he said. "Are you okay?"

His kindness threw me. I hadn't expected it. I said, "I'm okay, I guess." There was a long pause. I couldn't bring myself to ask for anything, but nor could I let the pause grow too long. Finally, I said, "I have nowhere to go."

"There was a call for you three days ago," Aaron said.

Who would call me? The phone was unreliable. Most people we knew didn't even have one. "Someone from a place called the Logo Moguls. She had a weird name—Darling someone or other. Sounded like lots of dough. Dad got the call."

"Dad's okay?"

"Of course not. He told them you'd call back."

"But he thinks I'm dead."

"Exactly."

"Where is he now?" I asked.

My brother said, "He's in the shop. Why don't you go say hello."

I made Aaron come with me. Karen was behind the counter, looking too unnaturally like Evie. In spite of my visit with the Sonias I still didn't like to look at her. My father was nowhere in sight.

"Dad!" Aaron called.

The old man's head popped up from behind a row of cough syrup and condom boxes. He saw me right away, but showed no sign of surprise. "Miranda," he said. "There was a call for you."

"Don't you want to know where I've been, Dad?" I said.

"Did you manage to get a shipment of durians from Dubinsky?"

That was how I knew he'd begun to see my ghost as well. Dubinsky the fruit man had died two years ago in a stabbing incident downtown. My father had been grief-stricken. "No durians today, Dad," I said.

"There was a call for you," my dad said. "It might not be too late." His eyes were a little shiny. With tears? He blinked and the shine was gone.

"What did you tell them?"

My father was silent.

Aaron said, "He just told them you weren't here."

I said, "I guess I'll have to call them back." And then, "I brought you this." I handed my father Evie's knapsack. He opened it, pulled out a box and examined the label carefully.

"Breakfast cereal?" he said.

"You better have come by that honestly," said Aaron.

Withers had come through after all, much to my surprise. The call came from an advertising firm called the Logo Moguls. They weren't based inside any walled city, but kept their offices in Bright Sea, in a newly fashionable part of the Unregulated Zone. You had to be careful on the streets, my brother said, but he thought the company would probably be operating in a high-security building with uniformed doormen to keep outsiders out and insiders in. It would be cheaper to run, less beholden to the strict regulations of the walled cities and therefore freer to be more creative both with their products and their labour practices. They were inviting me for an interview.

"Well, that's wonderful," said my father. "It would sure be nice if one of my children could make something of her life." He glanced unintentionally at my brother's hands. Somehow we all knew that he saw Aaron's nails were dirty. I grinned at my brother smugly.

"Nothing's happened yet," said Aaron.

My father got up and went to his piano.

In an elegant, high-ceilinged Thai restaurant, I met an elegant high-haired woman called Darling Tom.

"Actually," she said, "my great-grandfather changed it to Thomas in the 1950s as a friendly gesture to his new homeland. I just changed it back last year."

There was something feline about her, but it was more of the kitty-kitty variety than alley prowling tomcat. I found her mesmerizing.

"Show me what you've got," she said.

I produced a small portfolio of songs in the style of my mother's greatest hits. I had been writing them lately, to cheer myself up. She didn't seem particularly interested.

"I heard you had some drawings."

How could she have known? I had never shown my drawings to anyone, except, long ago, Ian Chestnut. I had only slipped them into the shiny new vinyl case my father had bought for the occasion as a last-minute afterthought. Since my last participation in Flowers' experiment my drawings had troubled me and I wasn't at all sure I wanted anyone to see them.

I pulled them out, feeling terribly exposed. How the drawings might look to this elegant woman, or any of the people she might wish to show them to, I could not begin to imagine. This stranger held the contents of my soul in her hands with an eye to turning them into marketing materials.

She looked through them gravely and thoughtfully, not at all with the dismissive eye with which she had regarded my sheaf of cabaret jingles. She paused for a long time over the *Little Mermaid* series. "These are interesting," she said. "The others are great, but these are a bit more accessible, I think."

Evie, I thought to myself, would have a lot to say to a remark like that, but I just nodded.

She reached into her sleek and fashionable brown leather bag and produced a small envelope containing photographs of three pairs of runners. Pallas runners. "I'd like to try you out," she said. "You think you can redo these images to show that the Little Mermaid wants legs and feet so that she can wear Pallas runners?" She smiled her most disarming smile. Unlike Evie's, her teeth were white and straight and evenly spaced.

I nodded weakly. "I'll try," I said.

When I told my father about it he said, "I thought you were studying opera."

"No, Dad," I said, puzzled. "I was going to be a doctor, remember?"

"Such a beautiful voice," he said. "Just like your mother's. Seems like a terrible waste." Then he turned around and slipped into the storeroom. The eerie piano started up.

"What's wrong with him?" I whispered to Aaron. For some reason I found it disconcerting that Karen should hear me, though of course she heard anyway, and whispering only made my unease obvious.

"It comes and goes," Aaron said. "Sometimes he's perfectly lucid. Just consider it a blessing he doesn't realize what a wreck you're making of your life."

"I'm doing just fine," I said.

"You'd be doing even better if you could bring us some more of that cereal," Aaron said. "It's selling like crazy."

From the storeroom, my father's mad music poured. "I'll try," I said.

Evie had boxes and boxes of that cereal. I saw it when she opened the cupboard to find me a spoon. I figured it was probably part of the seized assets of some bankrupt company that didn't have the smarts to do a little market research before producing vast quantities of the stuff. I had eaten a bowl. I couldn't imagine people liking it, but what do I know? People have strange tastes. At any rate, I wasn't feeling particularly interested in hunting Evie down for more. Not at that moment. It was obvious that she was the kiss of death to my family life, and besides, I didn't want her leaning over me as I set to work blackening my own soul.

Somehow the sanction of a job took the edge off my terror of Flowers' swimming world. I stayed up through the night reworking the drawings, re-engaging the Little Mermaid, the agony of her tail's splitting, the pain of giving up one's innocence. Hans Christian Andersen's tragic tale says that when the Little Mermaid walked it was like stepping on knives. But as I worked, the images took on the wicked sheen of parody. Shoes replaced the handsome prince as objects of desire and the mermaid's eyes glittered and winked. Perhaps she had the last laugh after all. When that thought crossed my mind, I imagined that something inside me turned and whispered, something long and coiled, a body that had not yet sprouted limbs, had not yet become definably human. I imagined I held a pomegranate seed in my mouth. I felt its presence, the small weight of it against my tongue. I envisioned it as a red crystal holding a microcosm of the world—minute versions of myself and Evie, my brother and Karen, my father and mother, Flowers and Seto, swimming in an ocean of blood. Waiting for me to involuntarily clench my teeth and crush us all in a single gesture. I could not push this thought from my mind, though I concentrated on the Little Mermaid's scales, the precise arc of their scalloped edges, their glittery translucent sheen. The strange sensation of something moving in my belly was so distracting after a while that I trundled down to the kitchen to warm myself a cup of milk. It helped for a few hours. I worked until the sun rose pale through the haze of an early morning rain shower. Then I crawled into bed and went to sleep.

It rained the afternoon I was supposed to go meet Darling Tom. By evening it had stopped, but the shoulders of the roads were slick and muddy and I had to be careful not to run into them because the mud made my tires skid badly.

I noticed the footprints when the unpaved shoulder gave way to newly poured sidewalk, all kinds of footprints from all kinds of shoes and boots. Because I was not on foot myself, however, I didn't notice that some left a textual imprint behind until after I had dismounted near the restaurant and locked my bike to a post.

When I stepped onto the sidewalk, the text became eminently clear. The soles of the shoes functioned like rubber stamps, the wet mud like ink.

The footprints said:

What does it mean to be human?
How old is history?
The shoemakers have no elves.

One set of footprints was just a price list:

materials: 10 units
labour: 3 units
retail price: 169 units
profit: 156 units
Do you care?

I clutched my little portfolio tightly and walked into
the restaurant. It was the swishy Spanish cowboy kind—
beat-up tables and chipped-paint cabinets belying an ex-
quisite taste, distanced enough from poverty to feel comfortable making chic from decay. Dim lights, big tall menus,
small amounts of food artistically arranged on large white
plates. In a quiet corner beneath a swinging ring of candles sat Darling Tom in a long white dress, somewhere
between avenging infanta and delicate snow goddess.

"Hun hao! Very good!" she said when she saw my
reworked mermaid drawings. "You're on." She winked at
me, lush eyelashes grazing silken-smooth cheek. I knew I
shouldn't but I let her buy me dinner. She ordered blue
martinis and encouraged me to eat as much as I wanted.
I let myself go soft inside with pleasure. Stuffed myself
with ceviche and roasted lamb, drank the berry-scented
wine she ordered by the bottle until the terra cotta walls
began to undulate.

Darling Tom pulled a neatly clipped sheaf of paper
from her smooth leather bag. "Standard contract," she
said. "Very fair to all concerned. We're so happy to have
you on board."

I tried to straighten up, tried to read the tiny swimming words in the restaurant's dim light, but gave up after a couple of clauses. "Everyone signs this?" I said.

She topped up my glass and ladled some wild mushroom fricassee onto my plate. "Everyone," she said.

I took a very big gulp of the berry-scented wine. "I don't know. Can I take it home and look at it?"

She shrugged. "If you want to. I'll try to keep the boss from giving it to this art school grad he's got waiting in the wings."

"An art school grad?"

"Mmm. Roger's really keen on him. I told him I'd really rather have you, and he did like your work very much, so don't worry about it. Just take your time. If he does end up giving it to the other guy something will come up sooner or later."

"I'm not trying to run out on you," I found myself telling her. "It's just . . . my head is swimming. I can't think right now. The wine . . ."

"It's a nice one, isn't it? This restaurant has one of the best wine lists in the city. A bit more expensive than the rest, but worth it, don't you agree?"

I nodded. "It's okay," I said. "I'll sign it now. I trust you."

"Good girl," said Darling Tom. She whipped the signed copy away from me and gave me another copy for my records. "Look it over tonight," she said. "I think you'll be happy with what you read. Can you start tomorrow?"

She drove me home in a sleek Japanese sports car, glittering silver green like an insect's wing.

It wasn't until I lay down that I realized how drunk I was. I closed my eyes and the bed seemed to hover beneath me and then fall away. I lay as though suspended in the air above a black pit until I considered the inevitability of gravity, and then I plummeted.

In the morning, I woke up on the floor with a pounding headache. But when I looked at the clock I saw it was not morning at all, but one-thirty in the afternoon. What time had I told Darling I would show up at the office? I dragged my sorry carcass to the bathroom and turned on the shower. It was a makeshift one attached to the faucet by silver tubing and suspended above the old-fashioned clawfoot tub stained green from the copper lining of the old pipes. I stepped in and turned on the cold only, grimaced as it hit my head and ran sharp and shivery down my back.

I pulled on my best office clothes, a navy blue polyester suit with a crepey sky-blue blouse underneath, hopped on my bike and pedalled towards downtown for all I was worth.

To get to the Logo Moguls offices, I had to pass through Chinatown. Just west of the last noodle house, I saw Evie, sitting in a doorway drinking soda pop and smoking. I wondered how much time she spent loitering on the streets. I waved at her as I sailed past. I had no intention of stopping, but she got up, tossed her half-smoked cigarette to the sidewalk and chased after me. I squeezed my brakes.

"Why are you in such a hurry?"

"I'm late for work. I got a job."

"Well, lucky you." She looked irritated.

Why did she flag me down if she just wanted to be rude? "That cereal you gave us is selling well," I offered.

"You want more?"

"That's not what I meant."

"There's tons of it. It's just sitting there. Why don't you come and get it?"

She would be furious when she heard where I was working. "It's okay," I said.

Her face softened a little. "Sonia 14 has been asking about you. Why don't you come by the house?"

"I don't know the way."

"What time do you finish work? I'll meet you here."

I pumped away down the road towards the Moguls' downtown address. When the traffic got bad, I jumped the curb and pedalled down the sidewalk. I didn't notice Darling ahead of me with a cardboard tray of cappuccinos in hand until I nearly crashed right into her. I clamped down on the brakes.

I smiled sheepishly, hopped down and began to stroll beside her. "Sorry I'm late."

"Good thing you already signed the contract."

Her sternness made me nervous. My instinct was to apologize further, but something held me back. I walked beside her in silence.

There were enough cappuccinos to go around the office, including one for me.

"This is Roger," said Darling.

I nodded hello.

"Only five hours and thirteen minutes late," he said. "I hope it doesn't get any worse than this."

"Extenuating circumstances," I said glancing at Darling. She scowled.

"The mermaid stuff was great," he said. "We're going to run it in a few city magazines to see how it goes over. Now, has Darling brought you up to speed on the new Trembling campaign?"

"Trembling?"

"It's a perfume," said Darling.

"That's what they've given us," Roger said. "We have to work with it. What does it make you think of?"

"I don't know. Romance. The instability of new love. Family values. The new helplessness for women."

"Right. Darling did say you were a bit of a socialist."

"Hardly. I'm here, aren't I?"

"It seems so," said Roger, irritated. "Well, come on, give us something we can work with."

"He doesn't mean right away, sweetie," said Darling. "I'll show you your cubicle." She led me to a little nook beside the photocopy machine. There was no window, but the space was big and bright, and there was a desk, as well as a small drawing board. "We're a small firm, so everyone does everything. Do your best. Pictures, text, whatever. Meeting to hash out ideas at four-thirty."

By four-thirty this was what I had come up with.

You think my head is full of percentages and decimal points
You think that all I care about is the bottom line
But what gets me through the day
Is not the thought of accomplishment
It is the thought of you . . .

                                                Trembling

"You could have variations for a series of ads over the course of a season," I explained, and unveiled two more.

> *You think I care only about Basqiat and Lichtenstein*
> *You think all I care about is the next big thing*
> *But what gets me through the day*
> *Is not the thought of the next record-breaking sale*
> *It is the thought of you ...*
> > *Trembling*

> *You think I only care about skating fast and shooting straight*
> *You think all I care about is the next big score*
> *But what gets me through the day*
> *Is not the thought of glory*
> *It is the thought of you ...*
> > *Trembling*

"Fabulous," said Roger.

"I told you she was good," said Darling, eyes gleaming greed-pride.

I said, "What does the stuff smell like anyway?"

But my great crime was not my participation in the banalities of the advertising world. It was not the slow undermining of women's self-worth through the glamour of passivity. My great crime was yet to come. It was committed in the seemingly innocuous staff lounge, where I sat with Darling at the end of the day to discuss the future. As I relaxed on the smooth neoprene couch in the back room and drank herbal tea, my thoughts drifted, for some reason, to Doctors Flowers and Seto and the rumour of the dreaming disease being contracted through the soles of the feet. It drifted to the kids with plastic bags inside their shoes, and the eyes of those who wandered barefoot, their eyes swimming with grief and history. I thought about the footprints on the sidewalk and the graffiti on the side of the concrete building that demonstrated how to seal one's feet inside plastic bags without the danger of infiltration from the ground, the danger of attack from the land itself, fighting back. To Darling Tom I said, "You know those Pallas ads I did for you?"

Darling nodded.

"I was thinking, suppose Pallas were to advertise shoes as protection against the dreaming disease. Memory-proof soles. I think they would sell really well. And there's this great wall that we could include as part of the ad campaign. They would just have to design a product to fit the concept . . ."

Darling smiled so that all her small white teeth showed.

3. The Sonias' Soles

I left the office hating myself. I did not want to see Evie. I hopped on my bike and took off in the direction opposite to the one I had taken in the morning, meaning to turn around a couple of streets up. In my despair, I did not notice where I was going until the toy store was right there, the one from which I had lifted countless objects and in which Evie had set that nasty fire just weeks ago. I pumped away from it as quickly as I could, but several yards down the way, she stepped out of a dark doorway and right into my path.

"How was your first day?"

"Fine. I have to go home."

"I thought you were coming to see me."

"I changed my mind."

"I thought you might. I brought you some cereal."

"I don't need you taking care of me."

"I'm not taking care of you. We need to get rid of it."

"Fine. Let's have it then. I need to go."

"I can't give it to you here."

We didn't see the Pallas Security coming for us until it was too late. "You can give it to me then," said a man's voice.

Evie pulled the bag close to her. "Get away from me, jerk. You have nothing on me."

The security officer shook his head as though at a wayward child. "I know who you are, Evie Xin. You may as well give me the bag."

There was another officer coming towards me from the right. If I bolted now I might still get away. A gap came up in the oncoming traffic. I leapt into it, or tried to. But the security man was quicker. He had me against a car and cuffed before I knew what hit me. "Miranda Ching," he said, "you are under arrest on charges of larceny and arson. . ." His moustache quivered as he spoke. I thought to elbow him, but it didn't seem it would do me any good.

In the meantime, the other policeman had snatched Evie's bag. He was just undoing the zipper as I turned. He shook its contents out onto the hood of the car. "Breakfast cereal?"

"Bad breakfast cereal," said his partner. "What are you girls up to?" He tore a box open and out fell a stack of thin rubber soles, with text in mirror image on the bottom face of each.

"What the hell are those?"

"Those weird footprints that have been showing up all over the city since last week.

"There's a big penalty to pay for economic sabotage, girls."

The evening found us sitting in a dark holding tank in the basement of the police station, bruised and furious, but not seriously hurt.

"You should have told me," I chided.

"You would have said no."

"You put my family at risk without their consent."

"At risk for what? My family pays for your family's ease and comfort."

"You are oversimplifying, and you know it."

She said nothing about my attempt to bolt, but I knew what she was thinking.

So I sat quietly in the dark and contemplated my crimes. For the first time ever I was glad my mother was no longer around. I thought of my father anxiously counting tins of cream of mushroom soup and boxes of dishwasher detergent to work out how much had been stolen that week. It always happened, no matter how vigilant we were.

Evie sat hunched in the corner, sharp face propped up on sharp hands, scowling. "They can't do anything to us. The evidence is entirely circumstantial. They can't do anything unless they find out what I am. Then that'll be it."

"Don't be so melodramatic," I snapped, suddenly frightened.

She fell silent, but her face grew darker. I chewed my fingernails.

The cell was dark and the only way to clock time was through the meals they brought us, mostly thin soup with dry crackers that turned to dust in the mouth. Mice scurried about with impunity, waiting like dogs for crumbs. They weren't frightened of us at all until Evie accidentally stepped on one in the dark, and then they just scurried about instead of waiting patiently, avoiding the bloody mess of fur and bones that remained of the one sacrificed.

After that it was hard even to keep the thin soup down.

We waited. In the next cell we heard the eerie high-pitched sound of a very young woman weeping. Then, in spite of the dark, we could not sleep either. Once, for comfort, we held each other, but I could feel this terrible hollowness inside her and it scared me. She seemed empty, I felt unbearably full. In spite of the poor nourishment, my body swelled, round and lazy, and I resented its swelling. I did not want this fullness and lethargy. I wanted to feel awake and furious like Evie.

When the guard came one day with a key instead of that dreadful lukewarm soup, we were both surprised.

"My father," I said. "He must have contacted one of his old banking colleagues."

Evie shook her head.

The guard slapped handcuffs on each of us and led us out onto the bright street. My eyes smarted and burned. The city seemed to glow with an angelic white light, but I shuddered. They could be taking us to another, darker prison, or to a football stadium or an empty field. I cowered in my soft vinyl seat.

"Where are you taking us?" asked Evie.

Neither guard nor driver answered.

"Where are you taking us? We have a right to know."

A short silence, and then the guard said, "I'm afraid you have no rights at all, Sonia 113."

They let us out in the middle of an abandoned highway, grass poking between the cracks.

"This makes no sense," said Evie. "No sense at all. We're very close to the house."

"I don't think we should go there. That guard knew who you were."

"That's why we have to go."

We made our way down the overgrown highway. It amazed me how quickly the earth can take over what humans have abandoned. The eager grass had shattered the highway into millions of shards. Dandelions and some small purple flowers I couldn't identify dotted the road like bright kisses on an ancient wound. At a large overpass we selected one of four cloverleaf exit ramps. It led down into the abandoned suburb where the Sonias made their home. We passed many crumbling stucco houses, some with torches burning in the windows against the rapidly falling dark.

The durian tree had been cut down and burned. Nothing remained on the front lawn but a charred stump surrounded by pale rocky earth, bits of moss and stray clumps of hardy razor grass, the only variety that thrived in this neighbourhood. We rushed around to the back. Sonia 14 was asleep in her rocking chair out on the porch, her grey head bent over, one hand in her lap and the other dangling loose. She had dropped her pipe onto the floor. It lay inches from her relaxed hand as though waiting for her to wake and bring it to life. Evie breathed a sigh of relief.

We hurried towards her.

"Good morning, Sonia 14!" called Evie.

Sonia 14 didn't move. Smoke wafted thinly from the mouth of the dropped pipe.

"Sonia," Evie said, placing a hand on her arm. Sonia 14's eyes blinked drowsily open. They were bloodshot and frighteningly dark.

"Shit," Evie said. "It didn't work, did it?"

"Worse," said Sonia 14. "The Sonias . . ."

"Where are they?"

We listened in horror as Sonia 14 recounted the tale. Because I had no idea what they were planning, the shock was double for me, and at the same time, less severe because they weren't my family. Evie and the Sonias had for months been planning a massive infiltration of shoe factories at Redemption, Murphy's Flats and Trough. In the basement of the Sonias' house they had been producing moulds for the soles of a special edition cross-trainer they dubbed "sabots." Some told the stories of individual Sonias' lives, some were inscribed with factory workers' poems, some with polemics, some with drawings. The day of infiltration had occurred during our stint in prison. The Sonias had decided to go ahead regardless.

But someone had ratted. The Sonias were ambushed, with months' worth of moulds in bags and boxes. These were all confiscated. The Sonias were in detention or had disappeared. Without a legal existence to begin with, they could not be reported missing. Sonia 14 combed prisons, abandoned schools, libraries and warehouses hoping to find them hungry but safe. Instead she found an empty field with newly turned dirt in a strip along the far edge beside the forest. Sonia 14 went home, returned with a shovel and dug. She recognized Sonia 148 by her hand, still wearing a ring cut from a bit of copper pipe. She recognized Sonia 116 by a mole on her heel, which also emerged early from the soil. After that, she couldn't bear to look any further. She shovelled dirt back over the bodies. She picked daisies in the field and strewed them over the grave.

When she got home that evening, the durian tree had been cut down and the garden destroyed.

As she told the story, Sonia 14 drew a small packet of tobacco from the inside pocket of her jacket. She packed a small wad into the bowl of the pipe, lit it and inhaled deeply. Her face relaxed as the agony that had marked it shifted. Evie's presence, and perhaps mine as well, seemed to soothe her.

"I'll kill him," Evie said, as the fate of her sisters became clear. I didn't know what she was talking about.

"Do what you need to," said Sonia 14, "but the daughters are still alive and well."

"They left them unharmed?"

"We hid beneath the floorboards. They found Dora 6 and took her away, but the rest are still here."

"You can't stay here," said Evie.

"It's all right," said Sonia 14. "We have a place to go."

"And the durian tree?"

"We saved three large fruits and a basket of radishes.

You and your friend could come with us if you wanted."
Her face was so old and wrinkled. I thought to myself if
it were up to me I would go. The thought of this very old
woman and those young girls taking care of themselves
did not sit well with me. It was likely the first altruistic
thought I'd had in my life. But Evie had other ideas.

"I don't think so, Sonia," she said. "But thank you. Me
and Miranda have stuff to do."

We returned to the highway and followed it until we
reached a part of the city that still had electricity and running water.

In this neighbourhood there were very few cars now,
parked along the side of the street. Evie looked at them one
by one, carefully, as though choosing fruit. She selected
an innocuous-looking blue family sedan and plunked her
knapsack down beside it. Out came the blanket and the
sledgehammer.

"Why do you bother?" I said. "You have nowhere to
run to."

"I'm not running," said Evie as she laid the blanket over
the window.

"What are you doing then?"

"You're not expected to follow me, you know."

"Follow you where?"

"To see my father." She swung the hammer against the
glass and it shattered without a sound. With a practised
hand, she brushed the glass from the seat, smashed the
casing from the steering column and jump-started the
car. She unlocked the passenger side and I climbed in
beside her.

"I don't want to bring trouble to my family," I said. "So I have nowhere to go either."

4. Zero Point Three Per Cent

I recognized the road. Up past the grey Zodiac compound and through a stretch of quiet green fields into the suburbs. Towards Flowers' office.

From the corner of her eye she saw me register recognition.

"My father," she said.

"Flowers?"

"He's been making people since the fifties. Sonias and Miyakos mostly. Miyakos have cat genes. Sent them all to the factories to work for Pallas. All except two. One for a wife and one for a daughter."

"That's sick."

"When the daughter turned out no good, he sent her to the factories and forgot about her."

"And the wife?"

"Chronically suicidal. That's why I was buzzing around the clinic. I was hoping to take her away."

"Dr. Seto?"

"Yes. She died last week, don't know if you heard. Hung herself in the blood lab."

"How do you bear it?"

Something inside me burned for her. Something struggled against the inner face of my skin. A latent power so tremendous it could overturn the world with a flick of its sinuous tail. That something frightened me. I sat paralyzed.

She drove.

I am your grandmother, I wanted to tell her. I am the maker of your maker. Both of us, such putrid origins, climbing out of the mud and muck into darkness. But I did not want to unmake what I had made, imperfect and wicked as it was.

The thing turned thirsty against my muscles, wringing them. I felt my heart, my liver, my kidneys and lungs shift and elongate ever so slightly in the dark cavities of my body. River music, my blood rushing, whispering *lengthen, lengthen*.

She drove, feverish with anger and fear. Sweat poured down her face, her fistulas ran with pus. I did not know what she intended to do.

The office building loomed in the sky as we approached. Taller than the surrounding buildings, less dilapidated, and less familiar somehow than it once had been, it towered. Still it was dingy and concrete and covered in the same spidery mildew I remembered. We pulled up and stepped through the double glass doors into the waiting elevator. Through its windows I watched the city fall away beneath us on one side and on the other watched the floors go by, one by one, sandwiched by layers of wiring and insulation. The elevator reached the fifty-third floor and scuttled sideways along the width of the building. It let us out in Flowers' main lounge, much plusher than I remembered. The floor was covered in a living carpet of the most expensive genetically engineered moss and the walls climbed with unusual brilliant flowers and succulent green vines. Whatever it was that Flowers had been dabbling in, he had been eminently successful.

Behind the receptionist's desk sat a lovely young woman with dark skin and smooth black hair. It took me a moment to recognize her as the same long-haired receptionist who worked there before. She blended into the lush atmosphere of the reception room much as a Gauguin nude might blend into hers. If I were not quite so skeptical about the natural to begin with, I would say she blended naturally into it. And the mind of the designer behind this paradise . . . I did not want to think about it.

Evie was unfazed. "I'm here to see my father," she said to the woman.

The woman raised a lovely, very natural eyebrow. "Dr. Flowers?"

Evie nodded curtly.

"Do you have an appointment?"

"I don't need an appointment," she said. She grabbed my arm and pulled me through a thin curtain of vines that fluttered a little in an artificially generated breeze, the source of which had been discreetly disguised. The tropical aura of the reception room gave way to a once-upon-a-time sort of European forest. We scampered down a hallway that resembled a forest path, beside which a little artificial brook bubbled, effervescent and poetic. The lovely receptionist followed us, looking suddenly terribly misplaced in the northern forest. Looking as though she had tumbled out of the wrong cartoon. We ran down the path to the large oak that loomed at the end. The base of the trunk was wide as a house, and there was a door in the centre with a handle of smooth brass.

"Such arrogance," muttered Evie, pulling it wide open.

The illusion ended there. Behind the door was the same sterile white lab I remembered from my earlier days working with Flowers. And hunched over a lab table sat Flowers himself, eye to the microscope, oblivious. After a long moment, he raised his head, relaxed, unflapped.

"Evie," he said, "I've been waiting for you."

Breathlessly the receptionist pulled the door open. "Dr. Flowers, sir, I'm sorry."

"Never mind, Miyako," said the doctor kindly. "No harm done."

"Thank you, sir," said the lovely receptionist. She pulled the door shut and was gone.

"Do sit down, Evie, Miranda," said Flowers, magnanimously.

"Like hell!" said Evie. "I know you killed them."

"They were not human, Evie. And it wasn't me who killed them."

"They were the same as me," she said.

"No, they weren't," said Flowers.

"You got rid of me. You put me back in the factories. I am not your daughter any more. I am the same as them. How could you . . ."

"Do you understand what those degenerate Sonias were doing at that house?"

"You gave the orders, didn't you?" The knife appeared in her hand so quickly I could not be certain where it came from. But now the cool blade pressed, razor-sharp, against the sagging white flesh of his throat.

"I had no choice, Evie," he rasped. "The tree . . ."

And in that moment I understood the secret of the trees, the clever Sonias, the depth of their subversion. That they were building a free society of their own kind from the ground up.

"The Sonias had been cultivating that tree, those cabbages and radishes for years. You had no right . . ."

"You don't know," said the doctor, "what monstrosities might have come of those births. Those trees have been interbreeding and mutating for at least three generations since the original work. The fertility those durians provided was neither natural nor controllable. It was too dangerous."

"But what you did to make me, to make us, was not? I should cut your heart out and eat it."

"I'm a scientist, Evie. Whereas those Sonias . . . not human . . ."

The blade nicked his skin and he began to bleed. Sweat poured down his forehead.

"Please, Evie," he said. "Didn't I save you?"

"I wish you hadn't."

"I saved you because I love you . . . daughter . . ."

Neither of us saw his hand slide discreetly into his pocket until the alarm began to ring. Immediately there was the sound of hard leather soles clicking against the floors of the hallway outside Flowers' office. For a moment we were both surprised and our guard dropped. Flowers used the opportunity to push Evie away from him. He fell on top of her, pinning her against the floor. The knife fell from her hand. Instinctively I jumped for it. My fingers closed around its warm grip. Evie and Flowers struggled, but he was bigger and heavier. I thrust the blade in through the fabric of his lab jacket and something soft— a wool sweater perhaps—beneath, and drew it down, cutting through the layers into his soft white flesh, felt it peel away from either side of the blade and the blood spurt up from his dark veins to drench all three of us. Evie pushed him off and we ran through the door. He was not dead. The last word I heard him yell was *traitor*. Covered in blood, we ran down the wooded path into the lush tropical reception area. The pretty receptionist was waiting. "In here," she said, and pulled back a curtain of climbing flowers to reveal a large stationery cabinet. We ducked inside and she closed the door. "I knew she was one of us," said Evie. We watched through the slit between the double doors and past the veil of leaves and flowers. Brown-booted men trooped through the glass doors on either side of the elevator. They pushed past the vines that separated the reception area from the cool forest. As soon as they were through, Miyako pushed us out of the office and pointed the way to an ancient service elevator through which we could exit safely.

Evie found us another car, and in moments we were in with the engine running. My head was reeling with new knowledge, with the secret of the trees.

"How long have you known?" I asked Evie.

"There were rumours, even at the factories. Of course, we had no means to find any validation, but it was a dream of ours that moved up and down the assembly line. We planned our escape and the search for a tree by writing on the inside faces of soles."

"Do you know how the trees came to be?"

"It's all conjecture, but Sonia 14 says it started a century ago. They were implanting human genes into fruit as fertility therapy for women who could not conceive. And of course the pollen blew every which way and could not be contained. And fertilized the fruit of trees bred for other purposes—trees bred to withstand cold climates, trees bred to produce fruit that would strengthen the blood. Perhaps some natural mutations were also involved. What we learned was that the fruit of certain trees could make women pregnant without any need for insemination. It was great for us, because, as you know, Painted Horse and Saturna manufacture only women."

"And the cabbages and radishes?"

"Support and strengthen the fetuses."

I thought about my mother, and the durian tree of my beginnings. I thought about all the durians that moved through my parents' shop and wondered how many of them were of this wonderful sort, since none of the durians we stocked came from certified sources. And then I remembered the one I had eaten at the Sonias' house. I remembered the creamy yellow flesh, the pepper-pissy flavour that seeped into the body before it registered as taste. Suddenly the strange movements I had felt of late within my body began to make sense. I had had no reason up till now to think of myself as pregnant, and so I did not. And now that there was this possibility, suddenly I knew. Suddenly I could feel my roundness, my body ripe as a pear about to drop. There was now a clear logic to the stretching, a soundness to the movement. Soft pear, succulent sweet. And ready to rot, already dreaming of the return to earth.

I thought, we are the new children of the earth, of the earth's revenge. Once we stepped out of mud, now we step out of moist earth, out of DNA both new and old, an imprint of what has gone before, but also a variation. By our difference we mark how ancient the alphabet of our bodies. By our strangeness we write our bodies into the future.

"Where can we run?" said Evie.

I was jolted out of my reverie. "We could go to the shop," I said. My father will be angry, but he will hide us."

"The Pallas police will find us."

We hustled down the steps to the car.

"Where then?"

"I know someone who will help."

I had not been to the aquarium since my mother was alive and I did not recognize it right away because Evie drove down a back road and pulled up at the rear entrance. The blood on our clothes and faces had dried by then, but the stains were obvious.

"No help for it," said Evie. She got out and thumped on the door.

A Chinese man opened it. He was very tall, but his face was gentle and the features fine. "Evie," he said, "you're a mess. Is this your little friend?" He nodded at me politely. "Come in, come in."

"Hello, Chang," said Evie.

It was warm in the lab. He let us use the shower in the back and gave us T-shirts with pictures of whales on them, and the words "Zodiac Aquarium" on the back. He gave us bowls of pork congee from a pot simmering atop a bunsen burner, opened the specimen cold box and took out a box of thousand-year-old eggs.

"I don't know why Rudy lets you get so dirty," he said. "I told him the Sonia series is special. You should give them interesting work so they don't get bored. The Sonias are a good-looking series. Don't make them do dirty work or abuse them. Guess he didn't listen. Where did you come from? A hog farm?"

"Cattle," said Evie, blowing on her congee to cool it.

"A girl working the kill floor," muttered Chang. "That's not right. I told him . . . but since when did Rudy ever listen to any sense?"

"Chang," said Evie, "we're running away. Can you get us some food?"

He stretched his hand out to refill her empty bowl. "Is it really that bad, Evie? I mean, they feed you all right, don't they? They don't beat you? I would hate to think of any of you suffering. I'm the one that made sure all the right DNA went into your little cells, you know. But then you were always the naughty one. Because you're smarter than the others, I don't know why. I gave you all the same stuff."

"Please, Chang," said Evie, "help us."

"Could never say no to you," said Chang. "All right. What do you want?"

"Bread, crackers. Stuff we don't have to cook. Those tins of Buddhist vegetarian are good. Dried fruit. Bottled water."

"All right," said Chang. "Okay. Anyone see you come in here? Rudy will be angry with me. He thinks you're not so good. Says if he didn't care for you so much he would have you put down. Aries William thinks it should have been done a long time ago."

"No one saw us," said Evie.

"Okay. I'm going. Why don't you go say hello to your mom while I'm gone?"

"Your mom?" I said as he stepped out the door.

Evie rolled her eyes. "The carp. My point zero three per cent. You wanna see? Come on."

We stepped through the back door of Chang's lab and into the darkness of the aquarium. It was quiet—just a few elderly couples strolling through and one young mother who appeared to be home-schooling her two sons. We looked into a large tank of tropical fish, their bodies bright and luminous, their faces set in permanent expressions of disdain.

There was one—a brown one with large white circles on its underbelly—that swam about at a furious pace, as though it might escape more quickly if it swam faster. There was an angel fish with a tattered wing. It seemed to be having a hard time keeping upright.

"What a terrible, sad place this is," I said.

"Don't say that. Many lives begin here."

On the other side of the tank, a well-dressed woman and her husband were staring in at the fish. Because of the tank between us and them, it looked as though they were standing under water. They were not remotely as beautiful as the yellow, blue and orange fish that swam between us and them or as the vibrant, translucent corals that shivered with a strange, barely animate life.

We moved on to a tall narrow tank in which an octopus lay, the brown bulbous body pulsing with a visceral, membranous sort of intelligence. Its wrinkled folds moved in and out and its tentacles furled and unfurled to their fine, sensitive tips. Its white suction cups pushed against the glass, not at all the slimy stuff of horror movies, but something infinitely more delicate and lovely. Its eyes, though, were glazed and stunned, but there was a chart beside it declaring that octopus eyes and human eyes were very similar in their construction and functioning.

"Hard not to believe in God, isn't it?" said Evie. "All this beauty and all this variety."

"I never thought about it."

"But if you look at this, and it makes you believe in God, then you also have to believe that it was all meant for human pleasure. Which makes it perfectly all right to shut these beautiful things up in tanks and bottles. The logic is built right into the architecture."

"Do you think they get depressed?"

"No doubt. Wouldn't you?"

"Their eyes are so different from ours. I can't tell what they feel."

We came to a large tank labelled "lungfish." There were a lot of sea anemones inside, pale ones with tendrils that started white at the base, slowly transmuted to pink and ended with brilliant tips the colour of blood. These stretched into the water and waved about, clutching for prey. The lungfish were huge—the same length as a human body. They weren't dainty like the tropical fish. They had large squat heads, wide faces and stunned eyes. But their bodies were beautiful, covered in large, rectangular scales, silver tinged with pink. Their fins rippled with the precise sensitivity that many of the underwater creatures we saw that day seemed to share. What piqued my interest was that these fish got their oxygen not from water, but from air.

I watched them and I did not notice Evie moving away until one lungfish angled up to a higher level, for a moment its body almost upright and almost superimposed over the watery shape of hers. Then it came horizontal again as Evie disappeared through the doorway.

And then the lights blared suddenly bright and there was the sound of police boots tromping on the concrete floor. A woman shouted through a megaphone, "Please gather in the main foyer. No one who complies will be hurt. Please gather in the main foyer."

I dashed after Evie into the next room, an arboretum. She stood on a bridge that arched over an artificial stream that rushed into an artificial pond teeming with flapping carp, golden and white, black, orange and spotted. She produced a biscuit from her pocket, crumbled it and scattered the crumbs over the water. The carp rushed for them, clambering over one another, making a wriggling island of their bodies.

"They're looking for us," said Evie. She reached for my hand. I took it and we moved away from the water towards the emergency exit at the back of the arboretum.

I followed her. "What about Chang?"

"Let's hope he forgets to come back." She pushed me

through the exit into a grey hallway. We heard boots clipping the hard floor. Evie pulled me through an unmarked door into what turned out to be a cold storage room where many fish lay in glass cases, trapped under ice. To my horror, I noticed several human beings as well, frozen in blocks and perched upright. We waited for the sound of boots to subside. Our teeth chattered.

When the hallway was silent again, we stepped out, ran for the nearest exit and prayed that the door would open. It did, but it also set an alarm screaming. We ran back along the road to the door where we had left the car. Climbed in quickly. With a deft hand, Evie jump-started it and we were off, only to see Chang pulling into the parkway.

"Turn around!" Evie yelled through her broken window. "The place is crawling with cops."

But Chang seemed not to hear her.

"We can't leave him," I said.

"We don't have a choice," said Evie. She turned onto the highway. The tires screeched.

Something happened as we turned the corner. As though the world behind had vanished. As though the minute we turned, it utterly ceased to exist. We turned the corner into mist. No matter how destroyed the land, the mist clings, hovers like a worried mother or a lover too far gone to know her love has long since died, that what clings to the body is no longer life exactly, but something much more hungry and desperate and strange. We turned the corner, and Chang disappeared, the aquarium disappeared, the terrible Pallas police in their brown uniforms and clicking boots disappeared when we turned the corner into mist.

And where we drove, amazingly, there were still trees, towering above us like that day in the mountains long ago. Trees green and living, exhaling their contemplative cedar scent and casting blue-green light over the crumbling road in a lacy pattern, making images that flickered and vanished beneath the wheels of the plain blue sedan. The mist and cedar air rushed through the broken window.

Evie drove very fast. So fast it felt like falling, felt as though some kind of gravity compelled us, not the tug of heavy earth, but another kind of gravity, close and pulsing. Evie drove too fast but I wasn't frightened. Evie's face was imbued with an awesome serenity, perfectly relaxed but not sleepy. Her brown eyes glistened alertly.

And if someone was following us through the wafting mist and the flickering patterns of light that the trees had scattered over the road, we did not notice, and we went on. We went on without ever re-entering the city, and the road slanted slowly upwards. The air grew cooler and fresher, though the mist never lifted. And Evie barrelled into the mist even though there were often moments when we could not see more than a few metres ahead. It didn't scare us. Perhaps we had simply moved beyond fear, having seen in the flickering light on the road reassuring images of what we were, or what we might become again.

The car wound up into the mountains. Night came and the mist did not leave us. We were not tired, our bodies tingled with alertness. We drove through the mountains to daylight on the other side. A valley flooded with mist and soft yellow light.

There, I saw the shacks for the first time, some abandoned and hardly shacks at all, but skeletons of shacks, the last tarpaper of the roofs flapping in the wind. But three had been fixed up, new boards nailed neatly to their frames, the tarpaper roofs replaced. Evie pulled up onto the grass beside them, stepped out of the car, put her feet on firm ground.

"Stay in the car," she said.

But I couldn't help myself. I climbed out of the car and followed her as she pulled open the worn grey door of the shack. One narrow window had been cut in the far wall, and through it poured a thin stream of daylight, filtered through trees, fog and snow.

Inside were three long rows of narrow beds, and in the beds, covered in institutional grey blankets, the rounded shapes of bodies, each curve of spine a slightly different curve, each grey mound heaving breath to a slightly different rhythm, all fast asleep. The room was cold and reeked of mothballs.

And then I noticed at the foot of each bed was a pair of shoes, a pair of Pallas runners, placed neatly side by side waiting for their owner to wake and fill them.

"People like you?" I asked, self-conscious of the euphemism.

"Yes," said Evie. "I think so. But these look like men. Flowers has never bred men before."

We tiptoed in so as not to wake them.

The first ten beds contained young boys, no older than five. In the second ten beds lay boys clearly grown from the same DNA, perhaps five years older. We examined the sleeping faces all the way to the back of the shack. The faces of the fifteen-year-olds looked familiar. When we saw the twenty-year-olds we felt more certain. In the faces of the eldest, around twenty-five years old or so, there could be no question. One of them let out a rumble of dream-laughter and rolled over in his sleep.

"Flowers," I said.

"The fountain of eternal youth," said Evie.

My stomach churned, as though something moved inside.

We tiptoed out of the shack as quietly as we had entered.

"We could torch it," I said.

Evie shook her head. "Those are my cousins," she said. "And I am not a murderer."

We walked a little way into the woods behind the camp. Creepy sound of an old tree moving under the weight of snow-laden branches. Why shouldn't the tree creak if it wants to? It was not the tree that thought *gibbet*, it was me.

And then the curious round cabin appeared. A ring of thick cedar logs for its sides and a roof that spiralled up and ended with a skylight at the top. "They commissioned a Native architect, Agnes Bishop, to design it," said Evie. "As though purchasing her labour would somehow connect their project to the land."

With a small electronic device she had obviously used time and again, Evie picked the lock and we were in. The cabin revealed its shape—a spiral, like a snail shell, or the body curled fetal, door where the head goes, toilet at the centre, where the tail could curve in. And the skylight directly above. Was I meant to make something of this, was the cabin design a riddle? After all, children also enter the world from the dirty end, poke their heads through the point of light. A stinking toilet as the end of the story? Why not? This is a story about stink, after all, a story about rot, about how life grows out of the most fetid-smelling places. I leaned into the wall of the coiled cabin, snail, the body curled in upon itself, spine coiled, a snake lying in wait.

Evie showed me the fridges where all the DNA was kept, the vials of fertilized and unfertilized eggs, the cold steel tables upon which the act of creation took place. All these tidy attempts to control the mud and muck of origins upset me. I hid my face. I closed my eyes and saw myself knife Flowers again, felt the press of the steel edge into his soft back and the flesh peeling away from the other side of the blade.

She said, "I want to show you something." She took my hand and led me out of the coiled cabin. Walked me across a flat frozen bog and up into the rocks.

There was a glossy hazardous blanket lying over the land. I imagined a thousand tiny ocean creatures swimming in the rock beneath, leaving the ancient imprint of their bodies to sleep beneath ice and snow, smelling faintly of salt. Here they lay on this dry, cold ocean, dead or dreaming, I couldn't quite tell. I felt a strange sort of longing, that feeling again of being on the verge of remembering something I did not know I had forgotten.

Night comes quickly in the mountains. It fell on us before we made it back to the snail cabin. We got lost. We stumbled nervously through the dark, getting cold and scared.

"The moon will come out," said Evie. "It is brighter than you would think."

We stopped and waited for it. The mist shifted invisibly in the dark and spilled tiny crystals onto our faces, blew cool breath in our ears. The breath made me tired. Sleep tugged at my sleeves. I longed to surrender.

"The moon is coming," said Evie. "Don't give in."

Slowly it rose, climbing an overhang of jagged black rock. It poured light over the edge, revealing a steaming pool beneath, a stone's throw from where we sat.

"A hot spring!" said Evie.

Yes, I thought, an ancient ocean bubbling up through the rocks, salty and full of minerals. I scrambled desperately towards it, shed my clothes and slipped in. No shame as the coils unravelled. And to my surprise, Evie too slipped out of her clothes and slid into the water. Her legs fused together, and where her skin met water, a thin layer of tiny silver scales began to form and glisten in the moonlight. She stretched her tail through mine and our coils interlocked and slid through one another and then all of a sudden I found myself breathing these great heaving breaths. My belly heaved and contracted. Blood streamed into the water, staining it. I howled with the pain of womb spasming deeply, and then a dark head emerged six inches below my navel, from an opening in my scaly new flesh. The head had a wrinkled human face. Evie reached under water, guided the thing out, black-haired and bawling, a little baby girl. Everything will be all right, I thought, until next time.

Acknowledgements

This book would not have been possible without the love and support of sisters and loved ones who got me through the day to day: Rita Wong, Lorna Boschman, Robin Tieu, and Debora O. Much gratitude for travel companionship, gross-out stories and friendship over short and long distances: Hiromi Goto, Ashok Mathur, Aruna Srivastava, and Tamai Kobayashi. To my ever-since-forever-in-spite-of-time-and-space writing buddies Monika Kin Gagnon and Shani Mootoo, many thanks. For meaty gossip and meatless meals, and for the epigraph, thanks Janet Neigh.

In England: Louise Tondeur, Isanna Curwen, Scott Wakeham, Donna Daley-Clarke, Mairi Contos, Neil Stewart, Dominique De-Light, Tom Corbett, and Juliet Sargent, each for your own particular brand of warmth and affection, thank you. Flatmates, especially Satoko Masuda, Yukari Tamazaki, Kumiko Ushida, Kazuyo Takeda, and Annelore Chauvin, much gratitude. From class to pub and back again, a tip of the nib: Jamie Harris, Rebecca Fortey, Christine Thomas, Paul Murray, and Tim Jarvis.

Many thanks and endless vowels to the gals at the Sea to Sky Retreat, especially: Fiona Lam, Rita Wong, Cathy Stone-house, Nancy (Pea) Pollak, Sue Leibik, Louie Ettling, Shauna Fowler, and Esther Shannon.

To the women from Pine Mountain, warm thanks, especially Monika Gagnon, Jill Holwager, and Margot Blair.

Truest teachers Ali Smith, Deena Metzger, and Olga Broumas, thank you.

I am very grateful to those who read drafts and/or generously gave suggestions: Scott Toguri McFarlane (especially for your elaborations on the firefly disease), Kathy-Ann March, Simone Lazaroo, Andrew Motion, Michele Roberts, Louise Tondeur, Hiromi Goto, Scott Wakeham, Rita Wong, and Janet Neigh.

Much appreciation across the ether: Eva Tai, Gregory Scofield, and Diana Atkinson.

I am very grateful for the kindness and support of Sandra Vida and the Steering Committee for the Markin-Flanagan Distinguished Writers' Programme during my year as writer-in-residence.

How to say this enough? An enormous bucket of thanks to my beloved editor, Katja Pantzar. Warmest thanks to the lovely and gentle Patrick Crean, publisher. Much gratitude to my intrepid agent, Anne McDermid.

Last, but most of all, huge gratitude to my family, especially: Tsui-Pun Wai-Chee, Yuen-Fong Woon, Whalen Lai, Yuen-Ting Lai, Tyrone Lai, and Wendy Lai. Thank you for believing in me.

I would also like to acknowledge the generous support of the Markin-Flanagan Distinguished Writers' Programme at the University of Calgary, the Canada Council, the Leighton Studios at the Banff Centre for the Arts, the Department of Canadian Heritage, and the Cultural Services Branch of the British Columbia Ministry of Small Business, Tourism, and Culture.